Son of a Witch

Crypt Witch cozy paranormal mystery
series - book 5

K.E. O'Connor

K.E. O'Connor Books

Chapter 1

I loved the familiar sucking pull of the magic as I slid through the barrier from the outside world back into Willow Tree Falls. It felt like home as I stood blinking in the late afternoon sunshine.

I'd only been away twenty-four hours. The demon I'd been tracking had been easy to capture. Easy but stinky.

My long hair stank like cheese that had been left on the countertop in the hot sun. And, no matter how tightly I tied the demon bag attached to my belt loop, the demon inside continued to ooze noxious fumes through the material.

I looked at my black pants and grimaced. They'd have to be burned. I doubted even my mom could remove the stench and stains on them.

Rolling my shoulders, I adjusted the bag on my hip and strolled toward Angel Force. They could deal with this pongy demon. Once they had him, I intended to kick back and enjoy a couple of lemon drops in Cloven Hoof before it got busy for the evening.

"Tempest! Tempest Crypt! Stop right there."

My shoulders hitched as I saw Mannie Winter racing toward me on his stubby legs, a bag in one hand. What did our local mayor want? We were far from friendly since I'd revealed his affair during the last mayoral election. He did nothing but glower at me and mutter whenever our paths crossed. Not this time. Mannie was smiling, and that made me suspicious.

"Phew! That's my cardio for the week." Mannie patted his round belly and blinked up at me. He was a sturdy dwarf, standing at just over five feet, with a long, well-oiled beard that trailed to his silver belt buckle.

"It looks like you need a sit down after that run," I said. "Something must be important to get you moving like that."

Mannie chuckled and smoothed his bushy eyebrows with his fingers. "Indeed, there is. I have urgent business to attend to. I haven't stopped all day."

"There's not another election coming up, is there?" Mannie had been in his role as mayor for less than a year. His vision for Willow Tree Falls was to turn it into a mecca for tourists who were attracted to our mystical stones and thermal spas. I couldn't think of anything worse than having the streets constantly thrumming with tourists. A lot of them found us anyway, but since Mannie had taken charge, the numbers had increased.

"Oh no. That's not for another four years. You're stuck with me for now." He chuckled heartily and slapped his belly.

"That's good to know. If you'll excuse me." I tried to step past him, but he matched my movement and blocked my way.

Mannie wafted his hand in front of his nose. "You've got a stinker in that bag. I hope he didn't cause you problems."

I shook the bag and more toxic fumes seeped out and wafted around Mannie. "Nothing I can't handle."

"Of course. A clever demon catching witch, such as yourself, is always in top form."

I raised my eyebrows. Why was he being so nice? "I need to be. Otherwise, I won't be alive for much longer."

Mannie chuckled again. "Absolutely. Quite right. How's the family? Is everyone keeping well?"

I wished he'd stop making small talk and tell me what he wanted. "They're all good."

"And Queenie has recovered from that terrible incident with her friends?"

"She's much better." Auntie Queenie had recently lost two of her biker gang members when one of the gang turned rogue. "She's just come back from a cruise. It's done her the world of good."

"Oh, I love a cruise," Mannie said. "There's nothing like sitting on the deck, a tankard of ale next to me and the sun on my face. Have you ever been on a cruise?"

"No. Mannie, I really must get on. This demon won't stay in the bag for much longer."

"Oh, of course. But, before you go." Mannie placed his bag on the ground and extracted a pink box with the Sprinkles bakery logo on the top. "I thought you might like a cake." He flipped the lid open to reveal a row of glistening doughnuts. There was every kind, from traditional glazed to luxuriant looking snickerdoodle.

I licked my lips. I was starving but still hesitated. Mannie Winter wanted something. All this sweet talk and now the offer of doughnuts. I raised a hand toward the doughnuts but didn't take one.

"Go on. One doughnut won't hurt." Mannie waggled his eyebrows. "You deserve it after keeping the world safe from another demon threat."

I tilted my head. "Are these treats being offered to make sure Frank doesn't come out and play with you?" Mannie knew me well, and he knew that feeding me sweet treats kept my incumbent demon from getting feisty.

Mannie shrugged and looked a little shamefaced. "It never hurts to make sure both of you are happy."

I stared at the doughnuts. They did look tasty, and you could never go wrong with a doughnut from Sprinkles.

"Wait for me!" The ground shuddered beneath my feet.

I turned to see Wiggles charging toward us, his ears flat against his head and a determined gleam in his red eyes.

My eyes widened, and I backed away. Wiggles was heading straight for the box of doughnuts in Mannie's hand. "You might like to—"

Wiggles launched into the air, colliding with the box and knocking it to the ground. He tumbled across the dirt, bounced onto his feet, and pounced on the first doughnut before it had rolled to a stop.

I sighed and looked forlornly at the fallen doughnuts.

"Well, I never." Mannie stared at the mess on the ground. "Your dog needs to go to obedience classes."

"What can I say? He's a demon when it comes to cake."

Wiggles glanced up, his mouth full of a glazed sugared doughnut. "A hellhound, actually."

Mannie glared at Wiggles as he munched on his second doughnut.

"Hey, Tempest," Wiggles said. "Good trip?"

I patted the bag. "I got the job done. Did you miss me?"

He made a muffled sound as he scooped up his next doughnut.

I took that to mean: *yes, very much. And I didn't race all this way just to eat the mayor's doughnuts. I was coming to see you and tell you how happy I am that you're home.*

Mannie was grumbling under his breath, his hands in fists by his sides.

"Apart from wanting to welcome me back to the village and offer me doughnuts," I said to him, "was there anything else you needed?"

"It's funny you should ask." Mannie adjusted his waistcoat. "As you know, I've been working on our exciting new tourist attraction."

My mouth twisted to the side. "The magic museum."

"It will be incredible. A history of magic and witchcraft. Dozens of exhibits, lifelike dioramas, and stunning history to enjoy. People will flock here in the thousands to see our interactive, fully immersive exhibits. I'll be unveiling a new exhibit every other month."

"I can't wait." I didn't mind a bit of history, but this museum would mean a lot more tourists, and I wasn't a fan.

"This will put us on the map." Mannie nodded. "It opens tomorrow evening. We have VIP guests and exclusive speakers attending. And we'll reveal our first exhibition. The Murder of Witches."

My eyebrows shot up. "Your first exhibit is all about how to kill my family?"

Mannie roared with laughter. "My dear Tempest, your family is indestructible. This is about the history of witch murders. The traditional methods used hundreds of years ago to hunt down witches and expose them."

I frowned. "Who wants to see that?"

"Everyone who doesn't have magic, of course," Mannie said. "There's always been a fascination from those who don't have our skills. They love to see how witches and other magical creatures were treated over the centuries."

"We were treated appallingly," I said. "Why not do a diorama about ten ways to kill irritating dwarves?"

Mannie shook his head. "No, murdering witches is all the rage."

I wouldn't mind seeing the dwarf exhibit. There was one dwarf who was tempting me to try a cruel and unusual method of killing him. "Willow Tree Falls is our haven. Why bring up the past? Here, we don't need to worry about ducking stools appearing by the pond and an angry mob with flaming torches dragging us from our beds."

"A ducking stool! It's as if you've read my mind. That's our opening exhibit."

I arched an eyebrow. "It sounds great. Best of luck with it."

"Oh, no. You misunderstand. I—"

"Mannie! Mannie! What are you doing?" A stick-thin, sharp-faced woman with a steel-gray bob strode toward Mannie, her green eyes narrowed and a pair of glasses perched on the end of her long nose.

Mannie's smile stretched across his face, but it didn't reach his eyes. "Gretel, I was about to extol your virtues to Tempest."

Gretel eyed me with suspicion. "There's no time for that. There are so many problems at the museum, I don't know where to start. You must come quickly."

Mannie chuckled, but I noticed his shoulders hunch to his ears. "Everything's running to plan. We've been over the arrangements a dozen times. It can't be anything serious." He turned to me. "Tempest Crypt, meet Gretel Le Strange. She's one of our VIP guests at the museum opening."

I nodded a greeting at Gretel. "Nice to meet you."

"Indeed." Her gaze ran over me. She wrinkled her nose when she saw the smoking bag on my hip. "What have you got there?"

"Tempest's a skilled demon hunter," Mannie said. "In fact, she has all kinds of marvelous skills."

"Good for her." Gretel turned to Mannie. "You must come at once. You have to see the disaster. If we open with the ducking stool exhibit looking like it does, we'll be a laughing stock."

"Just a moment," Mannie said. "Tempest, Gretel has been helping at the museum."

Gretel snorted. "Helping! The place would be a joke if I wasn't involved."

Mannie winced. "Gretel's a well-known historian, specializing in the history of magic."

"Congratulations," I said to her. I could do snooty too if needed.

Mannie's gaze turned anxious. "Gretel will be giving talks and demonstrations at the opening tomorrow."

I nodded and watched Wiggles with envy as he polished off the dirt-covered doughnuts. He would have such bad indigestion. I wouldn't be sharing a bed with him tonight.

"Since we're having VIP visitors at the museum," Mannie continued, "I'm in need of your expertise."

I glanced at him. "To do what?"

"To assist with the security. It's such an important event, and the place will be crammed full of guests."

"Okay, but it's a museum. Why do you need security?"

"Because of our important guests." Mannie tilted his head at Gretel, who stood tapping her foot. "Along with Gretel, we also have the author of the book who helped bring this museum to life."

Gretel snorted. "Isadora might have written some popular piece of fluff about the history of witchcraft, but it's hardly instrumental in creating the museum. In case you've forgotten, I've advised you every day for nine months on this matter."

Mannie's lips pressed together. "I haven't forgotten. Your input has been most welcome."

Gretel huffed and folded her arms across her chest. "We need to get a move on. Stop wasting your time with this witch."

"Tempest is going to help us," Mannie said, a pleading look entering his eyes. "I need her for the extra security at the museum."

I shook my head. "I'm no security expert. Why don't you ask the angels?"

Mannie scuffed a foot in the dirt. "The angels are lovely creatures, and they do their best. I'm not sure they can handle a security job of such importance. Things could get hectic. What if someone needs calming down?"

"Have you ever been hit in the face with an angel wing? They sting. It would calm anyone down." I didn't want anything to do with this. "If your museum guests get rowdy after their sherry, the angels can handle them. I don't run a security team."

"You've got experience from running Cloven Hoof," Mannie said. "You have door staff."

"What's Cloven Hoof?" Gretel sneered. "It sounds like some disreputable devil's den, a place for down and outs."

"You're pretty close." My smile felt more like a snarl. "We have a specific clientele we cater to."

"I doubt I'd enjoy your establishment," Gretel said.

"It's definitely not for you." My fingers flexed, and I took a step closer to Gretel.

Mannie grabbed my arm. "Please, Tempest, I need the very best for our guests. Whatever you need to make it a success, it's yours."

I pulled my arm from his grasp. "I need nothing. I'm not a bouncer. This isn't what I do."

"Money's no object."

Gretel scowled at Mannie and turned away from us, her foot continuing to beat on the ground.

Mannie leaned closer. "Please, Gretel's very demanding. I need somebody to keep an eye on her and make sure she doesn't take over and spoil things."

I stepped away from him and studied Gretel's back. She did look like a handful, but I didn't want to hang out with a rude magic historian for an evening.

"Try someone else. Rhett's gang is always good if you're looking for muscle to keep things under control."

"Oh, no. They're not the right kind of security." Mannie shook his head swiftly. "You can handle yourself in a professional manner if there's trouble." He nodded at the bag on my hip, which now oozed a green sludge from the bottom. "You look after the demons. You even have your own under control these days."

Gretel spun on her chunky-heeled shoes and scowled at me. "You own a demon?"

I shook my head. "No. It's a long story."

"There'll be canapés and champagne. You'd be free to help yourself," Mannie said. "You'll be doing me such a favor."

"Did someone say free canapés?" Wiggles belched out smoke, which was tinged with the smell of sulfur.

Gretel took several steps back and pinched her nose.

"Sorry, Mannie. I'm out. You'll have to find someone else."

He caught hold of my elbow, and his eyes glittered. "I wasn't going to mention this, but if you do this for me, last month's noise violation will disappear. What do you say? The paperwork vanishes, you get a decent bit of cash in your pocket, and you can drink and eat 'til your heart's content."

This time, it was my turn to scowl. That noise violation would cost me a few thousand in fines, and there was no way out of it. "Just one evening?"

"That's all I ask. Get there at six, and we'll be done by eleven."

I rubbed my forehead, not happy with Mannie's underhanded tactics. "Can I bring an extra body? Suki looks after the door at Cloven Hoof most nights. She's good at keeping order."

"Absolutely, bring whoever you like," Mannie said. "Same goes for them, free canapés and drinks."

"I'd better get out my smart bowtie," Wiggles said, "if I'm going to be a bouncer for the evening."

Mannie blinked at Wiggles before nodding. "Why not? A hellhound as security will be a fun bonus."

Wiggles strutted around us. "I'll take my payment in bones and cupcakes."

I sighed. It looked like I'd be adding bouncer to my resume. "We'll be there."

"That's excellent news." Mannie smiled at me before turning to Gretel, whose face looked set in a permanent frown.

"My time is precious," she snapped at him.

"Of course." Mannie nodded at Gretel. "Let's see about this museum exhibit you're not happy with."

I watched them walk away. "How were the doughnuts?" I asked Wiggles.

"Tasty. A bit gritty, but they were free."

"They looked lovely. Maybe save me one the next time you knock a whole box on the ground."

"You wouldn't have liked them. Some had coconut sprinkles on the top."

I stuck my tongue out. I wasn't a big coconut fan. "Come on. Let's get rid of this demon. Then we need to figure out how we're going to avoid falling asleep at this dull museum opening."

Wiggles nudged me with his nose as we walked to Angel Force. "It's good to have you back. I sort of miss you when you're not around."

I smiled down at him. "I missed you too, you greedy hellhound."

Chapter 2

"I didn't know my girlfriend was so rough and tough." Rhett Blackthorn grinned at me from the other side of the bar.

I returned his grin as I passed him a lemon drop. "Mannie Winter strong-armed me into it. You could say he blackmailed me."

"What with? Does he have some dark secret he's been keeping about you?" Rhett's gorgeous dark eyes sparkled in the bar light. He was dressed in his usual uniform of black, topped off with a battered leather jacket. He looked deliciously tempting.

"There might have been a small noise violation issue not so long ago," I said. "He said he would make it disappear if I did what he wanted."

Rhett's grin faded. "I never trusted that dwarf."

I shrugged. "He's also paying a decent amount and said there will be free food and drink. Besides, what can go wrong at some stuffy museum opening? We'll be bored most of the time."

"I'm looking forward to it. It should be fun."

My eyes widened. "You're going to the opening?"

"Sure. I heard that some exhibits are interactive. You can get involved and speak to characters from the past."

I laughed. "No kidding. I didn't think I was dating a secret history geek."

Rhett chuckled. "Less of the geek. History is cool. You can learn a lot from the past, mainly what mistakes to avoid in the present."

I brushed a finger across the back of his hand. Rhett was full of mystery, but then a fallen angel who led the local biker gang had to have hidden depths. "Don't cause any trouble tonight. You don't want me chasing after you in my role as a rough, tough bouncer."

His grin widened as he caught hold of my hand and tangled our fingers together. "I can't think of anything I'd like more."

I leaned across the bar and pressed a kiss to his lips. "I'd chase you any time."

"What do you think?" Wiggles bounded behind the bar. He sported a large black bowtie and a pair of wraparound shades.

"You look suitably bounceresque," I said.

"You should see Suki."

I glanced up as Suki shuffled out from the back room, her hands clasped in front of her. She wore a large, ill-fitting tuxedo, her black bowtie clipped on wonky. She also sported a pair of shades that masked her eyes.

"Erm, I don't think we're supposed to dress up for tonight," I said.

Suki raised her gaze from the floor. "I told you we don't have to wear this," she said to Wiggles. "I feel stupid."

"You look great," I lied. The pant legs of the tuxedo were too short for Suki and exposed a lot of ankle and some candy-pink socks. "It just needs a little adjustment."

"Are you wearing a tuxedo?" Rhett asked me, a smile on his face.

"Not a chance," I muttered.

"Of course, she is," Wiggles said. "I got it arranged this morning. I hired a tuxedo for Tempest and Suki and got myself a new bowtie. Watch what it does." He pressed his chin onto the bowtie, and it spun around.

"That's clever," Rhett said, his tone serious. "Does Tempest's bowtie also do that?"

"Stop it," I warned him. "I'm not wearing a bowtie or a tuxedo."

Suki's eyes widened. "I'm not wearing this on my own. You have to put yours on, or I'll feel ridiculous."

"You should have an outfit for the evening," Rhett said. "You'll look great in a tuxedo."

"And I got you a pair of shades, so we all match," Wiggles said. "If we're going to be bouncers, we need to look the part."

I looked down at my mostly black outfit. "What's wrong with this?"

"You heard what the mayor said. There will be VIP guests tonight. We're looking after academic royalty. We need to look like we mean business."

"Ill-fitting tuxedos and shades do that?"

Wiggles sat up, puffing his chest out. "Indeed, they do. Now, get a hustle on. We need to leave soon, and you're not changed."

"Why are you so excited about this?" I asked him.

"It's not every day you get to meet an important person, dress up in your best bowtie, eat fancy canapés, and quaff champagne."

"No champagne for you. I know what you're like when you get your paws on bubbles."

"I become even more fabulous." Wiggles jumped up and strutted around, posing now and again to show off different angles of his bowtie.

I groaned and shook my head. "Help me," I whispered to Rhett.

"Not a chance. I can't wait to see you in your tuxedo, guarding important guests. Who are you looking after?"

"Gretel Le Strange and some author. I met Gretel yesterday. She might be a clever historian, but she's not all that friendly."

Rhett's brow wrinkled. "I know that name. Gretel Le Strange comes from an ancient family of magic users. She's a popular university lecturer. Has she really come all this way for the museum opening?"

"It looks like it."

"She knows her stuff," Rhett said. "Gretel has studied the history of magic and witchcraft for decades. She's an expert in her field. Everyone speaks highly of her work."

I fanned my face with a hand. "Please, stop! I get so excited when you go all geeky on me."

"Hilarious," he said. "I wouldn't mind meeting her, though. Maybe you can make an introduction after the museum has opened?"

I wrinkled my nose. "You don't want to meet her. Gretel's rude and abrasive. Even Mannie was struggling to keep a civil tongue in his head when she was snapping at him."

"I love bossy women." Rhett winked at me.

"Tempest, hurry up and get into your tuxedo," Wiggles said. "We're leaving in ten minutes."

"Duty calls," Rhett said. "I'll catch up with you at the museum."

I gave him a quick kiss. "I look forward to it." I dragged my feet as I went into the back room to find my own tuxedo hanging on a door.

Wiggles bounced around as I changed out of my clothes and into the tuxedo. Despite the jacket being a little on the large side, it wasn't a bad fit.

"And the shades," Wiggles said.

I looked around and saw a pair of wraparound shades on the counter. "Really? It's evening. No one wears shades at night."

"Hard core bouncers do," Wiggles said. "Anyone who thinks about stepping out of line will stop when they see the three of us. We're like the magic version of the Three Musketeers."

"I think you mean the Three Stooges," I muttered.

Suki walked in and stared at me in my tuxedo. "You're really going to wear it?"

I shrugged as I adjusted the lapels of my tuxedo. "It looks like it. Don't worry. You look great. Focus on the food. You'll get first dibs on all the canapés. That will take your mind off of what you're wearing."

Suki's face brightened. "That sounds good. I'm still not sure about this jacket, though."

I hurried over and unbuttoned it before adjusting the shoulders. "Roll the sleeves up to your elbows."

"Great idea," Wiggles said. "That'll make you look much meaner."

Suki glanced at him. "I don't want to look mean. I'm not a mean person."

Suki had her moments of meanness. She was a giant wood nymph who was normally placid and easygoing unless you riled her. Then she turned into an unstoppable force. You needed to run in the opposite direction when Suki was in a rage.

She rolled up her sleeves and looked at me. "Any better?"

"Not bad. We'll do for the mayor and his cronies."

I waved goodbye to the staff behind the bar before we headed out into the cool evening air. The sun was dipping below the horizon as we headed toward the museum.

The museum was housed in a disused mansion that had been owned by Vincent Maldovic. The lovely Vincent had been chased out of Willow Tree Falls after he'd used a curse to turn a family to stone because they'd disrespected him.

Since then, everyone had stayed away from his mansion. There was a rumor it was haunted by the tortured souls Vincent had played with in his basement. Who said that money couldn't buy you happiness? It made Vincent happy by giving him the space to get away with murder for a very long time.

Once Mannie became mayor, the first thing he'd done was use public funds to take possession of the mansion for a fraction of its value, fund its refurbishment, and open it as Willow Tree Falls' first museum.

I slowed as we turned the corner, and my mouth fell open. A long line of people snaked around the building. "Why are there so many people here?"

Suki glanced down at me. "It's a big deal. Everyone's excited about this museum."

"Not everybody," I said. "It must be the whole village here."

"And some guests," Wiggles said. "I recognize that woman in the sequined dress. She promotes her psychic skills all over the place. A lot of big names use her services. I'd better get her autograph."

"No pestering the guests," I said. "We're here to keep order. Our job is to stay in the background and be discreet. We look out for trouble and stop it before it happens. Nothing more. No hound dogging the gorgeous women."

"We can eat the canapés, though?" Suki asked.

"Sure. Grab as many as you like."

Suki sighed. "I'll be happy, so long as I can eat."

We walked past the queue of people. I stopped as I recognized some familiar faces. "Mom! Granny Dottie? What are you doing here?"

Mom hugged me. "Don't you look smart. We wouldn't miss this. It's supposed to be amazing."

Granny Dottie grinned at me. "What are you wearing?"

"We're the security for the night." Wiggles bounced around everyone. "They needed to hire the best."

"But they got us," I said.

Mom patted my cheek. "You be careful in there. There's a big crowd tonight. Everyone wants to see what Mannie's been up to."

"It's a crowd of history geeks," I said. "I can't see them being trouble."

Grandpa Lucius and Uncle Kenny hurried over. "Sorry we're late. We've just finished at the cemetery. Aurora lost track of time and forgot she was supposed to take a turn."

"She's on her own?" I hadn't spoken much to Aurora since her announcement that she was getting married to Toby Matlock. I got the impression she was avoiding me. It was mutual. I had no clue what to say about how serious things were with Toby. I didn't trust him as far as I could throw him, but Aurora had blinders on when it came to her new fiancé.

"It's been quiet at the cemetery for a couple of days," Uncle Kenny said. "We made sure everything was secure before we left."

"We won't stay here long," Mom said. "We'll check in at the cemetery on our way home and make sure everything's fine. We're taking the next shift, anyway."

"Oooh! I think they're about to let us in," Granny Dottie said as the crowd stirred around them. "Hurry up, everybody. We don't want to miss our spot."

"We'd better go inside," I said. "Have fun."

We strode to the front door, and I banged a fist on it.

After a few seconds, it cracked open. Mannie peered out. "Tempest! Hurry! Everything's in place." He slid the door open, and we all walked inside.

His gaze ran over us. "You look very... official."

I quirked an eyebrow. "Who are we looking after?"

"This way." Mannie bustled along, his tartan suit stretched around his rotund gut. "Isadora, darling. Over here."

"That must be the famous author," Wiggles whispered.

A petite woman of about fifty with a blonde bob, wearing a tailored cream pantsuit, turned and smiled at Mannie as she walked over to join us. "How are we doing?"

"It's all looking good." Mannie clasped his hands together. "Isadora, this is your security detail for the evening. Tempest Crypt, Suki, and erm, this is Wiggles. He's small, but he's a hellhound and good in a fight."

"I'm excellent in a fight." Wiggles bared his teeth and made his bowtie rotate.

"I'm hoping there won't be any fighting tonight." Isadora chuckled and shook hands with all three of us, bending to shake Wiggles' paw. "It's lovely to meet you all. I'm Isadora Ash. I believe you were drafted in at short notice."

"Something like that," I said.

"I'm sure we won't need security," Isadora said. "Museums rarely get rowdy."

"You never know. It's important to ensure the safety of our valuable assets." A tall, narrow-faced man with slicked back dark hair strode over.

A quick glance at him suggested a hint of the undead. He wasn't a full vampire, but somewhere in his history, there'd been a vampire liaison with a human. It was the cheekbones and the pale skin, such a giveaway.

"Seth, I'm sure you're overreacting." Isadora smiled at him. "Seth Fellows, this is our security for the night." She introduced us all.

Seth glanced up from the papers he held. "We need to stop the rabble from getting too close to Isadora. She'll be signing books later, so you'll need to keep control of things. The fans can get over-excited."

"We can handle the rabble," I said.

Seth's gaze ran over me, and his dark eyes gleamed. "Make sure you do."

"This is Jonah Dragoon and Lotus Umbra," Isadora said as two more people approached. "Jonah's my right-hand man."

A serious-faced, broad-shouldered guy in his late twenties with bright blue eyes shook my hand. "Officially, I'm Isadora's personal assistant, but I also answer to right-hand man."

"And Lotus is my genius research assistant," Isadora said.

Lotus smiled and nodded at the three of us. She was a pretty, elven female with spiky blue hair and delicately pointed ears.

"Lotus and Jonah have been helping me manage all this craziness with my book," Isadora said.

"Craziness that's well deserved," Mannie said. "Isadora's book is nothing short of a work of genius. Her research is thorough and precise. It's all thanks to Isadora's book that this museum became a reality. I'd always had an idea for a museum but didn't have the right focus. Once I'd read a few papers written by Isadora on witchcraft through the ages and discovered a book was in production, I knew I had exactly what I needed."

"And, after some gentle persuasion," Isadora said, "I decided to consult with Mannie and help make the museum happen. It's exciting to see the dry words I wrote brought to life in such an amazing way."

"Your words are a delight," Mannie said. "I was captivated by the advance copy you gave me."

"It sounds like a good book," Wiggles said.

Isadora smiled down at him. "I'd be happy to give you a copy. Signed, of course."

Seth sighed. "Don't keep giving away your books. People are here tonight to spend their money."

Isadora's mouth drooped, and she shrugged.

"Wiggles isn't much of a reader, anyway," I said. "Tell us where we need to be, and we'll keep an eye out for any problems."

Mannie scratched his fingers through his beard. "There's one problem. Gretel's missing. She's a special guest, as well. I was hoping one of you could chaperone her for the evening."

"She needs chaperoning," Seth muttered.

"Does she usually cause trouble?" I asked him.

He smirked at me. "For other people. She might be a notable historian, but she's also a notable pain in most people's backsides."

"She's a woman who knows her own mind," Mannie said. "The plan was to have one of you look after Gretel, another would look after Isadora, and the third can mingle and keep an eye on the crowd."

"I'm up for mingling," Wiggles said. "It'll be easier to keep an eye on the canapés supply and make sure nobody's being too greedy if I'm on the move."

"Suki, how about you look after Isadora?" I suggested. Isadora seemed pretty easy going and much nicer than Gretel. I could handle her sharp tongue for an evening when she turned up.

Suki nodded. "I won't leave her side."

Isadora chuckled. "Just hang around in the background and keep an eye on anyone getting too in my face. Fans can be a bit full on, and it gets too much for me. I'm used to being on my own. Crowds make me nervous."

"We'll control the crowd. You don't have to worry about that." Mannie looked around. "I just wish I knew where Gretel was."

"I can look for her," I said.

"Have a quick hunt around but then stay by the main entrance doors," Mannie said. "Maybe she's running late. Isadora, you head to the podium with Suki and get yourself ready."

"And I'll mingle with the catering staff," Wiggles said. "Check they have enough food out."

"Yes, an excellent idea." Mannie clapped his hands together. "Places everybody. The doors open in five minutes."

I strolled into the first room of exhibits and froze. I'd walked into a twisted world of magic. The place looked incredible.

"Welcome, child of the night," a deep voice boomed.

I jumped and spun around. The skeleton in the corner was talking.

"Enjoy your time of freedom, fun, and frivolity. The time of the long night inverts the rules and desires your company."

I backed up and hit a witch. Her arms curled around me. I leaped away, batting at her bony fingers and ragged clothing.

The witch cackled before retreating into her exhibit. This was too creepy for its own good.

The skeleton's bones shook as he laughed. "The long night lures out our darker sides, offering a release from the everyday."

"I'm good with the everyday," I said. "It's weird enough."

"Expose your primeval self."

I shook my head. "I'm exposing nothing to you, buddy."

The skeleton laughed again before sliding behind a door.

I had to admit, it was an immersive experience. Mannie had spared no expense in pulling this together. I could sort of understand everyone's excitement if it was all like this. The glass cases around me glistened, and there were trays to pull out and inspect the artifacts. I was tempted to take a look.

I stopped by a display of witch hats through the ages. The sign said, 'try me on.'

I couldn't resist. I grabbed a typical black pointed hat and stepped in front of the mirror.

"Not your style." The wrinkled face of a witch appeared in the mirror.

Jumping back, I flung off the hat before laughing. It was a neat trick.

I'd almost forgotten what I was supposed to be doing as I wandered around, staring at the ancient torture devices used to extract confessions from witches.

Peering into a glass cabinet, I grimaced. There was a metal mask with spikes on the inside. It was described as a witch talker. It was used as an encouragement to get reluctant witches to reveal their abilities when interrogated.

"I'm glad they don't use that anymore," I muttered.

"Tempest! Any sign of Gretel?" Mannie bustled into the room.

I'd only gotten into the first exhibit room before getting distracted. "No sign of her in here."

"I hope she gets here soon, or I'll have to change the running order of the evening." Mannie frowned. "No matter. This way. I'm about to open the doors."

I followed Mannie into the main entrance foyer. Rows of chairs sat in front of a podium. Behind the podium was a long red curtain.

"Cleo! There you are. Get ready by the door to welcome our guests." Mannie gestured to a short, curvy brunette with tanned skin and silky dark hair who lingered by the chairs.

I'd not seen her in Willow Tree Falls before. She must be a member of Isadora's team.

Cleo nodded and hurried to the double doors to stand opposite me.

Mannie looked around before giving a satisfied nod. "Let the crowd enter."

I opened the doors, with Cleo's assistance.

Mannie stood to one side, shaking hands and kissing the cheeks of all the women.

I kept an eye out for Gretel, but she didn't enter with the crowd. Maybe she had stage fright.

"Take a seat, everybody," Mannie called as the crowd grew and people jostled for space. "We're having a wonderful reading from the renowned author, Isadora Ash, before the museum opens."

Waiters wandered around the crowd, passing out glasses of champagne and tiny filled pastry canapés.

I grabbed a couple of canapés and stuffed them into my mouth. Not bad, cream cheese and smoked salmon.

There wasn't much to do other than crowd watch. Everyone was mingling and making small talk. All the history nerds were behaving themselves as I figured they would.

The sound of a microphone squealing had everyone turning. "Sorry about that. If you'd all like to take a seat, we can get started." Mannie stood on the podium, smiling at everybody.

It took a few minutes, but everyone was soon settled in a seat and waiting for the talk to begin.

I edged around the side of the audience and stood next to Suki and Isadora.

"Is everything okay?" I asked Suki.

"Everything's good on my end," Suki said. "I didn't get much of a look in with the canapés, though. I heard the waiters complaining about a fat dog who keeps knocking them out of their hands."

Trust Wiggles to get in on the canapé action. "Don't worry. Once everyone's looking around the museum, we can eat the leftovers."

Mannie tapped the microphone. "Ladies and gentlemen, please welcome Isadora Ash to our new museum. Her research inspired the wonderful exhibits you'll see tonight. Make her feel welcome."

There was applause as Isadora walked to the podium and nodded thanks at Mannie, who moved to one side.

"Thank you for such a lovely greeting this evening. I'm sure I'm as excited as everybody here to be the first to reveal the exhibits at the Museum of Witchcraft and Magic."

"It's scary back there," Suki muttered to me. "Isadora showed me a couple of the exhibits. They did gruesome things to you witches back in the day."

"They probably still would if they knew we existed," I whispered.

Suki shuddered. "I got jumped on by a ghoul."

"What did you do?"

"Squished him in a headlock." Suki shrugged. "Isadora stopped me before I pulled his head off. He wasn't real, but he sure smelled like he was."

I nodded. The exhibits were pretty spooky.

"I'd like to read you a few passages from my new book," Isadora said. "But, before I do that, I'll reveal the first interactive exhibit of the museum to give you a taste of what's to come." She walked to the side of the curtain and pulled a cord.

The curtain dropped, and the crowd gasped.

Displayed in front of everyone was a small pond, complete with living plants and the deep croaking sound of toads. The stench of fetid water crept across the room. By the side of the pond was a full-sized ducking stool. On that stool was a dead witch.

Everyone applauded as Isadora presented the display with a flourish of her hand.

"This is our first exhibit, which is an interactive experience." Isadora gestured to the lever. "You can duck a witch. And for those brave enough, you can take your place on the ducking stool and see what it felt like to be a witch questioned by those who feared the magic we all possess."

"It looks a bit chilly to me," I whispered to Suki. "I bet that water's not warm."

"Not to mention the smell." Suki held her nose. "I've never been a fan of water. This reminds me of the swamp in the forest."

A movement by the ducking stool caught my eye. I stepped away from Suki and peered closely at the rushes planted by the pond. Wiggles was poking around in the middle of the display.

I gestured for him to come away, but he ignored me and continued sniffing.

Isadora had returned to the podium and was reading from her book, drawing the audience's attention back to her.

I inched closer to the display, not keen to draw any attention. "Wiggles! Get out of there before you break something."

He looked at me, and his red eyes glowed. He lowered his snout into the water and snorted loudly.

I shook my head. He most likely wanted to be the first to take a ride on the ducking stool.

When Wiggles' head emerged from the water, he held the witch's leg in his mouth.

That leg looked worryingly real. The skin was puffy and blotchy, nothing like a mannequin's leg.

Glancing at Isadora to make sure I wasn't disturbing her, I ducked and concealed myself with the plants as I crawled on my hands and knees marine-style toward Wiggles. As I got closer, my nose wrinkled. There was an unhealthy smell lingering in the water, and it wasn't pond scum.

"Put the leg down," I whispered to Wiggles.

He spat the leg out. "Happily. I knew I smelled something odd. They're using a real body for the exhibit. How true to life is that?"

True to life! I sat up and heard several of the audience members murmur as they saw me.

"Is that Tempest?" I heard Granny Dottie say. "Coooeeee! Tempest. I didn't know you were a part of this exhibit."

I ignored my embarrassing family as I lifted the head of the witch sitting in the ducking stool.

I gasped as I stared into the very lifeless eyes of Gretel Le Strange.

Chapter 3

The book fell from Isadora's hand as she turned and saw me beside the dead witch. "Is that Gretel?"

I lowered Gretel's head back to her chest. "I'm afraid so." That explained why she hadn't shown up for the museum opening. She was already here, but not in the role I imagined she wanted to be.

"Tempest, what's going on?" Mannie hissed as he hurried over. "You're making the audience worry."

"They need to worry." I stood and wiped my damp hands down my tuxedo pants. "This is a crime scene. The witch in the ducking stool is Gretel Le Strange."

Mannie gasped and staggered back. "That's not possible."

"You said she was missing. It turns out, she's not missing. She's dead." The audience was murmuring, and I felt the panic grow in the room. "We need to clear this place," I said to Mannie. "Any evidence that might show who did this to Gretel will be destroyed with so many people in the room."

Mannie stared at me. "What about the opening? It's been arranged for such a long time."

"What about the dead body?"

His lips pursed. "Of course. We need to move Gretel before the evening can continue."

I gaped at him. "There's not going to be any evening. Somebody's been murdered in the museum."

"Murder!" A woman in the front row rose from her seat and craned her neck. "What's that about murder?"

The word spread quickly, and soon the rest of the crowd were on their feet, pushing closer to get a better look.

"Suki! Wiggles! We need crowd control," I shouted.

They jumped in front of the podium and kept the crowd from getting too nosy.

"Get everyone out of here," I said to Mannie. "Now."

"Very well." Mannie huffed before hurrying to the podium. "Ladies and gentlemen, if I may have your attention. There's been a small accident. I'm afraid the evening will have to be postponed for a few hours."

The crowd murmured their disapproval and shuffled uneasily.

"What's going on?" someone shouted.

"It's nothing to worry about," Mannie lied. "A small technical difficulty."

"Is that a real body?" another person yelled.

"Of course not." Mannie's laugh sounded forced. "Everything is fine. You all need to leave for now, though. Perhaps we'll have a second go at the opening tomorrow night. I'll make sure we have extra champagne to make up for this unfortunate incident."

I shook my head as I stared at Gretel. There'd be no chance of opening this museum anytime soon. Not with a dead body on our hands.

The audience remained where they were as if expecting a show.

I moved away from the ducking stool and stood with Suki and Wiggles. "Let's clear this lot out. Herd them like sheep toward the door. Prod anyone who doesn't look like they're going to move."

Between the three of us, we forced the grumbling crowd to the main doors. After ten minutes of gentle shoving, everyone was outside.

I locked the door behind them. "We need Angel Force here."

"I'll send a message via the snow globe," Mannie said. "We have one in the back office." He bustled away.

"What do you need us to do?" Suki asked, her shades slipping down her nose.

"Nothing for now. Just try to avoid messing with the crime scene."

"Hey! Here's a plate of canapés," Wiggles called. "They've only been trodden on a couple of times. Plenty are undamaged."

Suki hurried over and sat on the floor with Wiggles to inspect the trampled food.

"Do you want one?" Wiggles glanced at me.

"I'm good." Wiggles would eat anything, and it looked like Suki wasn't all that fussy either.

A fist pounded against the door. I cracked it open and peered out to see Dominic and Sablo standing outside, their white angel uniforms gleaming in the gloom.

"That was quick." I pulled the door open wider and let them in before locking it again.

"What are you talking about?" Sablo's long blonde hair was wrapped in a thick coil on top of her head.

"Mannie only just sent the message."

Sablo exchanged a confused glance with Dominic. "We saw no message. We were passing on our way to grab a pizza and saw the crowd outside. We thought we'd better see if everything was okay."

"We can't be long," Dominic said. "Our pizza will be ready in five minutes." He grinned at me. "You're welcome to a slice of mine, Tempest."

"The pizza will have to wait," I said. "There's been a murder."

Sablo took a step back, and her wings fluttered behind her. "Are you sure?"

"There's the body of a witch on the museum's ducking stool. It's doubtful she ducked herself," I said. "You'd better take a look."

Sablo and Dominic hurried after me as I returned to the exhibit.

They stood staring at Gretel for a minute, neither of them saying anything.

"This is terrible timing," Sablo said.

"I'm sure Gretel will agree," I said. "She was here to show off her knowledge at the opening event, not be drowned on a ducking stool."

"Oh, it's not that." Sablo glanced at Dominic. "Dazielle's away."

"Then she needs to come back." Dazielle could be stubborn and sometimes followed the wrong clues, but she usually saw sense in the end. Sablo and Dominic, not so much.

"She's on an immersive course outside of the village. I don't think they get access to their snow globes."

"So, who's in charge?"

Dominic scratched the back of his head. "We sort of all are. We operate a cooperative system at Angel Force. When the boss is away, we all get a say in how things are run."

I repressed a groan. All that meant was no one would take charge of this murder investigation.

Mannie hurried over. He tugged at my arm and tilted his head to the side. "I need to speak with you in private."

I followed him, leaving the angels to puzzle over what to do next. "What's up?"

"You have to deal with this problem," he said. "The museum will be ruined if this doesn't get sorted quickly."

"You've got Sablo and Dominic here." I glanced over to see Dominic toying with the lever on the ducking stool. I could tell he was itching to give it a tug. "They'll figure things out."

Mannie curled his beard around his fingers. "Tempest, we both know what the angels are like when Dazielle's not here."

"Are you referring to the incident three years ago?" I grinned.

He nodded. "We were finding feathers six months after that party."

I held my laughter in. The last time Dazielle had been away, the angels had had the equivalent of a frat party at a thermal spa. Three hundred drunken angels had gate-crashed the party and run amok through Willow Tree Falls. It was epic.

"We didn't have a murder to deal with then," I said. "I'm sure they'll sort this out. They can be professional when they need to be."

Mannie's expression was pensive. "Dazielle knows how to take charge and get things moving. And these two are..."

"Pretty but ineffective?"

"Something like that," Mannie said. "You'll have to help them figure out what happened."

"Mannie, I've already stepped up as your security detail for the night. That's enough."

"And look what happened." Mannie gestured around the deserted room. "My audience fled in terror, and someone's been murdered. I call that terrible security work."

I scowled at him. "Gretel wasn't murdered on my watch. That body has been in the water for a while."

"You see! You know about this sort of thing, and you found the body. You're good at this. I know Dazielle complains about you—"

"What does she say?"

"Oh, the usual." Mannie wouldn't meet my glare. "She thinks you interfere."

"And I definitely will be interfering if I investigate this case when she's not here."

Mannie grabbed hold of my hands. "Please, you have to sort this out. What can I give you to convince you to step up and lead on this investigation?"

"Nothing! I didn't know Gretel. I only met her briefly yesterday. You need to find out who'd want to kill her in such a public way. Someone clearly didn't like Gretel and needed everyone to see what they thought of her."

"There you go. You're already thinking about the reasons for her murder. Anything you want, it's yours. I can pay for a holiday, or how about a car? You're always walking around everywhere. That must be exhausting."

I tried to pull my hands from his hot grasp, but he held on tight. "Mannie, I don't need a holiday or a car. I don't even drive."

"Someone has to lead on this. It doesn't need to be for long, just until Dazielle returns from her course."

My brow wrinkled. "How long will that be?"

"A day or two at the most. No time at all. You just need to do the basics. Collect evidence, talk to suspects, figure this out. A smart young witch like you should have no trouble dealing with this."

I finally extracted my hands from Mannie's grip. "If I'm investigating this, you'll be a suspect."

Surprise registered on Mannie's face. "Me! A suspect. I was friends with Gretel."

"If you want me to do this, I'm doing it properly."

He huffed out a breath. "Very well. I suppose it's only right you ask me appropriate questions, but I can assure you I'm not involved."

I looked around the room. Sablo and Dominic still stood looking perplexed by the body. If I did nothing to help, they'd probably leave Gretel attached to the ducking stool for anyone to gawp at.

"I'll do this. Just until Dazielle returns." I lifted my chin. "I get to question whoever I need to, and you don't interfere."

Mannie sighed. "Thank you, Tempest. Anything you need, it's yours. Gretel was a friend. It's terrible what's happened to her. I need a nip of brandy for the shock."

I nodded. "First things first, I need you to round up everyone close to Gretel. We might as well start there. Anyone who's been working with her at this museum could be involved. I must speak to them all."

"Of course. I'll get right on that." Mannie hurried away.

I was surprised he was following my orders. Maybe this wouldn't be so difficult to deal with.

I turned and walked back to Dominic and Sablo. "Good news. You have a new boss."

Dominic grinned at me. "Mannie's put you in charge of running Angel Force?"

I choked out a laugh. "Not for a second, and I'd never agree to do that. He wants me to lead on this investigation. Do either of you have a problem with that?"

"I think it's brilliant," Dominic said. "I always enjoy hanging out with you."

Sablo's eyes narrowed, but she nodded. "I don't see it being a problem. You've helped us in the past. With Dazielle away, we'd appreciate an extra pair of hands."

"What do you want us to do, boss?" Dominic asked.

I looked at Gretel, and my stomach clenched. I was never good with dealing with the more gruesome side of murder. "Secure the crime scene and control entry. It's been contaminated enough. No one else goes near the body. There might be clues as to who did this. Get photos of the scene, including pictures of Gretel before she's moved out of the water."

"Wow! Tempest, you know what you're talking about," Dominic said. "You sound just like Dazielle."

"I've heard her bark orders at you enough times to know the drill," I said. "Look around for any signs of who did this, but don't touch, just document. Gretel didn't put herself in that ducking stool, which means someone else is involved. They might have left behind a clue."

"No problem," Dominic said. "I'll head back to the office and grab the equipment."

"Get the pizza, too," Sablo whispered.

I glared at her but then shrugged. Pizza sounded good after only a few puff pastries. "Pizza too. Get extra for everyone. Be quick. When you get back, you need to keep everyone separate. We don't need our suspects fudging their alibis."

"Got it."

"Sablo, you stay with Gretel until Dominic returns."

Sablo nodded and clasped her hands behind her back, her gaze darting around the room as if looking for an attacker.

I walked over to Suki, who stood by the door with Wiggles, the tray of squashed food long gone. "You might as well head back to Cloven Hoof. There's not much you can do here."

Suki's nervous gaze shifted to the body before she grimaced. "If you're sure. I can stay if you like, but..."

"No, you've been great tonight. Go grab a coffee and take a break, make sure everything is fine at the bar. Some museum visitors might have stopped off there, so it could be busy. We won't be too long."

Suki nodded, her relief obvious, before hurrying out of the museum.

I turned as I heard footsteps.

Isadora walked over, her face pale. "Do you know what happened?"

"Someone wanted Gretel out of the way. Any idea who that might be?"

Isadora's hand went to her mouth, and she swallowed loudly. "Gretel was a strong woman. Whoever did this would need to be equally as strong."

"What were her powers?"

"She was an elemental witch with a liking for old magic. She had a collection of artifacts that had residual magic in them. She enjoyed indulging in the old stuff. It makes sense. That was where her passion lay."

"Her ability was strong?"

Isadora nodded. "And she was never one to be walked over. Gretel would have fought back if someone attacked her. It would need someone with strong magic to hold her in place and use the ducking stool to kill her." She looked away and wiped a hand across her cheek.

"Is everyone still here?" I asked. "I need to speak with you all."

"Oh, yes. Mannie asked us to stay. We're in the red exhibit room."

I took a deep breath. I wasn't certain where to start, but I recalled the comment Seth had made about Gretel being a problem.

Since he hadn't had anything nice to say about our victim, I'd start with him and see if he'd acted on his low opinion of Gretel Le Strange.

Chapter 4

I walked into the red exhibit room with Isadora and looked around at the anxious faces. Mannie stood with Seth and Jonah. Lotus stood apart from the group with Cleo.

It wasn't ideal that all the suspects and witnesses were together, but Dominic would be back soon to separate everyone.

"Seth." I gestured him over.

Isadora nodded at me. "I'll leave you to it." She hurried away and joined Lotus and Cleo.

Seth strolled over. "I hear Mannie put you in charge."

"Lucky me," I said. "I'd like to talk to you about your relationship with Gretel."

"There's not much to say. I'll help if I can."

"How well did you know her?"

"As well as I wanted to." Seth shoved his hands into his pants pockets and leaned back on his heels. "I know I'm the first person you're talking to about her, but I'll be honest with you. Gretel was a hard person to like."

"You didn't like her?"

"No one did. If they tell you differently, you've found your killer. Gretel Le Strange was sharp, rude, and full of herself." Seth shrugged. "In a way, she had a right to be. She was at the top of her field. If anyone had a question about some historical magic artifact, Gretel was your go to woman."

"Did she do anything, in particular, to make you dislike her?"

"She didn't go out of her way to target me. She was just a beast to anyone who got in her way. People let her get away with being obnoxious and rude for so long that it became her default mode. Gretel considered everyone else beneath her because they weren't as clever as she was."

"What did you mean when you said that Gretel was a pain in people's backsides?"

"Nothing was ever good enough for that woman. She drove me almost to distraction by her demands."

"What was she demanding from you?"

"Gretel saw this museum as hers. Mannie brought her in as an adviser because of her expertise, but she was soon claiming this was her idea. That sat badly with everyone who made this happen."

"That must have annoyed the whole team."

"Of course." Seth shook his head. "The worst thing is, Gretel demanded that she be interviewed about the museum."

"And she wanted you to set that up?"

"I'm a book publicist. I know how to arrange a few interviews, but I'd never arrange a single interview for Gretel. She'd annoy everyone because she'd be rude." Seth glanced at Isadora. "Isadora, on the other hand, is a dream to work with. She's my client. She was the one going in front of the cameras and talking about her book and its links to this museum. She has a way of making the dullest subject interesting."

"And Gretel didn't like that Isadora had all the limelight?"

Seth shrugged. "Professional rivalry, I guess. Call it what you like, but Gretel wasn't camera ready. I rejected her suggestion, and she made my life difficult after that. I kept out of her way, but the closer it got to the launch of Isadora's book and the opening of this museum, we couldn't avoid each other."

"Since she was making your life so difficult, did you do something about it?"

Seth smirked. "Sweetheart, you obviously don't work in PR."

I narrowed my eyes. "No, but I do hunt annoying demons for fun. And any magic using creature who gets on my wrong side."

Seth tilted his head. "Oh, you're the witch who hunts demons. I've heard of you. You've got an interesting reputation. I could make a book out of your story if you're interested."

"I'm not."

"And you're freelancing with the angels now? Even more of an interesting twist."

"It's a temporary thing," I said. "Who have you been talking to about me?"

"Word gets around. And I know Brogan Costin. We're old acquaintances. He mentioned you when I dropped by his café last night."

Half-vampires were a close-knit group, so I wasn't surprised to hear that Brogan and Seth knew each other. "Getting back to Gretel's death, where were you last night?"

"I grabbed a bite to eat. Brogan will confirm that, and then I headed to the local pub. I think it's called the Ancient Imp. I was there all evening."

"And after you left the pub?"

"I went back to the house."

"Where are you staying?"

"Mannie's rented us a place while we're here. We didn't fancy staying in the local hotel, so he got us a house for a couple of weeks. I'm there, along with Isadora, Lotus, and Jonah. It's a decent place, lots of space to work in. It's along Luminaire Lane. Number six."

I knew the place. "Who do you think would want Gretel dead and displayed so dramatically?"

"I can give you a long list of people who Gretel irritated. As for killing her, I don't know. You'd need to search back fifty years. There will be a lot of people who won't be sad she's gone."

"I'm more interested in the people here."

Seth's bottom lip jutted out. "It's a gruesome way to go. Killed by her own exhibit. Gretel was fascinated by witch trials. She's written several papers on that period in history. They're a bit dry for my taste, but Isadora used some of Gretel's research in her book. Sprinkle them with a little movie magic and they'd make a great fantasy production."

"I'm sure that would have made Gretel happy, seeing her research manipulated for a movie."

Seth chuckled. "I never mentioned the idea for exactly that reason. Now she's gone, the door's open to different income generating opportunities."

That gave Seth a motive. He saw Gretel as a cash cow, but only if she agreed to sell out. Something I doubted she would do.

"Who knew there'd be a ducking stool in the museum?"

"It was kept quiet, just between the team, so we wouldn't spoil the unveiling. We had parts made by different companies, so no one would figure out we were creating a working model of a ducking stool. Everyone you see in this room knew, but that's about it."

"What about other members of the team? Did Lotus or Jonah have much to do with Gretel?"

"Jonah spends all his time with Isadora. She works long hours, and he needs to be close by for whenever she needs anything. I expect their paths crossed, but I've never heard him complain about her."

"And Lotus?"

Seth grinned. "She's as sweet as apple pie. Lotus has never got a bad word to say about anybody."

I arched a brow. "The two of you are close?"

He smiled smugly. "As close as you can be. I met Lotus after I started working with Isadora to put together the publicity campaign. Lotus does background research for Isadora's books."

"It's serious between you?"

Seth nodded. "If she plays her cards right, we'll soon be married. She knows she won't find anyone better."

"You do sound like a catch." Not anything I'd be hurrying to grab anytime soon.

"Lotus does what I tell her because I'm always right. It's the perfect match."

"I hope you're happy together," I said. Seth's smugness set my teeth on edge. It wasn't an uncommon vampire trait, but he talked about Lotus as if he owned her.

"Can you think of anyone who disliked Gretel, who would act on those feelings?"

Seth looked around the room. "Well, I don't like to mention it, since he's such a respected figure in the village."

"Mention away," I said.

"I saw your mayor arguing with Gretel. She pestered him all the time about things not being right at the museum. Although he laughed off her comments, I could see they grated on him. I walked in on them two days ago in a fierce debate about the layout of a display. Gretel was in his face, shouting at him. Mannie's cheeks were bright red. I thought he'd burst a blood vessel."

"I know Mannie Winter well. I can't see him killing Gretel. As you pointed out, he's a public figure."

Seth smirked. "If you know Mannie as well as you say you do, then you'll know what he's like when it comes to his social status."

Mannie was a serious social climber but killing someone would do nothing to enhance that status. "What makes you say that?"

"Mannie mentioned how great he'd be in a documentary. He suggested we do a series in

Willow Tree Falls featuring local residents. A sort of faux reality series."

That sounded like a nightmare. "That won't interest anybody."

"You'd be surprised what trash people watch." Seth tipped back on his heels. "Mannie wants a starring role."

"Mannie has big ambitions. Was Gretel stopping him from achieving them?"

"She could have been. Mannie was jealous of Gretel and the respect her position gave her. He has himself up as some kind of know-it-all historian, but Gretel was quick to knock him on his behind if he got a fact wrong. They were competitive, and both hated to back down."

Could things have gotten out of hand with Gretel when they were arguing? Mannie was powerfully built even if most of his weight was stored in his expansive gut. It wasn't out of the question that he had the strength to hold Gretel on the ducking stool before drowning her.

"Did you see Mannie here last night?" I asked Seth.

"Only for a couple of minutes early on in the evening. He was running around trying to get this organized."

"Did you see him near the ducking stool?" Mannie might have investigated the stool to see how easy it would be to use.

Seth shook his head. "No, but he'd know how to work it. Mannie had a tedious argument with Gretel about the mechanisms of the ducking stool and how you'd get one to work, the kind of weight you need, and the..." he yawned. "Sorry, I'm boring myself. Anyway, they argued, and he knew what he was talking about."

This wasn't looking so great for Mannie. He knew how to operate the ducking stool, and he didn't like the victim. I couldn't rule him out just yet.

"You're wasting your time by quizzing me, gorgeous," Seth said. "I didn't do this. I've got an alibi, and it's a good one. If you're looking for a killer, go speak to your friendly mayor. I bet he's got a tale to tell. Are we done?"

I gritted my teeth but nodded. Gretel had rubbed Seth up the wrong way, but his alibi would be easy to check, and I could discount him as the killer. "You can leave. Are you staying at the house?"

"Sure. We've got a mess to sort out after tonight's event. I need to figure out the next steps for Isadora. Make sure her book doesn't flop."

I watched him saunter away. If everything Seth said was true, I had a problem on my hands. It was dwarf-shaped and had a huge beard. I couldn't go accusing Willow Tree Falls' mayor of murder without cast iron proof. If I did that and was wrong, the village would be in an uproar, and Mannie would most likely shove me on the ducking stool next.

I needed to be careful how I handled this. If I was seen interrogating Mannie Winter, there could be hell to pay.

Chapter 5

I decided to tackle the other members of Isadora's team before approaching Mannie, see if they supported Seth's theory that Mannie could be involved.

Walking across the room, I wasn't happy to find Mannie and Isadora talking quietly in one corner. I looked around and glared at Dominic, who was studying an artifact in the cabinet, a piece of pizza in one hand.

I hurried over to him. "You're supposed to be keeping the suspects separate."

He jumped and turned toward me. "Oh, sorry, Tempest. I got distracted. Have you seen this? It's a hand of glory."

I glanced at the mummified hand. "It is."

"Do you own one?"

"No. They're only for black magic." Although, I bet there was one covered in dust in Mom's attic. She loved collecting weird magic items.

Dominic continued to eat his pizza. "This is the severed hand of a hanged criminal."

"They all are. It makes them more powerful."

"Have you ever touched one?"

"Sure. Now, about this murder investigation you're helping me solve." I glanced at the suspects. "We have to get people apart. Use the extra pizza you got to lure them away."

"Extra pizza?"

I pursed my lips. "Yes, the pizza I asked you to get for all of us."

"Oh! Sure. That slipped my mind. I only picked up the order for me and Sablo. I guess I'm in shock over what happened to Gretel."

I sighed. "So, no pizza?"

He held out his crust. "You're welcome to this."

I wrinkled my nose. "I'll pass."

Dominic nodded. "It says here you use a blend of salt, long peppers, nitre, and zimat to pickle the hand."

"That's right." It looked like he wasn't budging until he'd educated himself on the hand of glory. I was tempted to get it out of the glass case and use it on him as a punishment for forgetting the pizza and not doing his job.

"It's creepy."

"It's dark magic. It's meant to be creepy. You get the hand to hold a lit candle. It enhances a spells power. If the candle was made from the dead person's fat, that's a bonus."

Dominic swallowed his pizza crust and grimaced. "Witches are strange."

"Angels can be too, especially when they're not doing the job they're supposed to do." I grabbed his arm and tugged him away from the display case. "Keep Mannie and Isadora apart. If they've got anything to do with what happened to Gretel, they could be fixing their stories while you're staring at a dead man's hand."

"Of course, all my fault." He tilted his head. "But you can't think Mannie has anything to do with this. He's our mayor. Everybody loves the mayor. He pays for the winter parade out of his own pocket."

"Everybody won't love the mayor if it turns out he killed Gretel. But I won't know that if he's fudging his story and getting Isadora to cover for him."

Dominic bit his bottom lip. "Dazielle's always telling me off for getting distracted on the job."

I raised my eyebrows. "Dazielle and I agree on that. Go over there and get Isadora away from Mannie."

Dominic's wings wilted as he walked away. He looked like a scolded puppy. It was hard to stay cross with him when he looked like that. There wasn't a mean bone in Dominic's toned body, just lots of foolish ones.

Mannie glanced up as Dominic spoke to him and then looked at me. I didn't like the determined expression on his face as he hurried over.

"Tempest, surely that's enough for one evening."

"You want me to stop questioning people who might be involved in Gretel's death? I've only spoken to one person."

"I know, but I've been asking around, and everyone's in shock." Mannie glanced over his shoulder. "And Isadora is feeling ill. She needs to lie down before she faints."

"Maybe she's feeling ill because she murdered someone."

"Shush! Don't say such a thing." Mannie grabbed my arm and pulled me out of earshot of Isadora. "She's a respected, talented author. Isadora has worked hard all her life to get to this point in her career. We're lucky to have her in Willow Tree Falls."

"That still doesn't rule her out as the killer," I said. "I have to speak to everyone tonight while the information is fresh in their minds. And, if someone here is the killer, what's to say they won't sneak away if we give them the night off to get over their shock?"

"No one's sneaking anywhere," Mannie said. "I know where everyone is staying. They've assured me they'll stay for as long as this needs to be cleared up."

I tilted my head back. That meant Mannie had spoken to everyone. So much for trying to keep people apart. I glanced at the ducking stool. "Where's Sablo?"

"I sent her to get a round of drinks and some muffins. I thought sugar would be good to calm everyone."

"Sablo agreed to that?" I spoke through gritted teeth.

"Of course. She trusts me. Everyone does." Mannie patted my arm. "Let's do this tomorrow morning. It'll give you time to think about the questions you need to ask, and we can all get a good night's sleep to help get over the shock. Poor Gretel."

Poor Gretel, indeed! This case wasn't going anywhere if everyone was chatting, sharing alibis, and covering for each other. "I need to take a step back from this. You agreed I could do this my way, but you're already interfering."

Mannie stroked a hand down his beard. "You do want that noise violation to disappear?"

"Hey! I agreed to do the security detail in exchange for that vanishing. You said nothing about having to solve this murder as well. That wasn't part of our agreement."

Mannie shrugged. "The deal's changed. I still haven't heard anything from Dazielle, so you need to stay on this until she's back."

"I'm trying, but you're suggesting we give up for the night. Dazielle wouldn't do that."

"We need to handle this carefully." Mannie patted his belly. "We're dealing with important people. People of influence."

"And one of those influential people is now dead," I said. "The sooner we clear that up, the better. Let me question everyone tonight, and this could all be over by tomorrow."

"My dear Tempest, while I appreciate your involvement, it's late and everybody's tired."

"But—"

"And, as Mayor of Willow Tree Falls, I insist we treat our VIP guests appropriately. Whatever happened here is unfortunate, but I think it highly unlikely that anyone involved with the museum would stoop to murder. We're a respectable bunch. We wouldn't sink to the depths of such depravity."

"Will you take responsibility if a suspect vanishes overnight? I'm not taking the fall for this if they make a run for it because you thought everyone looked a little stressed."

Mannie's eyes narrowed. "By suspects, if you mean Isadora's team, then yes. I have no qualms in vouching for any of them. I've gotten to know them all since they arrived. They're not involved in this."

I shrugged, stamping on my irritation. Mannie had dragged me into this, but he wasn't going to drag me down with him if it turned out one of his so-called respectable suspects had murdered Gretel. "Then everybody can leave, under your authority."

"That doesn't mean you give up on this investigation," Mannie said. "I still expect you to do your job."

My fingers flexed, and I sucked in a deep breath to stop from saying something I'd regret. "Of course, Mayor. I'm always happy to help."

Mannie patted his stomach and nodded. "Excellent. I'll send everybody home, and you can deal with the... situation on the ducking stool."

I watched him bustle around and share the good news that the suspects could leave and have time to sort out their alibis, so I'd never find out who killed Gretel.

"Tempest, is there anything we can do to help?"

I turned to find Dominic standing behind me. "We're putting this investigation on hold for the night."

"Oh! Sure. Great! My feet ache."

I pressed my lips together. "Have you gotten what you need from Gretel?"

"Not yet." His easy smile faded. "There is one tiny problem."

Of course, there was. "And that is…"

"We can't get hold of anyone to deal with the body," Dominic said.

"Can't you take Gretel to Angel Force?"

He shook his head. "It's always Cassiel who deals with the body. She's great at handling the gross bits."

"The gross bits!"

Dominic cleared his throat. "I mean, Cassiel knows how to handle the bodies and doesn't mind what state they're in. She's interested in dead bodies."

"If she's not around, you and Sablo will have to step up." I glared at him until he nodded.

"We won't move her, but we can preserve the scene. We'll use a spell to ensure nothing degrades."

"So, you turned up nothing useful at the crime scene?"

"Not yet. We can—"

"That's enough for tonight, Tempest." Mannie hurried over. "Everyone's on their way home. These fine angels can look after the situation here until the morning."

Dominic's eyebrows shot up. "You want us to stay here all night?"

"That won't be a problem, will it?" Mannie patted Dominic's arm. "A fine, upstanding angel like yourself is just what we need in a time of crisis."

Dominic's face paled before he nodded. "Whatever you say, Mayor."

I felt a little sorry for Dominic. He wasn't a natural in law enforcement. He was a big, feathery frat boy who was after an easy life and a good time. Weren't we all?

"Let's take another look at the scene now," I said to him. "It's quiet, which will help us focus."

"Start afresh tomorrow," Mannie said. "Dominic and Sablo will take care of things here. You go home. Sablo will be back soon with coffee and treats to keep them going."

"Five minutes," I said. "It's not a problem."

"No! The angels will guard the scene." Mannie gestured at Dominic. "Don't let anyone near the crime scene, not until the morning. I want to be here when you look around."

"Whatever you say," Dominic said. "No one gets in without us knowing about it."

"Good work." Mannie glanced at me. "I'll meet you back here tomorrow morning."

This investigation was a disaster, thanks to Mannie's interference. I should have accepted the noise violation and paid the fine. It would have been worth it to avoid this stress.

"You're the boss," I said.

Dominic looked almost panicked. "We really have to stay the whole night?"

Sablo walked over to join him, a large bag in one hand and a tray of paper cups of coffee in the other. "What's going on? Where's everyone gone?"

"We've got to stay here," Dominic said glumly.

Her eyes widened. "Is that necessary?"

"By order of the mayor," I said. "No one's allowed to come in until tomorrow."

Mannie nodded. "You two keep everything safe until then."

"Oh! Well, sure, we can do that." Sablo glanced at Dominic and shrugged.

Dominic turned his concerned face to me. "Any instructions?"

"Drink lots of coffee and try not to fall asleep." I turned and left the museum with Wiggles, eager to put distance between me and Mannie before I yanked his beard and called him all kinds of inappropriate names.

"That was some party," Wiggles said.

"We're never going to find out who killed Gretel." I stamped away from the building. "I don't know what Mannie's playing at."

"I do," Wiggles said. "Our dwarf could be guilty."

"Mannie Winter, a killer?" I shook my head. "Annoying. Full of his own self-importance. A pain in my behind but not a murderer."

"Why is he so keen on stopping you from talking to everybody?"

"Because he doesn't want to put his VIP guests' noses out of joint," I said. "Did you see how he was drooling over Isadora? Maybe she's on his list to be the next Mrs. Winter."

"Or, he's giving himself time to get his story straight." Wiggles trotted next to me. "If he killed Gretel last night, he'd need to firm up his alibi and make sure there's no chance of him coming under suspicion."

I looked back at the museum. "Mannie wouldn't risk his reputation as mayor to get rid of Gretel, would he?"

"Tempest!"

I turned and spotted Mom and Granny Dottie striding toward the cemetery. I walked over to meet them. "Hi, going to check on Aurora?"

"That's right," Granny Dottie said. "How's everything going at the museum? We tried to get a look at the body, but we were ushered out."

"It wasn't pleasant to look at," I said. "She'd been on the ducking stool for a while."

"Wrinkled up like a giant pink prune, I expect," Granny Dottie said. "That always happens to me when I've been in the tub for too long."

I grimaced. "Pretty much."

"How terrible," Mom said. "We heard someone say the name Gretel. Is that the woman who died?"

"Yes, she was a friend of Mannie's," I said. "Gretel Le Strange. She was something big in the history of witchcraft and magic."

"And why are you still involved?" Granny Dottie straightened my lapel. "I thought your job was security."

"Dazielle's not around, and Mannie twisted my arm to look into things until she gets back," I said. "Although, I'm beginning to think he's not being totally honest."

"Our mayor, not honest." Granny Dottie chortled. "As if there's such a thing as a dishonest public figure."

"He's acting shady. Mannie stopped me from talking to the people who knew Gretel, the people who are most likely to have killed her."

"Watch out for Mannie Winter," Mom cautioned. "He's always got a twinkle in his eye for an attractive young lady."

I shuddered. "I'll keep out of his reach. I don't think he'd dare make a move on me."

Grannie Dottie chuckled. "I'd like to see him try. I imagine a few fireballs aimed at that oiled beard of his, and he'd soon change his mind. He'd go up like a tinder block."

We all laughed, but I noticed Mom's attention was directed at the cemetery.

"Is everything okay at the prison?" I asked her.

"Oh, the prison's fine." She turned back to me, but her smile looked strained.

"Mom, what is it?"

"Aurora's lost weight," she said.

"She has? I hadn't noticed." But then, I'd barely seen Aurora. We were still treading on eggshells whenever we were around each other.

"And she didn't open Heaven's Door for two days last week."

"I noticed the store was shut," I said. "I wondered if she was having work done inside."

"Aurora hasn't said anything if that's what she's doing," Mom said. "In fact, she's been tricky to talk to. I want to discuss her wedding plans and see if she needs a hand with anything. When was the last time you spoke with her?"

Guilt trickled down my spine. I deliberately hadn't been talking to Aurora. I thought distance might do us some good. Every time I talked to her about Toby Matlock, I lost my temper, and that only drove Aurora further from me.

"Not for a while," I said.

"You haven't discussed any of her wedding plans?" Mom asked. "As her only sister, she'll want you involved."

Granny Dottie shook her head. "I still can't believe Aurora agreed to marry that wrinkly old warlock. He's as rich as the King of Sweden, but there's only so much money can smooth over."

"I haven't warmed to him either," I said. "There's something not right about Toby."

"Don't say that to your sister," Mom said. "She's besotted with him. I tried to corner him a couple of times in the crypt when they made their announcement. I wanted to get information out of him about their future plans, but he kept avoiding me. Toby also didn't let Aurora out of his sight for more than a few minutes, so it was hard to get him on his own."

"Aurora could just be nervous about the wedding," Granny Dottie said. "I would be if I was marrying Toby Matlock."

"Don't say they've set a date," I said.

"Not that we know of." Mom turned back to the cemetery. "Aurora's been so distracted. I wish you'd talk to her."

"She'll confide in her big sister if she's having problems." Granny Dottie patted my arm. "You two have always been close."

We had until recently. I needed to fix things with Aurora, especially if she was having a hard time. I hated the thought of her having doubts about her relationship with Toby but not feeling comfortable turning to me for advice.

"I'll look out for her," I said. "See what I can find out."

"Yes, we all will," Mom said. "Don't let that distract you from your business here. If you're involved in this murder investigation, you need to focus."

"I will if Mannie lets me," I said. "He's going to want to stick his nose into everything I do. If he does that too many times, I might find myself arrested by the angels for his murder."

"Tempest! Don't say such a thing," Mom said. "You don't go around telling people you're going to kill our mayor."

"I'm sure a lot of people have thought it," Granny Dottie said. "He can be an officious little toad."

There was a gentle rumble under our feet, and we all tensed.

"That came from the cemetery," Mom said.

Granny Dottie rolled her shoulders. "A new crack must have formed."

Mom grabbed her arm. "Let's go. Aurora's on her own."

"Do you need any help?" I called to their retreating backs, always amazed at how fast they ran when they sensed trouble.

Mom waved a hand in the air. "We'll be fine. Make sure you see your sister soon."

I watched them race toward the cemetery. As much as I loved Aurora, I wasn't sure how to make things right with her. We would never agree on her relationship with Toby.

I had to figure out how to have Aurora in my life without us exploding at each other every time Toby Matlock was mentioned. It was either that or dig up enough dirt on him to convince her she was with the wrong guy. So far, my attempts to do that had led me down several dead ends, and my sister wasn't talking to me.

"Those canapés didn't fill me up," Wiggles said. "I ate a whole tray, and I'm already hungry."

"We can have a late dinner if you like," I said.

"Now you're talking," Wiggles said. "What are you thinking?"

"How about the Unicorn's Trough? We can check Seth's alibi and see what Brogan knows about him."

"He was one smooth talking half-vampire," Wiggles said. "But he knows how to pick cute girlfriends. Lotus is adorable. We don't get many elves around here. She gave me a belly rub while I was waiting for you."

"You also don't get many elves interested in vampires," I said. "Let's get something to eat and see if we can figure out this murder before I end up committing one of my own."

Chapter 6

The Unicorn's Trough only had a few diners when we entered. It was past most people's dinnertime, so we had the pick of the tables. I strolled to the counter and checked out the specials board.

Brogan wandered over, his shirt sleeves pushed up to reveal the intricate tattoos on his forearms. "I heard about some fun at the new museum."

"News gets out fast," I said. "Mannie's grand opening plan ended in a watery disaster."

Brogan arched a dark eyebrow. "Was there really a dead witch on the ducking stool?"

"There was. No one from here, though. Gretel was helping Mannie to set up the museum. I didn't know her, but from what I've heard so far, she wasn't popular."

"Even so, it's a terrible way to go. Are you here for something to eat or to quiz my diners?"

"We're only here for the food," Wiggles said. "As soon as Tempest makes up her mind." He nudged me with his nose.

"And some information if you can spare us the time."

Brogan nodded as he looked around. "It's not busy. Everyone's order is in, and I haven't eaten. Mind if I join you?"

"Of course not," I said. "What's good tonight?"

He grinned. "Everything's good. I recommend the ham hock, cider, and green peppercorn pie with creamy mash and maple glazed carrots."

My mouth watered. "I'll have two of those."

"Be right back." Brogan strolled away to place our order.

I settled in a seat by the window, and Wiggles joined me.

"I know you're dating Rhett," Wiggles said, "but it's always good to keep your options open."

I looked down at him. "I know exactly what you're going to say. Don't waste your breath."

"Brogan Costin is a catch. He owns his own business. He can cook, and he's single."

"That you know of," I said. Although, I hadn't seen Brogan dating anyone.

"He makes a mean breakfast," Wiggles said. "All I get from Rhett are cookies."

"Rhett can stop giving you cookies if you're bored with them."

His ears shot up. "No! Cookies are excellent. I love Rhett's cookies. It's just that, well, Brogan's sausages are outstanding."

"Then you marry him."

"Who's getting married?" Brogan wandered over with a bottle in his hand and two glasses. He balanced a bowl of water on his forearm, which he set down for Wiggles.

"Oh, it's not important," I said, shooting Wiggles a warning glare.

"I thought you might be talking about your sister and her engagement to Toby Matlock." Brogan settled in the seat opposite me. "That's an interesting match."

"Tell me about it," I said. "I'm still trying to get my head around that one."

"Are you single, Brogan?" Wiggles asked.

I cleared my throat and grabbed the dessert menu.

Amusement crossed Brogan's face. "I was the last time I checked. Why, have you got someone you'd like to set me up with?"

"No, he hasn't," I said.

Brogan sat back in his seat. "It takes a certain kind of woman to put up with the habits of a half-vampire. Some get freaked out by my fangs."

"Fangs are cool." Wiggles bared his teeth. "Tempest is used to fangs."

Brogan chuckled. "They have their uses."

"What kind of woman are you looking for?"

"Maybe he's not looking," I said.

Brogan shrugged. "I always like to look. There are some pretty women in the village. I'm not sure if I'm ready to stop looking at them all just yet."

"Playing the field." Wiggles nodded. "I get it. I'm yet to find a furry friend to spend eternity with."

"Which will be shorter than you think if you keep prodding Brogan about his private life," I muttered.

Brogan's smile widened. He tapped his finger on the bottle he'd brought over. "This is sparkling apple juice. I got it when I visited Puzzlewood.

They make it locally and tell the tourists that the apple trees contain ancient magic, which is why their cider tastes so good."

"So, they're telling the truth." I smiled at Brogan. "I love Puzzlewood. Mom and Dad took us there a few times when we were kids." It was a tucked away magic community, much like Willow Tree Falls, but with more forest and a lot more fairies.

"Do you want to try their magic apple juice? Don't worry. It won't make you sparkle. Although you can buy a variety that does."

"That sounds great."

Brogan poured me a glass. "You're both dressed up for the evening."

I yanked off my bowtie and stuffed it in the pocket of my tuxedo. "I was doing our mayor a favor at the museum. It backfired."

"I'd have liked to have come to the museum opening," Brogan said, "but I didn't have cover here tonight."

"It was an opening that won't be easy to forget. Mannie wants me to poke around until Dazielle shows up. I'd most likely know by now who put Gretel on that ducking stool, but Mannie insisted I don't talk to key witnesses until tomorrow."

"Our mayor doesn't like to ruffle feathers. From the sounds of it, you're dealing with some influential people."

"That's what Mannie said. I don't care how influential they are if one of them killed Gretel. Murder is murder, no matter how high up you are."

"What about our lovely mayor? Could he be involved?"

"That's what I thought," Wiggles said. "He's covering up something."

"I'll have to talk to him," I said, "but I'm not looking forward to it. Mannie can make life difficult if you get on his wrong side."

Our food arrived, the plates piled with sweet smelling carrots, creamy mash, and pie.

The three of us stopped speaking as we enjoyed the food for a moment.

"Who else could be involved?" Brogan asked.

"That's the information I hope you can help with," I said. "Do you know Seth Fellows?"

Brogan's top lip curled. "I do."

"You're not friendly?"

"Seth pretends to be friends with everybody." Brogan shrugged. "He'll stab you in the back if it gets him what he needs."

"Would his murderous intentions expand to killing an annoying historian who made his life difficult?"

Brogan pulled on his bottom lip. "I've not seen Seth for a while, but he's got a past. He had some control issues when he was younger, almost killed a girl he drank from."

"He seems like a massive slime ball," Wiggles said.

Brogan nodded. "Seth has a high opinion of himself. He has vampire royalty in his lineage. It's what makes him such a... well, let's just say, a self-entitled individual."

"A slime ball," Wiggles said.

Brogan smiled and took a sip of the apple juice. "Yes, that as well. His father is Daray Plantagenet, although Seth kept his mom's surname. Daray has a liking for seducing stunning women, only to reveal what he is after they become pregnant."

"He sounds like a charmer," I said.

"Seth's inherited many of his traits. He idolizes his father but is half as powerful because, obviously, he's not a full vampire. His mother was human."

"What's he doing working as a publicist?" I asked. "That doesn't seem royal to me."

"This isn't his only job," Brogan said. "Seth's a freelancer, so he goes where the big bucks are. I suspect he's getting a healthy cut from the profit of whatever he's promoting."

"He's looking after the author Isadora Ash. She's also involved with the museum. It's her book he's promoting."

"You can make a decent amount off a book if it's a bestseller," Brogan said. "That must be why Seth's doing this."

"You don't consider him trustworthy?"

"No. He'll say whatever he needs to cover his back."

"Did he come in here last night?"

"He did. He had something to eat then said he was going to the Ancient Imp. He got here about eight and left within the hour."

"Did you talk to him?" I scooped up the last of my pie. I could manage another of these. It was the perfect blend of crunchy and peppery.

"As little as possible. Seth plays nice with everybody, but it's an act. He only looks out for himself."

"What about his girlfriend, Lotus? Do you know anything about her?"

"He wasn't with anyone," Brogan said. "He dined alone and didn't mention a girlfriend. I pity her, whoever she is."

I set down my knife and fork and wiped my mouth with a napkin. "I haven't spoken to Lotus yet, but she seemed sweet enough."

"Is it only Mannie and Seth in the frame for this murder?" Brogan asked.

"There could be others," I said. "Lotus, who works as a researcher. The author, Isadora, although she seemed nice when we spoke, a bit stressed about the launch of her new book, but who wouldn't be? There's also her assistant, Jonah. I don't know much about any of them."

"I'm pointing the paw at Mannie," Wiggles said. "He's a social climbing creep. He argued with Gretel and got his nose put out of joint."

"Everyone had access to the museum the night the murder took place," I said. "And with Mannie being so well-known in the village, he'd have a hard time killing Gretel and not getting spotted leaving the museum. There's always someone who wants to bend his ear."

"Not if he'd done it in the middle of the night," Wiggles said.

"True, but he'd have needed to persuade Gretel to be at the museum at the same time as him. She didn't seem like the sort of woman who'd be easy to persuade to do anything if she didn't want to do it."

"What's your next step?" Brogan asked. "Are you really planning to interrogate our mayor?"

I grimaced. "I'm going to try for as gentle an interrogation as possible. But yes, I need to speak to Mannie and everybody else."

"What about the scene of the crime?" Brogan asked. "Any clues there?"

"The angels are in charge of that side of things," I said.

"That'll be a no," Wiggles said. "Dominic's a good-looking angel, and I like Sablo well enough, but neither of them have a clue how to find a clue. Without Dazielle to direct them, they won't know what to look for."

"You should check out the murder scene, without any interference," Brogan said. "You might find something useful. I hear you're good at dealing with bad guys." He flashed me a smile.

I rubbed the back of my neck. "The angels won't let me take a look. Mannie put them in charge of guarding the scene until Gretel's body can be collected."

"I thought you were involved in this investigation?"

"So did I. But Mannie can't help but crack the whip and take over. No one's getting to the crime scene until tomorrow."

"Then you need a distraction," Brogan said. "Something to take the angels' minds off their jobs and let you do yours."

I grinned at him. "I'm listening. What do you have in mind?"

Chapter 7

The lengthening shadows of the trees around the museum made for a perfect hiding place as we prepared for our mission.

I carefully arranged the box of doughnuts on Wiggles' back.

"You realize that a few doughnuts might fall off," Wiggles said.

"Do not eat the doughnuts before you offer them to Sablo and Dominic," I said. "If you eat our distraction, this plan will fail."

"I'm just telling you the likelihood of what will happen," Wiggles said. "There are twelve doughnuts in this box. The angels won't want them all, and this box keeps wobbling. It's an accident waiting to happen."

I stood back and checked the weight of the doughnut box was evenly distributed. "That will have to do."

Brogan had donated the doughnuts to our good cause. He was right. We needed to get back in the museum and investigate the murder scene without Mannie or the angels getting in the way.

After finishing our dinner, I'd taken the doughnuts, and we'd headed back to Cloven Hoof for a few hours. After doing a bit of work and waiting until just gone two in the morning, when the bar was closing, we'd snuck back to the museum.

"I bet they're asleep," Wiggles said. "Those angels will have curled their wings around themselves and forgotten they're supposed to be guarding a crime scene."

"They'd better not be asleep."

"If they are, can I eat the doughnuts? They won't want them if they're sleeping."

"No! Wake them up and get them out of my way," I said. "Insist the doughnuts will go well with coffee and get them into the kitchen. I need time to check out the crime scene."

"I'm on it." Wiggles walked slowly toward the museum door, the box of doughnuts wobbling on his back.

I crept along behind him and pressed my hand against the door. It was locked from the inside, but a simple unlock spell unbolted the door, and I eased it open.

Wiggles crept into the darkness, and I kept the door ajar and pressed my ear against the gap. I didn't have to wait many seconds before I heard movement.

"Wiggles!" Sablo sounded surprised. "How did you get in?"

"Oh! Through the dog door at the back," Wiggles said.

"Dog door?"

"Yes, it's like a cat flap but a bit bigger." Wiggles' lie sounded convincing. "I come bearing gifts."

"Yum! Doughnuts." That was Dominic. "I'm dead on my feet here. It's so boring guarding a body."

"Why don't you have a coffee, as well?" Wiggles suggested. "It'll go great with these doughnuts."

"Good thinking," Dominic said. "Would you like to join us?"

"I thought you'd never ask."

I waited until I could no longer hear them talking before easing open the door and slipping inside.

There was a light on at the back of the museum. I kept an eye on it as I hurried toward the ducking stool exhibit.

I stepped over the barrier and scanned the surrounding area with a torch.

There were no footprints, but there were what might be drag marks around the pond. It suggested Gretel had been pulled along or fought back. Her attacker might be sporting a few bruises, which could help identify them.

The angels had moved Gretel from the ducking stool, so she lay on her back by the side of the pond. I was no expert on murder, but I saw bruising on her arms. Gretel had tried to kick butt before being ducked.

Her clothes were also damp and wrinkled, suggesting she'd spent a long time in the water.

I kept my attention from her face as I touched her cold arm. The angels' energy fluttered up my arm. It felt like a preserving spell, used to keep the body from decomposing and the evidence from being disturbed.

There was also another spell. It was the faint trace of a freeze spell. It made the tips of my fingers icy cold and numb. That spell could have been used to trap Gretel into place on the ducking stool. Her attacker might have forced her in here and used magic to hold her in place while she was ducked.

I removed my fingers and shook the magic off me. I'd need to take a few crime scene investigation classes if I had to keep doing this sort of thing. I usually left the more gruesome side of an investigation to the angels. But with Dazielle missing, I was out of options.

I jumped as I heard a crash from the back of the museum.

"Hey! That one was mine."

I ducked out of sight. Whatever was going on between the angels and Wiggles, it didn't sound good.

"He stole my doughnut!" Sablo yelled. "That's his third one."

Grimacing, I shook my head. I'd wasted my breath telling Wiggles not to steal the doughnuts. He could never resist anything sweet.

I had another quick look around the exhibit but couldn't see anything useful. It was time to get out of here before the angels returned.

I turned toward the door and yelped as a blast of hot, dust-laden magic slammed into my chest and knocked me off my feet.

My head hit the ground, and I gasped. Whatever had hit me had a weird feel to it. I felt itchy, and the air sparkled around me like fairy dust.

I struggled to my feet and peered into the gloom to see my attacker. I caught the gleam of someone's eyes. It was a woman, standing in the shadows.

"Who are you?" I held my hands out and sparked my magic to warn her I'd attack if she tried anything again.

"You must leave this place," the woman hissed. "This is my new home, and it has been defiled."

"Your home?" I edged closer and recognized the woman's face as she moved from the shadows. "You were at the museum. You helped with the opening."

She nodded. "I'm Cleo Jinx. What are you doing in my home? There's been enough destruction and pain here tonight. No more. Leave that witch alone."

"I'm not here to destroy anything or to hurt anyone," I said as I edged closer. "Do you live in the museum?"

There was another shout and the sound of pounding feet. The angels must be pursuing Wiggles and the stolen doughnuts.

Cleo continued to glare at me. I saw fear mingling with the anger on her face. She seemed terrified, and I was certain it wasn't my presence causing her such concern.

"Murder and angels have spoiled this pristine place." A sob caught in her throat.

"Murder is a bad business," I said. "But the angels are only doing their jobs. You were around when Gretel was discovered, right?"

She shook her head. "I don't like crowds, so I skipped out as soon as I could. I came back when I heard what happened. The angels must leave my home. I didn't invite them to stay." She raised her hands as if to attack again but then lowered them and sighed.

"The angels have to stay here to protect Gretel." I glanced over my shoulder as I heard more yelling. "Come with me, and we can talk about it."

"I want the peace back. I want my museum back. I don't want a body polluting such a sanctuary."

I tilted my head as I studied her. She had an exotic look. Cleo would look perfect in ancient Greece, with her tanned skin and glossy dark hair. "Are you descended from the Muses?"

She blinked at me before nodding. "From Kleio. Did you know her?"

"Not personally," I said. Kleio was the muse of history. Her father was Zeus. There was a lot of ancient power surrounding the muses. It was no wonder her ability felt so tangled and old. "I can see why you'd be interested in the museum, given your family connections."

"History runs through my blood," Cleo said. "It's why I'm here. It's why I must protect this place. It's why you and the angels must leave."

"I was about to," I said. "You'll get no trouble from me. I would like to talk to you, though. I'm also not happy that someone's been murdered in your museum. We can work together and figure out what happened."

Cleo wiped her hands across her cheeks. "I'd like that. I would like the peace back. If you can help me achieve that, then I will answer your questions."

"Incoming!" Wiggles raced past. "The angels are on their way."

Cleo's mouth opened, and a huge smile spread across her face when she saw Wiggles. "Oh! A puppy!" She ran after him, her arms open.

I hurried after her. "He's not exactly a puppy. He's pretty old and grumpy most of the time."

"I love puppies." Cleo giggled as she chased Wiggles.

I could hear the angels searching for Wiggles, getting closer by the second.

My gaze ran over Cleo as we followed Wiggles to the door. She didn't seem like a threat and had acted much like Fallon and Suki did when defending the forest. Cleo seemed to think she had guardianship over this museum and protected it from any perceived threat.

"Would you like to pet the puppy?" I asked her.

Cleo slowed and clapped her hands together. "I'd love to." She did a little jump and floated in the air for several seconds.

"That's great." I grabbed her hand and pulled her to the ground. "The puppy is about to leave, and we need to chase him." I gestured Wiggles to the door.

"When I catch the puppy, I'm giving him a big squeeze and lots of kisses."

"Wiggles loves cuddles and kisses."

Wiggles' expression turned scary as he overheard Cleo and me talking, and he slowed. "I do not—"

"No time!" I pulled open the main door and ushered him out. "We need to leave, Cleo. We don't want to lose sight of the puppy."

Cleo laughed, all trace of her sadness gone. "Let's chase the puppy."

I raced out the door, keeping a tight grip on Cleo's hand as we slipped into the night.

The door clicked shut behind us, and I let out a sigh. That had been a close call. I'd found a few clues at the crime scene but nothing conclusive. Nothing that pointed me toward anyone other than a strong magic user who might be concealing a few bruises.

But I had found a new witness and maybe even a new suspect. Since Cleo seemed so involved with the museum, she might have useful information about what had happened to Gretel. Or maybe, Gretel had done something to the museum that Cleo considered harmful, and her urge to protect it had led to Gretel's death.

From my short time with Cleo, she'd bounced from a magic flinging protector to a sparkly, hand-clapping puppy hugger. I needed to learn more about Cleo Jinx.

Chapter 8

"I don't see the puppy anymore," Cleo whispered as we hurried along the silent streets toward Cloven Hoof.

"I know exactly where he's going," I said. "Come on. I see him."

Cleo floated through the air again as I ran. I caught hold of her hand. It felt like I was tugging a heavy balloon behind me, but I was worried she might float away or simply change her mind and return to the museum if I didn't watch her.

"I asked Mannie if I could have a puppy in the museum, but he said no. He said not everyone likes puppies. What kind of monster doesn't like a puppy?"

"Beats me," I said.

"I do have my familiars. They keep me company."

I glanced at her. It was only witches who had familiars, and Cleo was no witch.

Wiggles was waiting by the front door of Cloven Hoof as we arrived. The place was locked and silent, all customers and staff gone.

Cleo stared at the building as her feet touched the ground. "Is this where you live?"

"Yes, I live here with the puppy."

"I'm not a puppy," Wiggles grumbled as he dodged out of Cleo's way when she made a grab for him.

"Do you have more than one puppy? Can I have one?"

I unlocked the door and ushered her and Wiggles inside. "I just have this one. He's more than enough. He's like ten puppies squashed into one."

Wiggles trotted ahead of us, casting a curious look over his shoulder. "What's all this about a puppy?"

Cleo skipped over to Wiggles. "I'm going to give you the biggest snuggle of your life."

Wiggles ducked out of her way as she tried to grab him again. "Sorry, cutie, I don't snuggle."

I bit my bottom lip to stop from smiling. "Maybe you can do a little snuggling. Cleo works at the museum. She might have useful information for us."

Wiggles turned to face Cleo, who still stalked him. His eyes glowed red, and he bared his teeth.

Cleo giggled and clapped her hands. "You clever puppy. You can do all kinds of tricks." She waved a hand in the air and a rainbow of sparkles floated out of her fingers and settled on Wiggles' fur. "Now you're a puppy who sparkles."

Wiggles growled and shook the sparkles from his fur. "Do we have to do this?" His glare cut to me.

"It might be helpful to the investigation," I said.

"I'm so great at snuggles that, once I've got you, you won't want to leave." Cleo opened her arms wide.

"I'd better get a big treat after this." Wiggles stopped growling and sighed. "Fine, you can snuggle me."

Cleo squealed and scooped Wiggles into her arms. "Oomph! You're a heavy puppy. I bet your owner feeds you all kinds of treats for being so adorable."

"She will after this." Wiggles slung his front paws over Cleo's shoulder and wrinkled his nose at me.

Cleo wrapped both her arms around him and squeezed. "You're so soft. Although, you smell like you need a bath. I have rose scented bubbles at the museum."

Wiggles wheezed. "I'm not a soft toy. If you keep squeezing me like that, you'll get more than my unique hellhound scent filling your nose."

"Let's take a seat." I gestured to a booth. "I've not seen you in Willow Tree Falls before."

Cleo's face was glowing with happiness as she settled in the booth with Wiggles still in her arms. "I'm new to the village."

I sat opposite her. "I saw you at the museum opening."

"That's right. I've been here a month. Mannie hired me. I've not had a chance to leave the museum since I started. It's been really busy." She rubbed her cheek against Wiggles' side. "I love it there."

"What do you do at the museum?"

"I'm the museum assistant. Well, that's what I signed on for, initially. But when I arrived, there were problems with on-site security."

"What kind of problems?"

Cleo's bottom lip jutted out. "The site is haunted. Did you know the building was owned by Vincent Maldovic?"

"Sure, everyone knows the tales. He was supposed to conjure dark spirits to make them do evil things. I even heard there's a hidden entrance to a dark magic dungeon. It's an urban myth. I've lived here all my life and have never seen anything dodgy happening in that house, not since Vincent was run out of the village for illegal magic use."

"It might not be an urban myth." Cleo stroked a hand down Wiggles' fur. The color changed to bright pink. "He's such a pretty puppy."

I decided not to mention the new fur color to Wiggles. It would only make him mad. "He is lovely. Does that mean you got involved with the museum security?"

"It was my idea," Cleo said. "I was renting a room at the hotel, but my assistant salary doesn't stretch to much. I offered to stay at the museum and make sure the place was secure. I've got a few tricks of my own to keep evil spirits at bay. It meant a bit more money and free accommodation. It was a win-win all round."

"Did you see any evil spirits?" I asked.

"Oh, yes! That place is haunted. There are loads of ghosts there. Not all of them are evil. I often get awakened by banging noises and icy drafts at night. Whenever I go to investigate, there's never anything there, so it has to be ghosts."

"It's an old building. It could be loose pipes in the basement or the wind knocking a tree against the glass."

"No, there's something dark in that museum. But it's such a beautiful place, and there are so many incredible artifacts there. I have to keep them safe. I patrol at night to make sure everything's secure, and so far, it's worked. But, with what happened to that witch on the ducking stool, I don't think I've been doing a good job. I let someone commit a murder."

"You were there the night Gretel was murdered?"

"I was in the building, but I didn't see anything." Cleo buried her nose in Wiggles' fur. She removed it just as quickly. "He's such a stinky puppy."

"I smell great." Wiggles shuffled his butt in Cleo's arms. "Can I get down yet?"

"A couple more minutes," I said. "Do you check the exhibits during your patrol?"

"The glass cabinets, yes. But the ducking stool was hidden by the curtain, all ready for the reveal on opening night. I'd been told not to touch it."

"By whom?"

"Mannie."

I tilted my head. We were circling back to Mannie as a suspect. First, he didn't want me interviewing everyone, and second, he'd stopped Cleo from checking on the ducking stool. Was that because he'd planned to use the stool to commit murder and didn't want anyone to disturb the scene?

"Did you hear anything odd on the night of Gretel's murder?"

"Only the usual ghostly noises. The bangs and whistles. One ghost laughs a lot. It's a deep, menacing sound, but I don't think he means any harm by it. There is a dark presence in the museum. If a ghost wanted to, it could have moved silently and attacked Gretel. That makes sense. It's the only reason I can think as to why I didn't hear anything."

"Hold on. You think a ghost killed Gretel?"

"Oh, yes! That's the only explanation. Gretel must have upset a ghost. If you're not polite to them, they can be mean. I always leave milk and cookies for the ghosts every night."

"Milk and cookies every night?" Wiggles turned his head, so his nose was next to Cleo's ear.

She giggled. "Absolutely. You can have them too if you want a sleepover."

"I'll consider it. What kind of cookies?"

"I bake all kinds. Apple and cinnamon. Chocolate chip. Maple syrup and marshmallow."

"You're winning me over," Wiggles said.

"Getting back to your ghost theory, you believe Gretel was killed by a ghost because she was mean to it?" I'd seen Gretel in action, so I knew she was sharp. Could she have riled a ghost enough for it to attack her?

Cleo nodded. "Ghosts can be powerful, especially the older ones. And when they've been tampered with by dark magic, you never know what you'll encounter."

"How long was the ducking stool exhibit in place before the museum opened?"

"It was one of the first exhibits to arrive. Mannie was determined to get that right because it was a part of the grand opening."

"Was the ducking stool always empty?"

Cleo shook her head. "No, there was a dummy of a witch in it. That's why nobody panicked when they first saw the body. We expected to see a drowned witch on the ducking stool. It wasn't until your beautiful puppy pulled the leg out that we realized something was wrong."

"Which means the killer removed the dummy from the stool and replaced it with Gretel at some point in the night."

Cleo nodded as she played with Wiggles' ears. "They must have been there late. But I guess ghosts don't need to sleep."

"Is that water deep enough to drown in?" I asked Cleo.

"If you jumped in, you wouldn't fully submerge. There's a couple of feet of water in that pond. It was staged so that part of the witch's body would be in the water as if she'd just had her final duck before dying."

"Enough water to drown a person in?"

"Definitely. The ghost must have seen its opportunity and attacked."

"Did you let Gretel in that night?"

"No, but she was in and out of the museum a lot before the opening," Cleo said. "She was an exacting woman. She knew what she wanted and wasn't giving up until she got it. I was working until eleven before the opening to get everything right."

"So, she died sometime after that?" It was a question I asked myself more than Cleo.

"She must have. That's when the ghosts are most active. They don't come out when the place is full of people. I wonder if they're shy."

"Shy ghosts, whatever next?" Wiggles muttered.

Cleo kissed the side of his face and nuzzled him with her nose. "Don't worry, puppy. I'll protect you from the ghosts. I protect the whole museum. That's my job."

"I feel so much better knowing that," Wiggles said.

"What did you do after you finished work that night?" I asked Cleo.

"I was exhausted. I'd been up since dawn, taking in last-minute deliveries and checking everything was where it needed to be and, of course, patrolling to make sure the ghosts weren't a problem. I passed out as soon as I fell into bed. I snuggled with my three companions and didn't wake until it was time for my first patrol three hours later."

"Your companions?"

"My three familiars. They live at the museum with me. Puppy, do you like cats?"

"They're fun to chase."

"No, you don't chase them. They can be a little... feisty when they don't get their own way."

"Have you had them long?" I asked.

"All my life." She kissed Wiggles' cheek again. "Much like your special puppy here, they'll be with me my entire life. We're joined by our powers, and our lives are linked. It will be nice if you join them, puppy. We can have fun together. My familiars are always looking for new playmates."

"I'm not looking for new playmates," Wiggles said. "I don't play nicely with others."

Cleo gasped. "Don't tell me you're a bad puppy! I can't imagine it, someone as cute as you. I'm sure you'll become close friends with my familiars."

"I'm giving you a hard pass on that offer."

"Getting back to Gretel," I said, "did you see or hear anything out of the ordinary when you did your patrol?"

"Nope, nothing. I was tired, though, so it was a quick look around and then straight to bed."

"How well did you know Gretel?" I asked. "Did you get along?"

Cleo shifted in her seat. "Not well, and I wouldn't say we were friends. She could be a bit bossy. Sometimes, I got scared of her. Gretel was always shouting that nothing was good enough."

"You didn't like her?"

"I didn't dislike her. I just kept out of her way. It made my life easier. I admired her passion for history, and we had good conversations about ancient times. She knew of my ancient lineage and respected my knowledge. Gretel wasn't always respectful of Isadora or Mannie, though. She'd mock them when they got their facts wrong and was quick to correct them."

"Did you see Gretel argue with anyone in particular?"

"Mostly Mannie and Isadora. There was bickering and a couple of stand-offs over aspects of different displays, but it wasn't serious. Providing Gretel got her own way, there were never any problems."

"And no rows on the day of her murder?"

Cleo tilted her head and rested it against Wiggles. "She was causing Seth problems. I overheard him talking on his snow globe. I wasn't sure who he was talking to, and a lot of it sounded like legal jargon. He was saying that Gretel was being difficult, and something had to be done."

That was interesting, but Seth had an alibi for Gretel's murder. "Did Seth mention what the problem was?"

"Something about a lawsuit. It sounded serious. I was tucked behind an exhibit adjusting the backdrop, so he couldn't see me when he was talking. I listened in because I was worried. I don't want anything to happen to the museum. Sometimes, these legal issues drag on for years. That could close the museum, then no one will see the lovely exhibits and immerse themselves in my history."

If Gretel was gunning for the museum to be closed, for whatever reason, that could lose Seth money. This was the launch pad for Isadora's book. If things got delayed, it would affect sales and mess with the opening of the museum. There were also implications for Mannie, given how hard he'd worked to make this museum happen. Seth and Mannie still had a lot to gain by getting rid of Gretel.

"Seth kept talking about the bottom line. He said it couldn't be impacted. He'd do all he could to stop Gretel getting her own way." Cleo tilted her head back. "The promotion was to go as planned, and he'd sort things out this end. He was adamant they weren't going to lose their investment. He used some rude words about Gretel, which I won't repeat in case it upsets the puppy."

"The puppy likes rude words," I said.

"I do. I have several favorites I use every day. They include bu—"

Cleo wrapped a hand around Wiggles' muzzle and shook her head. "You're a cheeky puppy. No swearing allowed."

I raised my eyebrows as I watched Wiggles squirm, indignation on his face. Cleo had been helpful, but her information meant I had to consider Seth and Mannie as suspects. What I really needed was evidence that ruled out suspects.

"Is that everything?" Cleo asked. "I'm having fun with this gorgeous puppy, but I need to get back to the museum. I've been keeping an eye on those angels. They're bad at their jobs. They were asleep most of the time, and the cute one with the dark hair, he kept wandering off and looking around. He spent an hour trying on witches' hats."

That didn't surprise me. "We're done for now. If you think of anything else, let me know."

"I'll keep an eye out for whichever ghost killed Gretel," Cleo said. "I'll speak to them and see if they know anything."

"You can speak to the ghosts?"

"I speak to them a lot. They don't answer back."

"Well, anything you find out, pass it on." I stood from the booth. I didn't think a malevolent ghost had anything to do with Gretel's murder.

"You're sure I can't keep this puppy? He likes me." Cleo held onto Wiggles tightly as he squirmed in her arms.

"I'm not up for adoption," Wiggles said. "And I'm beginning to sweat."

Cleo giggled before raining kisses on his face and lowering him to the ground. "Anytime you're looking for a new home, my familiars and I will be happy to accept you. They'll love playing with a puppy."

"Good to know." Wiggles shook out his fur, more sparkles flying off him, and backed away from Cleo.

I showed Cleo out and locked the door behind her before turning to Wiggles.

"That was torture," he said. "I smell weird, and I've got glitter in my fur. It itches."

"You also have a pink stripe down your back," I said.

Wiggles growled, and his eyes flamed red. "She's some kind of freaky magic user. She smells like lemons, cinnamon, and dusty books. The old kind of books that get covered in mold."

"I also got the ancient magic vibe off her," I said. "Her magic is mixed with something else."

"Madness," Wiggles said. "As if she'd think for one second I'd move into that haunted museum with three cats who want to scratch my eyes out."

"Not even for nightly milk and cookies?"

"Nope. I'd have to fight the killer ghosts and the evil cats to get those cookies. Not worth it."

"It could be fun," I said. "You might like a holiday there when I go demon hunting outside of Willow Tree Falls."

"I'd rather sleep in the gutter in the middle of winter, without having had a hot meal, than spend a night in that mad house."

I laughed. "Fair enough. I won't suggest you stay with Cleo and her fluffy gang the next time I'm away."

"What do you make of her story about the ghosts?" Wiggles turned, trying to get a look at his new pink stripe.

"Not much," I said. "And Cleo's alibi isn't great. She was alone in the museum at the time the murder happened. If she's as protective of the museum as she claims to be, she might have taken offense to Gretel poking around and being unkind to everyone."

"Cleo was trying to squeeze the life out of me, so I'm happy to point the paw at her as a suspect."

"I didn't get the murdering vibe off her. She's more kooky than criminal. What about the conversation she overheard with Seth? He sounds unhappy with Gretel. They could have locked horns if she threatened legal action against him or the museum."

"Or Isadora's new book," Wiggles said. "That's what Seth's interested in, getting money out of this publicity tour."

I nodded as we walked out of the bar and headed up to the apartment. Mannie, Cleo, and Seth all had plausible motives for wanting Gretel dead.

"As much as I hate to admit it, I need a bath," Wiggles said. "And you need to sort the pink stripe on my back. No self-respecting hellhound goes out with pink fur."

I smiled down at him. "I'll get the bath running and look through my spells to see if I've got anything to reverse what Cleo's done."

As I dwelled on what Cleo had told me, my interest in Seth grew. What would he do to protect the money he'd sunk into this publicity campaign? Might it stretch to murder?

I needed to talk to him again and find out what our smooth-talking half-vampire might be hiding.

Chapter 9

After our late-night adventure in the museum, Wiggles and I were late getting up the next morning. After a leisurely breakfast, I showered, dressed, and headed to the Ancient Imp.

There was a scent of wood smoke and dried hops in the air as I opened the door. The pub hadn't long been open, but some early lunchtime drinkers had already taken up residence at the bar.

I slowed as I passed one table and heard the words ghost and museum.

"They're talking about a murderous ghost."

"It's no surprise. Everyone knows what that place is like."

"It's a wonder a ghost hasn't crept out and caused trouble in the rest of the village. That place should be burned to the ground. It might need to be if the ghosts keep causing problems."

I shook my head as I walked to the bar with Wiggles. Rumors spread fast in this place. "Hi, Petra."

Petra Duke, the owner of the Ancient Imp, smiled. "How's it going, Tempest?" She looked at Wiggles and nodded. "I heard you've gotten tangled in this ghost murder."

"If you mean the murder at the museum, then I am. But don't believe the rumors about a ghost being involved."

"That's all everyone's talking about," Petra said. "It's hard to know what to believe. Can I get you both a drink?"

"A sparkling lemon water will be great. Water for Wiggles. What else are your customers talking about?"

Petra pursed her red lips and flipped her dark, silver-streaked hair over one shoulder. "I don't like to gossip, but I heard the woman who was killed wasn't popular. I even saw her bending Mannie's ear the other day with some complaint. The poor guy looked defeated, his shoulders slumped and head down as she berated him. If she treated everybody like that, it's no surprise she ended up in the ducking stool."

I accepted my lemon water and took a sip then placed the bowl of water on the floor for Wiggles, which he ignored as he snuffled for dropped potato chips. "That's the reason I'm here. One of the suspects in the investigation claims he was here the night of the murder."

Petra arched an eyebrow. "Who would that be?"

"A half-vampire called Seth Fellows. Tall, sort of handsome in an overly confident way. Nice cheekbones. Pale skin."

Petra smirked. "I'd hardly forget a handsome guy like that. He was here, flashing his money around and bragging about what a big shot he is. I've never heard of him. He kept talking about what a success this book he's promoting will be. I asked if I could have a free copy, and he said I'd have to buy one."

"Seth was here all evening, until closing time?"

Petra tilted her head. "Yes, until last orders. He ordered a whiskey for his final drink. As for being here all night, I can't confirm that. I wasn't watching him all the time, even though he sure is cute."

"Cute with a big order of arrogance thrown into the mix."

"You know me. I like my men with a bit of sass."

I shrugged. So did I. "Could Seth have disappeared for say half an hour without you noticing?"

"It's possible. It was busy that night, and it was just me behind the bar. I have to pay all my customers the right level of attention."

"Did you leave the bar unattended?"

"Sure. A lady has to powder her nose." She winked at me. "I also had to change a barrel. That took about ten minutes. My regulars don't mind waiting for a refill if I need to duck into the cellar. You don't think our cute half-vampire is involved in this murder, do you?"

"Seth knew Gretel. They weren't all that friendly, but there are other people I need to speak to."

"He was smooth. I can imagine somebody like that would pay to have the dirty work done. And he wears those lovely designer suits. If this witch drowned, as everyone says she did, he wouldn't want to get his designer clothes ruined with pond slime."

That was a good point. I could hunt around and see if anyone had discarded a fancy suit. I imagined Seth had his suits tailored, so it would be one of a kind and easy to match to him.

Seth's alibi wasn't cast iron, and with his great motive for wanting Gretel gone, my attention remained on him. He'd also mentioned nothing about her trying to torpedo this book launch and lose him money when we'd spoken.

"Anything else I can help you with?" Petra asked.

I shook my head as my attention went to the window. Aurora strode past, her blonde hair flying out behind her as she hurried along.

"Thanks, Petra." Leaving money on the bar, I hurried out with Wiggles. Mom was right; Aurora looked skinny. Her clothes hung off her, and her usual cheerful smile was gone.

I kept a little way behind her as she continued to walk. I didn't know what to say. I'd never felt awkward around Aurora before, but there was a growing divide between us, and I wasn't sure how to repair it.

"Aurora, wait up." Wiggles bounded away before I could stop him.

Aurora turned, glancing over her shoulder at me. Her expression hardened, but she smiled when Wiggles reached her and gave him a belly rub.

The rumble of a bike engine had me turning. Rhett rolled to a stop beside me, looking windswept and gorgeous. "I've been looking for you. I've heard interesting rumors about what happened at the museum."

"I thought you were coming to the grand opening?" I kissed his cheek before glancing back at Aurora. She still petted Wiggles, who rolled on the ground, exposing his belly.

"I got caught up in a bit of business. I'd just arrived when I saw the crowd pouring out. People were saying all sorts of weird things."

"The whole thing is weird. The historian Mannie used to help with the museum was murdered. The killer used the ducking stool in an exhibit to drown her."

Rhett's eyes widened. "What a way to go. Any suspects?"

"Several. And Mannie's got me figuring out what happened until Dazielle returns." I looked over my shoulder to see Aurora striding away, Wiggles watching her go. I sighed and shook my head, feeling guilty that a part of me was glad I hadn't had to speak to her.

"Still not having luck with getting through to your sister?" Rhett squeezed my hand.

"Honestly, I've been avoiding the issue. I don't know how to get her to open her eyes about Toby."

Rhett scrubbed his chin. "I've been digging into Toby Matlock's past. The more I find, the less I like."

"What have you found out?"

"He's a suspect in a fraud investigation. Not just one case, five separate incidents of fraud."

"You're kidding? What did he do?"

"He conned five million out of several women."

"Why? Toby's already rich. What does he need other people's money for?"

"No idea. But your sister needs to be careful. When Toby Matlock wants something, he goes after it and keeps fighting until he gets it."

"If it's money he's after, then he's chasing the wrong person. Aurora has her store and the apartment above it, but that's it. And the family isn't rich. All we have is the demon prison." I sucked in a breath. "You don't think..." I shook my head, not believing what had just crossed my mind.

"He wants the demon prison?" Rhett raised his eyebrows and nodded. "I've been thinking along those lines too. Toby's not after money from Aurora. But those demons your family looks after would pay a lot to be free. And they have friends in low places who would pay to get them out."

I took a step back, and my heart pounded. "Toby wouldn't dare. If the prison becomes compromised, it would destroy Willow Tree Falls."

"And your family's reputation."

"You think Toby wants to ruin the Crypts?"

Rhett stroked a hand down my arm. "Toby could be using Aurora to divide your family and weaken you all. It could be an old grudge he's chasing, or he's after something you have."

I wished that Rhett hadn't agreed with me about this possibility. It would be easier to accept Aurora simply had lousy taste in men and not that the creep she was involved with was far sneakier and deadlier than I'd realized.

"If the prison is badly damaged, the demons could get out and find a way through the barrier. Thousands of people would be harmed."

"We all know Toby's shady. He's old and well-connected, and he has a lot of power." Rhett frowned. "Power hungry people often don't know when to stop. They always want more."

My fingers went to the ends of the hair that Toby had trimmed off. I needed to be careful, or he might focus that power on me.

"I won't mention this to Aurora," I said. "Not yet. She didn't believe me when I told her about Toby's underhanded behavior the last time we tangled. She's never going to believe this. Even if we had solid proof that Toby was going after the demon prison and using her to get it, she'd ignore it. He's got a hold over her, and I don't like it."

"I'll keep looking into his past. Maybe we can find a chink in his armor, a way to convince him to leave your sister alone."

"Toby seems so sure of himself," I said. "I bet he's covered up his dark past. That's why the angels have had no luck with their investigation of him."

"I'm not the angels," Rhett said. "Well, I'm a fallen angel, but that means I don't operate under their constraints. I'll keep digging and let you know if I find anything that can help."

"Thanks." I kissed his cheek again. "I need to sort things out with Aurora. We can't go on avoiding each other. Ever since the announcement that they're getting married, things have changed. Aurora's distanced herself from all of us, and it has to do with Toby."

Rhett caught hold of my hands. "Be careful around him. He's up to no good. I don't want you getting hurt because he realizes you're looking into him."

"Right back at you. But if he tries to hurt me, I'll hurt him right back."

Rhett brushed a finger down my cheek. His gaze shifted over my shoulder, and his eyes widened. "What is that?"

I turned and looked down at Wiggles as he trotted toward us. Sticking out of his mouth was a charred human hand.

Chapter 10

My mouth fell open as I looked at the gruesome discovery Wiggles had hold of. "Where did you get that?"

Wiggles tilted his head before spitting out the hand. "The trash in the alleyway behind Sprinkles. I thought I'd have a look to see if there were any cakes that needed eating. I was digging around, and I found this."

I peered at the hand. "Wait! It's not real." I knelt and gingerly picked up the hand. It was plastic. "This must be from the museum dummy that was on the ducking stool."

Rhett studied the hand. "Is that all there is?"

"No, there are loads more body parts," Wiggles said. "No cake, though."

"Let's take a look."

Rhett climbed off his bike, and we followed Wiggles to the alleyway. Buried beneath several trash bags was the rest of the burned museum dummy. She wore the remains of a black linen dress. Her head had been taken clean off and sat on its own in the corner of the alley. She was also missing a foot, and the hand Wiggles had been chewing on.

"The killer must have dumped the dummy here," I said. "They hoped the trash would be collected before it was found."

"And burned the dummy to conceal evidence by the looks of it," Rhett said.

"It wouldn't have been difficult to sneak here and dispose of the dummy, but I'm surprised no one saw the flames when the plastic burned." I poked the remains around but saw nothing helpful. Whoever had burned the dummy had done a good job. "I need to update the angels about this."

"Are you in charge of all of Angel Force?" Rhett grinned.

"Not a chance. And Mannie's interfering whenever he can, so I might throw in the towel if he gets too annoying. I'm just a placeholder." I pursed my lips. "I don't like to say this, but I miss Dazielle. She needs to get back to Willow Tree Falls and take over this investigation. Maybe she'll be in the office when I get there, and I can hand this charred mess to her and forget about it."

Rhett scuffed a foot on the ground. "If you don't mind, I'll duck out of coming with you."

I smiled at him. "Are you sure you don't want to spend an afternoon with the angels? They're such fun."

He returned my smile as he shook his head. "They're anything but fun." He kissed me lightly on the lips. "Keep me informed and stay out of danger."

"The same goes for you," I said. "As soon as you learn anything about Toby, let me know."

He nodded as he waved goodbye and strode back to his bike.

"Wiggles, look after this hand. We can take it to Angel Force. It might be useful." I held it out to him.

He wrinkled his nose and shook his head. "It tastes funny."

"I can see your teeth marks in this, and it's covered in drool. You've been chewing on the evidence. It can't taste that bad."

"You look after the hand. You're used to a bit of dog drool." Wiggles hurried out of the alleyway before I got a chance to shove the hand in his mouth.

I pinched a finger of the hand and held it at arm's length as we made the short walk to Angel Force's headquarters and headed into the reception. There was nobody there. That was unusual. There was usually someone looking after the reception desk.

I waited a few moments before walking around the desk and knocking on the door at the back that led into the interview rooms and main office.

After a minute, a surprised looking Jophiel poked her head out. "Is there something I can help you with?"

"Is Dazielle back from her training course?"

She shook her head. "No word from her. It's strange. She should have checked in by now. You must be here about the museum murder."

"Yes. Has Gretel been collected from the museum yet?"

"No, we've had no bodies brought in today."

I shook my head and sighed. That meant Sablo and Dominic were still at the museum. I felt a bit sorry for them. Without Dazielle barking orders, the angels had no direction and no drive to do anything.

I held out the dummy hand. "I doubt there's any evidence on this, but you might like to bag it. It's probably from the dummy that was removed when Gretel was murdered. You'll find the rest in the trash behind Sprinkles."

Jophiel stared at the hand, a look of disgust on her pretty face. "Is this pertinent to the investigation? It looks like it's been chewed by a wild animal."

"It might be, but then I'm not the expert. You are." I dumped the hand on the reception desk.

"Oh, well, of course we are. I'll see if the others can deal with the dummy." She tilted her head. "Anything else I can do for you?"

"No, all's good here." I turned and walked out. No one seemed to want to take the lead on Gretel's murder, which left me concerned. I couldn't do this on my own.

I hurried to the museum with Wiggles and banged on the door.

A few minutes later, Sablo opened it, looking bleary-eyed.

"You've been forgotten about by the other angels," I said.

Dominic appeared behind Sablo and pushed the door open wider. "We're so glad you're here. I'm starving."

"I'm not here to feed you." I walked into the museum with Wiggles.

"Hey, you haven't been forgiven for last night." Sablo glared at him. "Tempest, did you know this greedy hellhound stole four doughnuts? He said he was making a special delivery. We were happy to share a single doughnut with him, but he ate one and grabbed three at once. No one can get three doughnuts in their mouth."

Wiggles puffed his chest out. "I can. At a push, I could probably get in four."

I composed my face into what I hoped looked like an angry expression. "You naughty dog. Stealing from the hardworking angels."

"We had to chase him out," Dominic said. "He's fast for a tubby little guy."

"I could run rings around you, Feathers." Wiggles puffed out smoke.

"I'll get you more doughnuts to make up for it," I said. "Has Mannie been by yet? We were supposed to meet to arrange interviews with the rest of the suspects."

"Not yet. You're the first person we've seen for hours," Dominic said.

"I discovered the missing dummy from the exhibit." I gestured to the ducking stool.

Wiggles loudly cleared his throat. "Who discovered it?"

"Okay, Wiggles was cake hunting in the trash and found the dummy behind Sprinkles."

"Excellent work," Dominic said. "That could be useful."

"I've also spoken to Seth and Cleo about their whereabouts on the night of the murder and if they saw anything suspicious."

Dominic nodded encouragingly. "So, who's the killer?"

I glanced at Sablo, who looked equally keen to know the answer. "I can't tell you. I've only interviewed those two, and no one's come forward with a confession. The body hasn't been examined, and we've got no clear evidence as to who did this."

"That's disappointing." Dominic looked at Sablo. "What shall we do now?"

Sablo scratched her chin. "Wait until Dazielle comes back?"

I suppressed a snarl of frustration. "Or we can interview the people most likely to have murdered Gretel before they all vanish and we lose track of them."

Dominic pulled on his bottom lip. "That's not a bad idea either. Hey, Tempest, maybe you can apply for Dazielle's job if she doesn't come back."

I grimaced. "What makes you think she's not coming back?"

"She'll be back." Sablo glared at Dominic. "Dazielle just needed a time out."

That sounded ominous. "Are you sure?"

Sablo shrugged. "Pretty much."

Dominic leaned closer. "Dazielle was told she had to go on this course."

Sablo fluttered a wing at him. "No one's supposed to know."

"Know what?"

Dominic ignored the evil glare Sablo gave him. "Dazielle has anger management issues."

My eyebrows shot up. "I thought she'd been a bit snarky. What did she do?"

Sablo smacked Dominic in the face with her wing. "Nothing! She's a great boss."

Dominic staggered back. "Ouch! That hurt. Tempest is Dazielle's friend. She'll want to help."

Sablo gaped at him, and I shrugged. I was no friend of Dazielle's, but I still wanted to know what she'd done to be forced to go on this course.

The door behind us opened. Mannie bustled in. "Excellent. I'm glad you're here, Tempest. What's going on with this investigation?"

I smiled sweetly at him. "I need to have a few words with you."

"How delightful," Mannie said. "Have you got it all figured out?"

"No, and this won't be a delightful chat," I said. "I need to confirm what everyone was doing the night of Gretel's murder. That includes you. Your name's been mentioned a lot and not in a good way."

The smile on Mannie's face faded, but he nodded. "We all need to prove our innocence. Why don't we make this more pleasant, though? This doesn't need to be a witch inquisition." His gaze went to the ducking stool, and he winced. "Maybe that was a bad choice of words."

I tilted my head. "What do you have in mind?"

"Let me take you to lunch. We don't need to be savages while we're completing this investigation. Everyone thinks better on a full stomach."

"That sounds good," Dominic said. "We've not had a break all night."

"Oh, no. Just Tempest," Mannie said. "You need to get to work on the scene. Do, well, whatever you'd normally do in this situation."

"And me," Wiggles said. "I'm coming to lunch. I'm an essential part of the team."

Mannie glanced at Wiggles and shrugged. "Your mutt can come too."

Wiggles didn't even growl at being called a mutt. His thoughts must be on his stomach. "Let's go to Bite Me."

Mannie patted his belly. "Why not? And it's on me. My treat."

I arched an eyebrow. "I hope you're not trying to bribe me, Mayor."

He took a step back. "What do you mean?"

"You've made me lead investigator in a murder that you're implicated in." I smirked. "Now, you're taking me to an expensive lunch while we discuss your alibi. Some people might find that suspicious."

I noticed Sablo and Dominic exchange a worried glance and almost lost control of the smile I was fighting.

"I've never given a bribe in my life," Mannie said. "I'm not about to start now."

"That's good to know." It was also completely unbelievable.

He sniffed before turning to the door. "Shall we?"

I looked over to see Sablo and Dominic still looking confused. I decided to cut them some slack. "One of you go to Angel Force and get the others to take over here. See if Cassiel is around to deal with Gretel. If she isn't, get her moved and back to your base. It doesn't matter who does it, just get it sorted."

Dominic looked even more perplexed, but Sablo nodded. "Yes, we can do that."

I wasn't convinced, but they seemed to operate better when given clear and simple instructions. I hoped they wouldn't mess them up.

I left the museum with Mannie, Wiggles walking beside me.

"Tell me your progress," Mannie said.

Talk about a conflict of interest. I was about to share information about a murder with one of the suspects. "There's not much so far. I only got to talk to Seth last night. I checked his alibi, and it's unlikely he's involved, although he has a small window of opportunity."

"Seth's a smart fellow." Mannie nodded as people walked past and greeted him. "I suggested he work for me on my next campaign. Do you know what he said?"

"That he'd be thrilled to run the campaign for the mayor of a small village?"

Mannie chuckled. "He said I wouldn't be able to afford him. I was tempted to show him my bank balance, but that seemed crass."

"I'm still considering him a suspect. He's too smooth for his own good."

"As you should, my dear."

We arrived at Bite Me, and Mannie held the door open for me.

I looked at Wiggles and shrugged. "You know the deal."

Wiggles snorted a cloud of gross smelling smoke. "I know. Not every diner wants a free fur ball with their meal. So long as I'm fed, I'll stay out here."

Mannie wafted his hand across his face before deciding he'd had enough of being a gentleman and hurried inside.

Most of the tables were occupied, but we found one at the back that gave us a little privacy.

Tilly Machello hurried over, her expression one of curiosity as she saw me with Mannie. She knew we weren't the best of friends. "It's lovely to have you here, Mayor and Tempest."

"Thank you. What can you recommend, Tilly?" Mannie asked.

"We have a delicious chicken and leek pie. Or there's our usual lasagne. That's always popular."

"Lasagne for me," I said.

"That sounds perfect. And garlic bread," Mannie said. "And two tankards of Imp's Claw ale."

"Not for me," I said. "I'll have water."

Mannie chuckled. "The ale is all mine."

"What about Wiggles?" Tilly tilted her head. "He's already making my heart bleed by giving me his abandoned puppy face through the window."

I grinned. "Whatever you've got spare. He loves your cooking."

Tilly nodded before hurrying to the kitchen to put the order in.

"From what you've said, you don't consider Seth your main suspect," Mannie said.

"Not yet. I need to speak to Isadora and her assistants, Jonah and Lotus, to get a better picture of the group dynamics. One of them could have seen or heard something suspicious."

"Leave that to me," Mannie said. "They're staying in the same house, so it's easy for me to arrange a meeting. I'll get in touch with Isadora, and you can all meet later today. Now everyone is rested, this nasty business will be much easier to handle."

"I appreciate that. Although, I shouldn't discuss any of this with you," I said. "I need to discount you as a suspect. You knew Gretel. You brought her in on the museum job. And, you were seen arguing with her."

Mannie stroked a hand down his beard. "Arguing is a strong word. Our professional disagreements were not uncommon, but we never fell out about anything serious."

"How heated did these professional disagreements become?"

Mannie played with a button on his green waistcoat. "We both maintained our dignity, even if there was a little yelling. But if you need my alibi, I'm prepared to give it to you."

"I'm guessing you have a good one."

His smile was a little on the smug side. "I was at the museum that evening. There was a lot going on the night before the grand opening. I walked around the exhibits with Gretel. She showed me what she was unhappy with. I arranged for the museum assistant, Cleo Jinx, to deal with the final adjustments. Have you met Cleo?"

"We bumped into each other. She was very helpful."

"Yes, she's a good girl. On the flighty side and somewhat obsessed with ghosts but very reliable."

"What time did you leave the museum?"

"We were all there late that night. I must have been there until around ten. Then I went home."

"Your wife can confirm that?"

Mannie smoothed his hand down his beard again. "No, I've gone my separate ways from the first Mrs. Winter. As you'll remember, she discovered my little... mistake, just as I was elected into this role."

I pursed my lips. His little mistake involved an affair with a much younger woman. One I publicly outed. "You're still with Star?"

He shook his head. "Sadly, we've also parted ways. She's a lovely woman but focused on her career. And I like to see a lady who knows how to dress like a lady. Star spent most of her time in workout clothes. All that lycra and those dance shoes aren't for me. I bought her new clothes and some delightful high heels to tempt her to change her style, but she wasn't having it. Star said heels damage your feet." Mannie leaned closer. "You should see the state of her feet after so many years practicing ballet. I have nightmares about those feet. Dancers don't have beautiful feet, and I'm partial to a pretty foot."

"Your foot fetish aside, if you weren't with your wife or your mistress, who does that leave?" Mannie might be a man of influence, but he was no stunner. Women shouldn't be falling at his flat feet.

"I have a new lady friend." He grinned at me. "Trixie Vermouth. We've been together two months."

Trixie sounded more like a cocktail than a person. "I don't know her."

"She's a new resident. She works with Abigail at the Fur Baby Emporium. I helped her to get the job.

It's just part-time, but she's talking about staying and taking on more hours."

"Trixie can confirm you were with her that evening?"

"Absolutely. I got home around ten-fifteen, had a late supper, and we sat listening to new music from Draygar. He knows how to work a dwarfen drum. Then we went to bed. That's where we stayed until the morning."

"I'm discovering Gretel annoyed a lot of people. And when I met her, she was bending your ear about the problems in the museum. That must have been wearing."

Mannie nodded. "Gretel was an exacting woman. You don't get to her position without treading on a few toes. She was head of her department and held that position for more than a decade. Whenever there was a conference on the history of magic, everyone wanted Gretel's input. She could charge whatever she liked to give talks."

"Does that mean you didn't like her?"

Mannie toyed with his napkin. "I respected Gretel. Her knowledge was outstanding, and I admired that. Were we best friends? No, but from one professional to another, I appreciated her input. I was the one who insisted she become a part of this museum development because it has to be world class. It wouldn't be without Gretel's input."

Tilly walked over with our food and drinks and set everything on the table. "Is there anything else I can get you?"

"No, this all looks lovely." Mannie flapped his napkin over his lap and grabbed a hunk of garlic bread.

The sound of frantic scratching came at the restaurant door.

I turned to see Wiggles giving me the stink eye through the glass. I chuckled. "You'd better serve his majesty before he barges in and starts stealing from customers' plates."

Tilly shook her head. "Will do. He's also getting lasagne." Her gaze went from me to Mannie before she walked away.

I gave the interrogation a rest as I sampled the rich, savory layers of lasagne and dunked my own hunk of garlic bread in the juice.

"Tilly has outdone herself." Mannie smacked his lips together.

"She always does."

We ate in companionable silence. Mannie had a good alibi, and it would be easy to check. It looked like I could discount our mayor from this investigation.

He lowered his fork. "Did you see the museum display about your family?"

"No, but Mom told me you've been asking to see old family documents." I wasn't keen about the Crypt family secrets being publicly displayed. Our demon catching lineage went back centuries.

"You should be proud of your family and what they've achieved."

"I didn't say I wasn't." Long before Willow Tree Falls existed, the Crypt witches hunted demons all over the world. For years, our home was wherever we laid our hats until an ancestor set down roots in the village and the demon prison was established.

"It's fascinating," Mannie said. "The research is meticulous, and it's all thanks to Gretel and Isadora's hard work that the exhibits are so impressive."

"Speaking of the exhibits, Cleo mentioned that Gretel was exacting in what she wanted to be displayed. Would that have irritated anyone?"

Mannie nodded as he brushed garlic bread crumbs from his beard. "It could have. In fact, I discovered Gretel making fun of one of Cleo's displays. She's a charming creature and an absolute font of knowledge, but her display ideas can be eccentric. I walked in on them, and Gretel was furious with Cleo. She was telling her she had no idea what she was doing and mocking her amateurish display."

Cleo hadn't mentioned that when I'd talked to her. "Was Cleo upset?"

His brow wrinkled. "It's tricky to know what Cleo's thinking. She's a strange one. Her ability is like nothing I've encountered before. It's a mixture of pixie magic and something much older. She feels like an old soul."

I nodded. That was exactly how I'd felt when I was around her. Cleo had an eclectic power. Maybe her act of being ditzy and cute was just that.

"Did Cleo complain about the way Gretel spoke to her?"

"She never mentioned anything to me," Mannie said. "While Gretel was ranting at her, Cleo was disassembling the exhibit and putting it back together the way Gretel wanted it. She was humming as she worked, which makes me think she was happy."

"And Cleo does the night security, as well?"

"That's right. I don't know how she does it. She patrols three times a night, which means her sleep is disturbed, but she's always full of energy. I've had to warn her a couple of times about all the sparkles she leaves around. It's as if she sweats glitter."

"Cleo said she's descended from the Muses. She could draw power from the artifacts around her. If she's regularly handling old items, they're often tinged with power. That would energize her, so she could manage both jobs."

"That's very possible. See, I knew you were the right witch for this job!" Mannie finished his last mouthful of lasagne and sat back in his seat. "How about dessert?"

"Tilly does a mean cookies and cream pie." As far as questioning murder suspects went, this wasn't a bad way to spend a lunchtime.

"We'll get three servings of that." Mannie nodded and smiled at me. "I know we've had difficult times in the past, but I appreciate your help with this. We must get the murder solved quickly. I have to get the museum opening rescheduled."

"I'll do what I can," I said, "but I'm only standing in until Dazielle returns. There's no guarantee I'll solve this."

"You're doing a splendid job. Dazielle will be back anytime now. Until then, you keep going. It's a pleasure to be interrogated by someone so charming." Mannie blinked his beady eyes at me.

It looked like Mannie and I were now friends. I never thought I'd see that happen.

After we placed the dessert order, I sat back and listened to Mannie regale me about a new tourist promotion he had planned for the thermal spas, but my mind was elsewhere. I was worrying about Cleo. With her mix of powers and obsession with history, she could have taken Gretel's criticism badly.

What if her sparkles and giggles were a front? I'd thought Seth was involved, but having learnt more about Cleo and more or less confirmed Seth's alibi, it might be that I'd focused on the wrong person.

There were a lot more questions to ask before I made progress with this mystery.

Chapter 11

I knocked on the door of the detached redbrick house Isadora and her assistants were staying in. It was three hours after my lunch interrogation with Mannie, and he'd been true to his word, arranging for me to see Isadora that afternoon.

"Mannie can't be short of money if he's rented this place for them." Wiggles snuffled around the outside of the door.

"That must be why he's so attractive to women in Willow Tree Falls," I said, "including his new girlfriend, Trixie."

"That's a pet's name."

I waggled my eyebrows. "Maybe she's his new pet."

Wiggles snorted. "It can't be the beard they find attractive. Even from where I sat outside of Bite Me, Mannie ended up with half his lunch nestled in that forest around his face. He'll be enjoying leftover garlic bread for days."

"I was trying not to look," I said with a grimace.

The door to the house opened. Isadora stood there, her eyes looking glazed and her hair unbrushed.

"Hi, is this a bad time?"

Isadora blinked at me, and her eyes snapped into focus. "No! Sorry, I was expecting you. Mannie said you were stopping by. I'm in the middle of writing a new chapter of a book and got distracted. Please, come in." She stepped to one side, and we walked into a dark oak hallway.

"You're working on something new?" I asked as we followed her along the hallway and into a cream colored lounge.

"I'm always working on something," Isadora said. "Too many ideas in my head, that's the trouble. I'm promoting my new book, but my focus is on one I'm yet to write. It's always the same. Take a seat. Would you like some tea?"

"If it comes with cake," Wiggles said.

Isadora scratched her head. "Oh, I'm afraid not. The cupboards are bare. I keep meaning to go out and get something, but with everything that's going on, I'm not sure whether I'm coming or going." She ran her hands through her hair before perching on the edge of the seat opposite me.

"I understand how distressing this is," I said. "Gretel's murder, the book launch being postponed, the museum opening on hold."

Tears filled Isadora's eyes. "My hard work could be ruined. I spent years working on that book. I worked long hours, only slept maybe five hours a night for months leading up to its release, checking final proofs and double-checking the facts to make sure nobody could complain that I got something wrong. Then Mannie came along with his proposal about the museum. At first, I thought it was wonderful. My historical teachings coming to life in a museum to share with everybody."

"That's a lot of pressure." I noticed Isadora hadn't mentioned Gretel's murder and how distressing that was.

"I let my ego take over my senses," Isadora said. "I wanted everyone to know about my work. I understand that not everybody reads books, but a museum is a wonderful, interactive way for people to learn. I couldn't turn Mannie down and came on board to consult on the project. It got so big, so fast. I'd expected a couple of exhibits, not a whole museum full of history, and for Mannie to use my research as inspiration for it all."

"You'll still be able to launch your book, though," I said.

"We have thousands of copies printed, so I hope so." Isadora sighed. "Seth's working on a new deal and finding other ways to generate a buzz about the book."

"Gretel's murder will generate plenty of buzz."

Isadora clasped her hands together. "Yes, I suppose it will. Not the right sort, though."

"Isadora, I've been checking over your schedule." Jonah stopped in the doorway, a sheet of paper in his hand. "Oh! I didn't know you had guests."

"Come in, Jonah," Isadora said. "This is Tempest Crypt. You might remember her from the museum opening. She's helping with the investigation into what happened that night."

Jonah nodded. "Nice to see you again. Can I get you anything?"

"I don't suppose you've got any cookies?" Isadora asked. "I need something sweet to calm my nerves."

Jonah smiled. "Of course. While you were busy in your room this morning, I went out and got a few provisions. How about I make everyone coffee and cookies?"

"You're an angel," Isadora said. "Leave me the schedule, and I'll take a look at everything."

Jonah passed her the sheet of paper before hurrying out.

Isadora watched him go. "Honestly, I don't know what I'd do without him. Jonah's so organized, whereas I'm so..." She waved her hand around. "Sometimes, I forget to brush my teeth I'm so caught up in my work."

"Has Jonah been with you long?"

"Five years. I'd be a disorganized mess without him."

Jonah returned with the coffee and cookies and poured cups for us all before leaving and pulling the door shut.

I took a sip of my coffee. "Is your new book also on the history of magic?"

"Yes, it's what I specialize in. I find the past much more interesting than the present. But I will be including a chapter on modern day witchcraft."

"Not our kind of magic?" I asked.

Isadora's smile was benign. "No, our secrets will remain safe. There'll be no mention of the magic associated with Willow Tree Falls or anyone who lives here. I find an increasing number of people, who have no magic ability, turn to our ways. The modern world leaves people wanting for something, and they think knowing about magic will help them."

"Were you working with Gretel on your new book?"

"Gretel hasn't got the patience to write a book. I consulted with her a few times on my book, and we worked together on the museum, but that's as far as our collaboration goes."

"What was your working relationship like?"

Isadora tilted her head as she dunked a cookie in her coffee. "I respected Gretel. She was dedicated to historical accuracy."

"She was a pedant?"

A smile filtered across Isadora's face. "It could be annoying at times. Gretel had this ability to rub people up the wrong way. She didn't do it deliberately, but she could be spiky. Borderline rude."

"Did you tell her that her behavior was inappropriate?"

"Tell Gretel Le Strange how to behave?" Isadora shook her head. "I'm not that brave. She was a no-nonsense sort of woman. Her passion for history meant that she cared for nothing else. She never married. Never had a family of her own. Her work was her life. Gretel didn't mind if she offended someone by telling them they were wrong. All she cared about was historical accuracy. She had my professional respect, and until recently, I thought we were friends of sorts."

I took a cookie and broke a small piece off for Wiggles, who'd been begging by my knee ever since they'd arrived. "What happened to end your friendship?"

"My new book," Isadora said, "the one that's about to be released. I talked through the idea with her years ago, and she supported my efforts. She said it would be a worthy addition to current literature."

"She changed her mind?"

"When she saw an advance copy, Gretel called it a work of fiction." Isadora's mouth turned down. "She said it shouldn't be on the historical shelves. It was a joke. I couldn't believe it at first. It isn't fiction. It's full of factual information and has source references to support my ideas. I insisted she apologize."

"That didn't go down well?"

Isadora sighed. "Gretel refused. She said she'd have no part in this book and couldn't endorse it. In fact, she went as far as to say that she'd recommend people didn't waste their time on it. That was spiteful and unnecessary. After that, I stopped talking to her."

"Which must have been difficult, since you were working on the museum together," I said.

"We had our moments, but most of the work was done. Gretel was stomping around barking at everybody and telling them they were doing things wrong, and I left her to it. I was ready to launch the book and leave as soon as possible. It doesn't look like that will happen now."

I sipped my coffee, and my gaze went to a stack of boxes in the corner of the room. "Are your books in those boxes?"

Isadora nodded. She stood and collected a copy before handing it to me. "You can have it autographed if you like."

I flicked open the first page. "Thanks. Do you focus on particular magic topics?"

"I mention it all. I've always been most interested in the history of witchcraft and how others have treated witches."

Isadora grabbed her own copy before returning to her seat. "Take a look at the chapter headings. You'll see I focus on different periods when magic was acknowledged and what happened to send it underground and lead to the establishment of places like Willow Tree Falls. Not that I mention the village, but to those without abilities, they simply believe that magic transformed into something more benign. Something that could never affect them."

"There's nothing benign about what goes on here." I scanned the chapter headings. "Death of the witches?" I flipped to that chapter.

"We all know about the persecution of our kind," Isadora said. "And the specific methods used when forcing confessions from witches or killing them so they couldn't return and terrorize the local villagers. Not that we ever would."

I scanned the text before flipping the page. My eyes widened as I saw a picture of a witch on a ducking stool. "Is the museum exhibit modeled on your description?"

"That's right. There were five main ways to kill a witch. The ducking stool was used to force confessions and see if the woman was a witch. The ridiculous thing about that was, if she drowned and floated, then she wasn't a witch."

I grimaced. "I never understood that. If she lives, she's a witch, so they'd kill her anyway. If she drowns, she's not, and an innocent person dies."

"Exactly. The second method is stoning. The witch was crushed to death by heavy stones. Then there's hanging, which was the most common way to kill a witch. Everyone thinks it was burning at the stake, but that was rare. Hanging was the most popular method but is rarely talked about. I guess it's not glamorous. There's also being trapped behind a wall and bricked in. That was even rarer but equally unpleasant."

"And there'll be a museum exhibit of each of these methods of killing?" I asked.

"Yes, the ducking stool was our pièce de résistance because it's so stark and dramatic. There will also be an exhibit of a witch buried under stones. You'll see glimpses of the witch underneath, with a hand sticking out. It's gory, but it happened. We have to portray the past accurately. We can't learn and change if we don't know what we did wrong."

I stared at the picture in the book of the witch on the ducking stool. The way the body was posed in the stool was just like Gretel had been left. She'd been slumped forward, her hair covering her face. Her legs had been in the water, and her hands tucked in her lap. It was eerily accurate.

"How many people have seen this image?" I asked Isadora.

"Me, of course, the illustrator, and everyone who works for me, the publishers. Mannie and Gretel have seen a finished copy, but I don't know if they've looked through it all. The public hasn't seen it yet. The book doesn't go on general sale for another week. Why do you ask?"

"It might be nothing, but Gretel's death looks like this picture, even down to the way her hands were placed."

Isadora's eyes widened. "Do you think the killer used that picture as the inspiration to murder Gretel?"

"That's something only they can answer. Looking at this picture, I instantly thought of Gretel."

"I trust everyone I work with. It makes no sense that the publishing house would have anything to do with this. No one from the company was at the museum event, so they can't be involved. It must be a coincidence."

I closed the book. "Do you mind if I keep hold of this?"

"No, call it a gift. It might be the only one I give away any time soon if the museum launch is scuppered."

I nodded. There was still no sign of sadness from Isadora about Gretel's murder. "Returning to your publishing company, I've heard legal rumblings about the book."

Isadora pressed her lips together. "What have you been told?"

"Gretel wasn't happy with some information in the book and was considering legal action."

Isadora waved her hand in the air. "I know what you're talking about, but everything's under control. Gretel was causing a fuss, but it was about nothing. Seth's looking into it. The book launch won't be delayed by Gretel's unreasonable behavior."

Gretel definitely wouldn't delay anything now since she was dead. "What was Gretel unhappy about?"

Isadora sighed. "Nothing. Silly details. Things that no one else cared about."

I raised an eyebrow and waited for her to continue.

Isadora huffed out a breath. "Factual inaccuracy, but everything was inaccurate as far as Gretel was concerned. She'd find faults where there were no faults to be had. My team is excellent at what they do. Her complaints were small wrinkles that are being ironed out."

"And now Gretel's not around, anything she was planning to do won't happen," I said. That was an excellent motive for wanting Gretel dead. If she'd been threatening to take Isadora to court because of this book, Isadora would be desperate to prevent that from happening.

"With everything that's gone on between me and Gretel, I can't say I'm shedding tears over her death. She was slowing everything down and making everybody stressed. With her gone, it removes roadblocks, and that includes her questioning my research. I wasn't afraid to go up against her in court. If she'd pursued it, I would have won the battle. Gretel was in the wrong."

I drank more coffee. Isadora seemed confident about her book, but her dislike of Gretel and the problems she was causing her had jumped Isadora to the top of my list of suspects.

"What were you doing on the night of Gretel's murder?"

"The same as everybody else involved with the museum," Isadora said. "I stayed there until around eight in the evening, came back here, and had a late dinner with Jonah, and then had an early night. I wanted to be ready for my big launch."

"Was Jonah with you the whole evening?"

"We were in the house together, but after dinner, I went to my room. I didn't see him after that. You can confirm with him that we had dinner together." Isadora checked the time and jumped from her seat. "Oh! I'm so sorry, but I must get back to work. I'm expecting a report to arrive that I must read for a new chapter in my book. Do you have any more questions for me, or is that enough information?"

"No, thanks. That's been helpful," I said. "Do you have plans to stay in Willow Tree Falls for much longer?"

"If we can get the museum launch going again quickly, we'll stick around and try for book launch part two." Isadora clasped her hands together. "Mannie assured me everything will be ready to go by the end of the week."

"It might take longer than that," I said. "We must make sure we find out what happened to Gretel."

"Oh, do you think so?" Isadora's shoulders drooped. "I need quiet time to focus on my new book. Trying to work in a strange place is unsettling."

"You do want us to catch the murderer, don't you?"

Her eyes widened, and she blinked at me. "Of course. But you can't think anyone here did it. We all had our differences with Gretel, but none of us are killers. We're researchers, historians. Book nerds. We're not murderers."

I patted the book she gave me. "I look forward to reading this."

Isadora's smile was tentative as she led me and Wiggles to the door. "I hope you enjoy it." She opened the door, and after saying goodbye, I walked away with Wiggles.

"Isadora seemed nervous," Wiggles said.

"She did. And she couldn't have cared less about what happened to Gretel. All she was worried about was people taking her book seriously and selling a ton of them."

"She's one of those typical professor types," Wiggles said. "The ones that have their brains engaged in something else, even when they're talking to you. She kept getting a weird, faraway look in her eye when you were asking her questions. It's like she can access a part of her brain us mere mortals can't."

"Or she was trying to hide her guilt," I said. "Isadora has a lousy alibi. Even with Jonah in the house, it would have been easy for her to sneak out and go back to the museum when it got late. She had a lot to lose, and Gretel was a massive problem for her."

We reached the end of the lane, and I slowed when I heard rustling coming from a nearby bush.

"That sounds like a big rabbit." Wiggles' eyes glowed as he stared at the swaying bush beside us.

"I don't think it's anything you want to eat." I heard a muttered curse from behind the bush.

Jonah pushed his way through the bush, brushing leaves off his pullover. "Tempest, I'm glad I caught you before you went too far. I have to talk to you. There's something wrong with Isadora."

Chapter 12

I approached Jonah, noting the worry on his face. "What's wrong with Isadora?"

He glanced back toward the house. "I didn't want to say anything while you were inside in case Isadora overheard. It's why I snuck out when you left. She thinks I worry too much, but I'm around her all the time, and I'm really concerned."

"Does her stress have to do with Gretel's murder?"

Jonah shook his head. "They didn't get along, but Gretel being out of the picture is a good thing for everyone. The problem is this book that's about to launch. It's been Isadora's obsession for years. Five years of almost full-time research to make sure it's the best book ever written on the history of witchcraft and magic. It's like her baby, her one true love. Now, she can see everything she's worked for collapsing around her. She's falling apart because of it."

"It's her book launch worrying her?"

He nodded. "She's not sleeping. I hear her at night, pacing her room and talking to herself. She's never been like this before. Isadora does get anxious before a deadline, but that's normal. This is a new level of stress."

"Isadora sounds obsessed," I said.

Jonah wrung his hands together. "She's got a right to be. It's a masterpiece. You should read that copy and see for yourself." He nodded at the book in my hand.

"I'm planning to. Do you do any of the research for her?"

"No, I'm her personal assistant, not a researcher. I do everything to ensure Isadora's daily life is as smooth as possible and she can focus on her passion. I'm on call all the time. Whether it's making sure there are cookies in the cupboard or reminding her of her dental appointments."

"That must be hard on you," I said. "You're running your life and hers."

"If it was anybody else, I wouldn't be around." Jonah shrugged. "Isadora is a good boss. And history is an interest of mine. I studied it at college and planned to go into teaching, but then this opportunity came up to be Isadora's assistant, and I grabbed the chance. Working alongside such a popular magic historian and helping get her book out seemed like a dream. I'd love to write myself, but I don't have the intellect to write a book."

"Is Isadora a demanding employer?"

"Not usually, although she keeps odd hours. It's mainly that she forgets about things when she's deep in her writing. For example, no food in the cupboards when you visited. It's the little things she forgets about; that includes remembering to eat regular meals. I give her a routine, and she sticks to it so she can maximize her productivity."

"Since Isadora is focused on making sure her book is a success, I imagine she'd do anything to ensure it didn't fail."

"Oh! Of course. There's a countrywide book signing tour planned. The museum's opening was stage one before she heads off to other venues. Isadora's also got a number of TV appearances booked when she leaves Willow Tree Falls. Lots of radio interviews, and she's appearing on numerous blogs. We have it planned out."

"I thought Seth handled the publicity."

"He does. We work side-by-side to make sure there's never a clash with Isadora's schedule. She has to have time to produce new work. A genius like Isadora never stops working."

To me, it sounded like Isadora wouldn't let anything stand in her way to ensure her book was an epic success. Maybe that included murder.

"How was Isadora the night before the book launch?" I asked him. "She said she had an early night after eating dinner with you."

He nodded. "That's right. She came back from the museum around eight. I was with her. They'd been working on last-minute problems Gretel had identified. Isadora wasn't happy about it. I ordered in dinner as a treat. We ate together and ran through the schedule for the launch, then she said she was tired and was getting an early night."

"Was that unusual? Does Isadora often go to bed early?"

"It depends on her work schedule. When she's close to a deadline, she'll often stay up until gone midnight working on a book. But all she needed to worry about was her talk at the museum and the launch event. There wasn't much she could do. I wasn't surprised when she said she'd have an early night."

"Did you see her after she went to bed?"

Jonah raised his eyebrows. "I'm not sure what you're implying."

"Nothing improper. But did Isadora come out to get a drink or use the bathroom?"

"Oh, no, not that I saw." Jonah smiled self-consciously. "I sat up until around ten-thirty. The house was quiet, so I did some work undisturbed. Then I went to bed."

"Did you hear Isadora in her room?"

He tilted his head. "I heard some noises early on, so I assumed she was getting ready for bed."

"You said that Gretel had issues at the museum that Isadora wasn't happy about. Did they often argue?"

"It was common. After the fallout over her book, Isadora stayed away from Gretel. Every time they met, they clashed. Two alpha females in the same room, you see, it's always going to be fireworks. Gretel thought she was better than Isadora because of her qualifications and the papers she'd published in a few dry academic journals."

"It sounds like Gretel rubbed Isadora's nose in it."

"All the time, but Isadora is smart. She does her research and goes back to the source material. She's not sloppy like many of these popular historical writers. They embellish the facts with nonsensical romance or ideas about historical figures that they can't know about. Isadora's an excellent historian. Gretel hated the fact that she'd never back down when they argued. It was a shock to her system when she didn't get her own way."

"When was the last time you saw them argue?"

Jonah tugged on his bottom lip. "Outside the museum, the night before Gretel died. It got quite heated. I was about to intervene when Gretel stomped away."

"What were they arguing about?"

"I didn't hear the details of the argument, but there were only ever two things they argued about, the museum or Isadora's book. It was all either of them cared about."

It wasn't looking so good for Isadora. She'd had an ongoing feud with Gretel, who sounded like she was trying to ruin Isadora's book launch, and no one could confirm where she was after nine o'clock on the night of Gretel's murder. It wouldn't have been difficult for her to slip out and confront Gretel at the museum. Jonah would have been none the wiser.

Isadora and Gretel both sounded passionate and headstrong. Gretel might not have considered it strange to meet Isadora so late if she believed there was a problem with an exhibit. She'd have wanted everything to be perfect for the opening event.

Jonah touched my arm. "The sooner you figure out what happened to Gretel, the better. I'm so worried about Isadora. She can't cope with more stress. Mannie is pushing for a second launch event, and Seth keeps adding more book signing dates to the list. Anything else, and she might break."

"I'm doing what I can, but I still haven't spoken to all the witnesses. And everyone who knew Gretel is under suspicion."

"You can't believe any of us are involved, do you?"

"Someone who knew Gretel killed her. She wouldn't have met just anybody at the museum that night. Can you think of anybody who'd want Gretel dead?"

Jonah's shoulders sagged. "Sadly, lots of people. I don't know of anyone who had kind words to say about Gretel, other than the fact that she was a genius when it came to the history of magic."

"Does that include you?"

He nodded. "Sure, but I'm used to dealing with high-powered types. Isadora mixes in a particular social circle. There are often experts and people whose egos need careful management. Difficult people are my bread-and-butter. It didn't bother me that Gretel was abrasive. I've handled people a lot worse than Gretel Le Strange. Academics are an odd breed. You learn to ignore their bluntness and eccentricities once you're used to it."

"Would you hazard a guess as to who'd most benefit from Gretel being out of the picture?"

He was silent for several seconds. "I'm not sure."

"What about the rest of the team you work with? I've spoken to Seth, and he confirmed that Gretel was tricky to work with. Did anybody else have problems? Was there any division within the team?"

"On the whole, everyone's happy." Jonah rubbed his chin. "We all like working with Isadora. Although, Lotus has just handed in her notice."

"Why is she leaving?"

Jonah puffed out a breath. "It's got to do with her relationship with Seth. I imagine he's mentioned her to you."

"He did," I said. "He said they might be getting married. Are members of staff not supposed to date?"

"It's got nothing to do with whether they're dating or not," Jonah said. "Lotus wasn't happy because of Isadora's handling of the relationship."

"Isadora isn't happy that Seth and Lotus are involved?"

"Jonah!" Isadora's voice drifted along the lane. "Where are you? I need you."

Jonah snapped to attention and stepped away from me. "I have to go. I can't leave Isadora alone for long or she starts to panic."

"Wait! What do you mean about Lotus and Seth's relationship?"

Jonah's fingers flexed. "Lotus isn't into Seth. She wants nothing to do with him."

"Jonah!" Isadora sounded like she was close to tears.

"I have to go. If you want to learn more about their relationship, you'll need to ask them." Jonah turned and dashed back to the house.

I rubbed the back of my neck as I processed this information. Seth had been so certain about his relationship with Lotus, but it seemed like there was trouble in paradise.

"Isadora sounds ambitious," Wiggles said as we turned and walked slowly along the lane toward the main street.

"Ambitious enough to kill Gretel," I said. "She sounds like a woman on the edge. How can somebody get so stressed about writing one book?"

"Have you ever written a book?"

"No, but I've read a few."

"Her book sounds like her whole life," Wiggles said. "Gretel threatened Isadora's livelihood, and she snapped."

I glanced back at the house. "Jonah seems worried about her. The team can't fall apart now, or they'll all lose out. If Isadora can't do this book signing, Seth will miss out on the publicity deals, and future sales will be affected. Lotus might not have a job if Isadora stops working, and Jonah won't have anyone to assist."

"You don't think they're all covering for her, do you?" Wiggles asked. "Maybe the team knows what Isadora did to Gretel and is providing her with an alibi, so they keep their jobs."

"If that's what they're doing, they're not doing a great job," I said. "Isadora's alibi is flimsy. Nobody can vouch for where she was at the time of the murder. Being in bed alone isn't a great alibi."

"And she's got a great motive," Wiggles said.

"I need to speak to Isadora again. But let's give her a bit of time to calm down. She sounded frantic when shouting for Jonah. I don't want to be the one to push her over the edge. How about we tackle Lotus next?"

"And find out if that smarmy half-vampire is telling the truth about their relationship?"

I nodded. "Somebody's not being honest, and we need to figure out why."

Chapter 13

I'd visited the museum in my search for Lotus, but there was no one there. I was pleased to see Gretel's body was gone, and there were no signs of the angels. It looked like they'd followed their orders.

Lotus hadn't been at the house when I'd visited Isadora, so there was no point in going back there. I wandered through the village, hoping I'd bump into her.

As I passed Mystic Mushroom, I did a double-take.

Lotus sat at a table on her own with half a giant pizza in front of her. Grease from the cheese was smeared down her chin, and her expression was glum as she sat alone eating.

I walked into Mystic Mushroom and over to the counter. "Hey, Tate. How's everything going?"

"No complaints." He grinned at me. "Are you after an early dinner?"

"Actually, just a few questions." I tilted my head toward Lotus. "How long has she been here?"

"She's been eating alone for the last hour," Tate said. "That's her second large pizza. I get the impression she's comfort eating."

"I could do with some comfort eating right about now," Wiggles said.

I ignored his nose as it stabbed into my leg. "She didn't mention why she needs to eat two huge pizzas on her own?"

"You mean other than the fact that I make incredible pizzas?" Tate smiled. "She didn't say anything, but I can tell she's upset. Her eyes are red, and her nose is puffy as if she's been crying. I asked if everything was okay, but she clammed up and said she wanted to eat alone. I decided not to bother her. If customers want to deal with their feelings on their own as they eat my pizza, they're welcome to."

I turned and looked at Lotus. I did need to bother her. I ordered a coffee and walked to Lotus's table. "Mind if I join you?"

Lotus looked up and blinked at me, recognition crossing her face. "Oh, you're that investigator."

"Tempest Crypt." I nodded at the chair opposite Lotus.

"Sure, help yourself." She stuffed a large piece of pizza in her mouth, her gaze shifting to Wiggles.

"That's Wiggles," I said.

Lotus tossed him a dough ball, which he grabbed in mid-air.

"Thanks." Wiggles swallowed after a single chew, his gaze on the remaining dough balls.

"Anytime," Lotus said.

"Tate makes incredible food, doesn't he?" I said.

She made a muffled sound of agreement around the pizza.

"How are you doing? It must be a shock what happened to Gretel."

Lotus shrugged and wiped cheese grease off her lips. "Not really. I'm surprised no one killed her years ago. She was an old hag. She always tried to pick apart my research simply out of spite. She kept on about lack of experience and youth as if that's a factor. I'm amazing at what I do. It always riled her when I proved her wrong."

"I thought Gretel was the font of all knowledge when it came to the history of magic."

Lotus snorted. "Gretel did old school research, sticking to books in dusty libraries. I investigate using two different methods. I go to the original source when possible, and I go online. Although, my computer's been playing up since we got here."

"Blame the magic. Electricity and magic always have fun together."

"Figures. Anyway, I fact check using specialist search sites. I leave questions in online chat rooms and use mapping programs to investigate sites I can't physically get to. Add that to my source data review, and my research is more comprehensive than Gretel's. The only issue with age was hers. She was too old to keep up with new ways of researching. She was a dinosaur. I'm a genetically modified super computer."

"I can imagine how much Gretel liked accepting that."

"She hated it, not that she'd ever acknowledge I was better than her. I think that was why she was so spiteful to me. Not that I cared. I knew I was better than Gretel Le Strange. It gave me a thrill to make her mad."

For a cute looking elf, she came with a mean streak. "I heard that you won't be working with Isadora anymore."

She nodded. "It's time to move on."

"Have you got a new job?"

"No. It's not easy to pick up research positions for this kind of work, but I've got my eye on something."

"You must have gained useful experience doing research for Isadora's book."

"And it's all for nothing." Lotus grimaced and looked away. "I worked alongside her for such a long time. I would say two thirds of the research in that book is mine."

"I'm surprised your name isn't on the cover."

Lotus scowled and ate a dough ball. "Exactly. Isadora doesn't even mention me in her acknowledgements. I'm always there for her, looking up obscure facts, finding information, and checking source material. Sure, Isadora did some of it, but she did the glamorous stuff. She got to have lunch with the fancy professors and give talks at museums and universities all over the world. What did I get? A dusty old room with no window in a library. I barely left that room for months when we did the initial research. Isadora only cares about the finished product. She wants her name all over this book, so she can be rich and famous."

"That must have made you mad," I said.

"For all the good it did me," Lotus said. "It doesn't bother her if her team isn't happy, so long as she gets what she wants."

"Is that what prompted you to resign?"

"It was the final straw. I was angry with the way she treated me, but when I asked for her help, and she saw I needed it, she turned away."

"What did you need help with?"

Lotus frowned. "Have you met Seth?"

"He was the first person I talked to about what happened to Gretel," I said. "Things aren't going well between you?"

She snorted a laugh. "Things have never gone well between us. Seth's so full of himself. He's been working with Isadora for nine months, getting this book launch in place. The first day we met, I knew he'd be trouble."

"What happened between you?"

"Seth assumed too much. He was overly friendly and acted like I should be grateful for his attention."

"And you weren't?"

"I have no interest in Seth. He's asked me out dozens of times, and I always turn him down. I've made it clear there's nothing romantic happening between us. Not now, not ever."

"Seth doesn't buy that?"

"He doesn't believe it. The guy lives in a fantasy world where we're blissfully happy together." Lotus pulled the pineapple off her pizza and ate it before flicking a piece at Wiggles. He ignored the pineapple offering. He wasn't a fruit fan. "Every time I say no to Seth, he comes up with another suggestion for a date or another reason he's perfect for me. At first, it was cute. It's flattering when someone's interested in you, but it got boring. He wouldn't stop asking."

"He sounds like a pest," Wiggles said. "Feed me a few more of those dough balls, and I'll bite him for you."

Lotus managed a small smile as she threw him a dough ball. "Be my guest. Anyway, I began to find reasons not to be around when Seth was about. Isadora was flexible and let me work anywhere, but I still couldn't get away from Seth. He'd turn up when I wasn't expecting him. No matter how discreet I was. I only ever told Isadora where I worked, but Seth still figured it out."

"What did you need Isadora's help with?" I asked. "If you didn't want her to okay your relationship with Seth, what else could she do?"

"Seth was interfering with my work. I asked Isadora to keep him out of my way, but she said Seth had a job to do, and she wasn't letting him go. But I'm not a part of his job. I have nothing to do with the publicity side of things. We have no reason even to speak."

"Isadora overlooked Seth's inappropriate behavior because he's so good at his job?"

"That's the problem. Isadora's determined her book will be a massive success. Seth isn't cheap to hire, and she wants the best." Lotus' mouth twisted to the side. "And, although he's a creep, he does know how to run an excellent publicity campaign."

"What did Seth do that made you want to leave?"

"It's not so much what he did." Lotus' shoulders slumped. "I'm used to batting away his advances and keeping his hands off me. But one afternoon, Isadora walked in on Seth making a pass at me. He had me pinned against the desk and was trying to kiss me. I looked right at Isadora and asked for help. I said I wasn't happy and Seth needed to leave. Isadora did nothing. She shrugged her shoulders, turned around, and walked out the door. She left me when I needed her."

My eyes widened. "How did you stop Seth?"

"I kicked him somewhere very delicate, very hard. He was limping for days." Lotus grinned at me. "I knew I only had a temporary reprieve. It wouldn't be long before he tried again. I'd had enough. What stung the most was that Isadora knew I needed her, and she hadn't helped me. If I didn't know how to handle myself around Seth, I'd have been in serious trouble that day, and Isadora knew that. She doesn't care enough about me to make sure I'm safe."

"What did she say to you about the incident?"

"That's the horrible thing. She never mentioned it. Isadora acted like she'd seen nothing."

"Seth sounds more like a dangerous stalker than a boyfriend."

"That about sums him up. And I'd never date him. Seth's a creep, and I don't trust him." Lotus chewed on a piece of pizza crust. "I like my work with Isadora, and I love doing research like this, but I had to resign. Isadora let me down. I can't forgive her for that."

Isadora seemed solely focused on making her book launch a success and had neglected her staff, even when they desperately needed her help.

"I understand why you want to leave. It's a shame you can't get rid of Seth and keep your job."

"I sometimes dream about bumping him off and getting rid of him permanently." Lotus chuckled. "I shouldn't have confessed that to you since you're investigating Gretel's murder. I promise I might dream of murder, but that's as far as it goes."

Lotus' openness made me trust her. She had enough problems in her life without going after Gretel and trying to conceal the murder. "There's no way to get Seth fired?"

"I've thought about it several times, trying to make him leave, but he's sticking around until he gets paid. Isadora also won't let him go. She can get another researcher easily enough. I'm replaceable."

"Did you see Seth the night of Gretel's murder?"

"Unfortunately, yes. There's not much for me to do at the moment, and everyone is focused on the new book launch. Isadora's working on something new, so I'm helping with bits and pieces, but I have free time and usually get to finish early."

"Was Seth working with you that night?"

"No. I finished work and went for a drink in the Ancient Imp. I'd been there a couple of hours and was thinking about getting dinner when Seth came in. Immediately, he came over, offered to buy me a drink, and started sweet talking me. I wasn't in the mood for his nonsense. I left the Ancient Imp and came here." Lotus sighed. "I love pizza. It takes away all your worries."

"There's something magic about what Tate does to his pizza. How long were you here that night?"

"Late. I stayed as long as possible to avoid Seth when I went back to the house. We're all staying in the same place, and he's knocked on my bedroom door a couple of times to see if he can give me a good-night kiss and a mug of cocoa."

My brows shot up. "I hope you never let him in."

Lotus wrinkled her nose. "The door is always locked. He's never getting into my bedroom. I left here at closing time and got back to the house around midnight. I went straight to bed. I didn't see anyone, and I was quiet because I didn't want to alert Seth if he was listening for me coming home."

"You're too good for Isadora and definitely too good for Seth." Lotus seemed like a decent person who'd been treated badly. "Who do you think wanted Gretel out of the way?"

"You can take your pick out of anyone here. Isadora hated her; Seth thought she was trouble and not worth the hassle. I even saw your mayor arguing with Gretel, and I thought they were friends. Even Cleo got the sharp side of Gretel's tongue more than once. Gretel made enemies wherever she went. There will be plenty of people raising a glass when they learn that Gretel Le Strange is no longer hassling them."

I nodded as I stood from my seat. "Thanks for the information. Enjoy the rest of your pizza." I wandered back to the counter where Tate was serving up a large deep pan stuffed crust with extra sausage and mushrooms.

"Did you get everything you needed?" Tate asked.

I nodded and licked my lips. "I don't suppose that's for me, is it?"

"Sorry, special order. I can always make you one."

"Make that two," Wiggles said. "And some dough balls."

"Maybe another time." I leaned closer to the counter. "Do you remember Lotus being in here the night Gretel was murdered?"

He nodded. "Of course. She's hard to miss with that cute blue hair."

"What time did she come in?"

"Just after eight. She had a large pizza, a side order of garlic bread, and a triple fudge sundae. She can sure pack away the food for such a tiny thing."

"How long was she here?"

"All night. I had to ask her to leave because I was ready to close the shop. She looked like she was settled in and would have stayed as long as she could."

"Lotus didn't say anything about why she wanted to stay?"

"No, she wouldn't open up." Tate glanced at her. "Did she tell you what's wrong?"

"Guy trouble," I said. "And employer trouble."

"That'll do it. Everyone enjoys comfort food when they've got problems like that." Tate shook his head. "I locked the store and walked Lotus almost back to her house. I didn't want her walking home on her own when she was clearly troubled."

I smiled at him. "You're a decent guy, Tate."

"And he makes awesome pizza," Wiggles said. "You can make me one of those deep pan extra sausage pizzas to go."

"No pizza," I said. "We've got work to do."

"Not even a small one?"

"We can treat ourselves to pizza when we've solved this murder." I nodded thanks to Tate and left

Mystic Mushroom before I was also tempted by the alluring scent of garlic bread and melted cheese.

My thoughts swirled as I considered what I'd just learned. Everything I heard about Isadora was bad news. She'd stop at nothing to ensure her book was a success. She'd ignored a staff member who needed her help, walked all over everybody else, took advantage of her assistant, and maybe even killed Gretel to rid herself of the woman who could ruin her hard work.

Isadora Ash was my number one suspect. It was time to bring her in for questioning.

Chapter 14

"Do you know when she's coming back?" I stood outside the house Isadora was staying in.

Jonah shook his head, his expression apologetic. "I insisted she take a break. She's gone for a walk to get fresh air. I'm hoping that will calm her. You're welcome to wait inside if you have more questions."

"No, thanks. We'll take a walk around and see if we can spot her. Did she say where she was going?"

"I suggested the stores. Isadora can have a browse around and take her mind off work."

"Thanks. I'll see if I can find her there." I said goodbye to Jonah and walked back into the village, hoping I'd see Isadora in a café or checking out one of the stores.

"Where do you think she's hiding?" Wiggles asked.

"I'm hoping she isn't hiding." If she was, it only added to my suspicions.

"Someone has a guilty conscience." Wiggles sat and scratched his belly with a back paw as we surveyed the people wandering past.

"It does seem odd. Maybe we spooked her when we first asked questions. Isadora might think we're onto her."

"I could try sniffing her out, but my nose is full of the delicious aroma of pizza. I have pizza on the brain. The only way to cure that is to eat pizza. We should get a pizza. Ten minutes to order a pizza. I can eat a whole pizza in five minutes."

"If you say pizza one more time, it's off the menu for a month."

"Piiiizzzzza." Wiggles snorted and turned his back on me.

I had to make this search for Isadora official. I needed to bring the angels up to speed on what was going on. They had more bodies than me and could help me look for her.

I walked to their headquarters to find the reception desk empty again. I didn't wait this time and went through into the back room with Wiggles.

A blob of something white and fluffy smacked into my forehead. "What the—"

"Oh! Tempest!" Sablo froze, a ball of what looked like sticky white feathers balanced on one outstretched wing. "We weren't expecting you."

I wiped my forehead and found it covered in white feathers and something that smelled like melted sugar. "What's going on?"

Dominic hurried over and handed me a cloth. "You know what it's like. When the boss is away..."

"You throw sticky balls of feathers at each other?" I wiped my forehead clean of feathers.

"It's Angel Ball." Sablo wandered over, tossing the white ball in the air.

"That's right," Dominic said. "We use our wings like bats. We each spare a few feathers, mold them into balls and bat them back and forth. Whoever drops the balls first is the loser and has to buy doughnuts."

"I'd love to play," Wiggles said. "I'm great with balls. And I love doughnuts."

"Angels only," Sablo said. "And I'm not trusting you anywhere near doughnuts ever again."

"We've been playing for three hours," Dominic said. "And we won't count your involvement because you aren't an official member of the crew. The pause in the game doesn't matter."

"No, we'll have to start again." Sablo flicked the ball in the air and caught it on her wing. "Previous time score void, thanks to intruders."

"Before you focus on this crucial task," I said, "you might be interested in what's going on with Gretel Le Strange's murder."

"Oh! Of course." The ball of feathers disappeared into Sablo's hand as she tucked it behind her. "What have you found out?"

I shook my head. I wasn't sure why I bothered. All the angels wanted to do was bat their balls around and munch on doughnuts. "I've spoken to everyone who has a connection to Gretel. Some alibis aren't great, but we need to focus on Isadora Ash."

"The author?" Dominic rubbed his chin. "Why would she ruin her book launch by killing Gretel?"

"Isadora isn't as straightforward as she appears. For one thing, her alibi is lousy. She was seen going into her room the night of the murder, but it would have been easy to return to the museum unnoticed. Isadora's also fiercely ambitious. She'd stop at nothing to make this book a success. Gretel was causing her problems. I've heard mention of a possible lawsuit against Isadora. Gretel was threatening legal action."

"That sounds serious," Dominic said. "You think Isadora killed Gretel to stop her from taking her to court?"

"It's looking increasingly likely. Although, no one has a nice word to say about Gretel. We need to bring Isadora in for questioning. I believe she had the most to lose if Gretel kept interfering."

"Make it happen," Sablo said. "We have an empty interview room if you want to use it."

Anger bubbled inside me. "I've been trying to, but there's a problem. She's missing."

"Is she on the run?" Worry flickered across Dominic's face.

"That's what we need to find out. Can you get the angels to be on the lookout for Isadora?"

"Sure," Sablo said. "We can pause Angel Ball and have a look around."

"If it's not too much trouble." I hoped I didn't sound too sarcastic. "Is there any sign of Dazielle coming back?" I never thought I'd be pleased to see Dazielle, but I now understood why she walked around with a sour expression on her face. It was all thanks to having to deal with this bunch of feathery fools on a daily basis.

"There's still no word," Sablo said. "We've sent three messages. She must be enjoying her training."

"Until she returns, we focus on Isadora. Get a team out looking for her. Whoever finds her first, bring her in for questioning."

"Are you leading on the questioning?" Sablo asked. "You know a lot more about this case than anyone else."

"Sure. You find her, bring her in, and we'll talk."

"We'll get right on it, boss." Dominic hurried away.

I looked around for Wiggles and saw him with his paws on a desk, chewing furiously.

"Quit it," I hissed at him. "You know what the angels do to you if you steal their food."

He took another big mouthful of whatever leftovers he'd discovered before racing over to me. "They always leave food around. I don't understand these angels. Why leave perfectly edible food to go stale? I'm doing them a favor by eating it."

I rubbed my forehead as I left the angels to get organized. If I came back to find them playing Angel Ball in a couple of hours, I was turning in my unwanted investigator badge and letting Mannie deal with the fallout.

Until the angels found Isadora, there wasn't much else I could do. I'd spoken to all the witnesses and suspects and needed to let the angels do their thing and track down Isadora.

I slowed as I walked past Aurora's store. The lights were off and the blinds down. "Why's the store shut? It's not closing time."

"Maybe she's got wedding business to take care of," Wiggles said. "I bet she's tasting wedding cake. That always sounds like the best bit of getting hitched. All the free cake you want to sample."

I peered through the window. Most of the shelves were missing stock. That never happened. Aurora was always getting new stock and special deals in for her customers. That was one of the things that made her so popular; she was rarely missing an item if somebody needed it in a hurry. Whether it was a calming spell or a healing crystal, Aurora always had something suitable.

"I don't like this," I said to Wiggles. "Maybe Aurora's not well." I took a step back and peered at the apartment above the store. There were no lights on, and the curtains were open. It didn't look like anybody was home.

"She'll be at Toby's house," Wiggles said. "I bet that creep's convinced her to move in with him. Not that I blame her. Twelve bedrooms, a heated pool, acres of ground for me to run around in. I'd be tempted to move in if he asked."

I glowered at him. "You love our apartment."

"The apartment's great, but it would be nice not to have to run up and down the stairs every time I need a bathroom break. I've told you I'm happy to use a litter tray if you can find a big enough one."

"You're not a cat," I said. "You don't go to the bathroom in the apartment."

Wiggles grumbled under his breath. "Maybe I should get Toby to ask me to move in with him. I bet he'd give me a litter tray. It would be gold-plated. No, it would be solid gold."

"He'd never do that. Toby has allergies, and he's particularly allergic to you."

"He will be after my gardening efforts the last time we were at his house," Wiggles said.

"We need to pay Toby Matlock a visit. I want to see what he's up to with my sister."

We hurried past the stores again. I kept an eye out for Isadora as we walked, but she was nowhere to be found.

We walked along the long lane toward Toby's house, passing increasingly grander houses as we approached his driveway.

I headed to his front door, which was flanked by two menacing stone dragons. I paused before I knocked.

"This needs discretion," I said to Wiggles. "We don't want to bump into Feodor and be stopped from getting in. Let's see what's going on inside before we try to get through the front door."

Wiggles stood to attention, his tail in the air. "Stealth mode activated."

"Let's head around the side. Maybe Aurora is inside and nothing bad is going on. They might be having a nice dinner and I'm worried about nothing." I didn't believe my own words, but I hated to think Aurora was being exploited by Toby.

We crept around the side of the house, passing manicured bushes pruned into animal shapes. I peered in the first two windows and saw the hallway.

Wiggles hummed the theme tune to Mission Impossible as he scuttled beside me on his belly, his eyes darting from left to right.

I raised my head and looked through the window. My breath caught in my throat. "She's in here."

Aurora was in Toby's study, a smile on her face as she sat perched on the couch. She was staring into space, looking at nothing in particular.

Toby sat behind his desk, bent over some paperwork.

I stared at Aurora. Although she was smiling, the expression on her face was vacant, and her eyes looked glazed.

"Let me see." Wiggles pulled himself onto the frame with his paws and peered through. "I've never seen her in that dress before. It's low cut for your sister. She's showing a lot of, well, I don't like to leer at Aurora. She's showing some skin."

"I'm not worried about the dress." My fury mingled with Frank's energy as his power pushed up my spine. He sensed Aurora was close, and something bad was happening to her. "Toby's used his magic on her. Look at her face."

"She looks spaced out." Wiggles shuffled his butt closer. "Is that goofy look because of Toby?"

"It has to be." I studied her neck and saw her magic eraser pendant in place. How was Toby influencing her so easily?

"Eeek!" Wiggles tumbled backward. "We've been spotted."

I froze as Toby's gaze met mine. It was too late to do a Wiggles and hide. I stared at Toby for several seconds, neither of us blinking.

Rather than seeming surprised at my appearance outside his window, a sly smile spread over Toby's face.

Frank's energy burned at the back of my neck. His desire not only to have Aurora but destroy the man who was manipulating her fueled his anger.

"Tempest! Get down," Wiggles whispered. "Aren't you worried that Toby's seen you?"

"It's Toby who needs to worry." I drew back my fist, not entirely sure who was in control of my actions as Frank's energy pounded through me.

Just before I slammed my fist through the window of Toby's study, everything went black.

***

The world felt like it was spinning too fast. I held my hands out to stop from toppling.

"Tempest, you look beautiful in this color." Aurora knelt in front of me, adjusting the hem of the floor length yellow satin gown I wore.

I blinked slowly as my vision cleared and sucked in a breath. My ears were ringing, and my head throbbed with every movement of my eyes.

I was inside Toby's house. He'd used his sleazy magic on me.

"Say something," Aurora said. "Don't you like it?"

I stroked my hands down the soft fabric of the dress. "Why am I wearing this?"

Aurora giggled and clapped her hands together. "Stop fooling around. You're not getting away with wearing jeans and boots for our wedding. There are other color options, but the yellow makes your dark hair look incredible."

"The wedding?" My gaze went to the full-length mirror I stood in front of. The dress was high-waisted and off the shoulder, with lace sleeves running down the length of my arms. I had no idea how much time had passed or how I'd ended up in this dress. If Toby had helped take my clothes off and put this dress on me, I'd delight in setting Frank on him.

"I was thinking yellow and cream for the flowers," Aurora said. "They'll set your dress off perfectly. As my only bridesmaid, I want you to feel amazing."

Another wave of dizziness hit me, and I swallowed, my mouth feeling sandpaper dry. "It looks fine, and the flowers sound great." I glanced over my shoulder to see Toby sitting at his desk.

He raised his head and nodded at me. His eyes narrowed as if daring me to confront him. I took a step toward him. Toby wasn't getting away with this. I had to break Aurora free from his twisted clutches.

Aurora grabbed my hands and squeezed before I could go any farther. "I'm so happy you came. I've hated not being able to talk to you about the wedding preparations. There's so much to do, and now you're here, it will be easier to manage."

I nodded slowly. At least I was with Aurora again, and we were talking. Whatever Toby was doing to her, I couldn't leave her on her own to deal with him. She was oblivious to how manipulative he was. If I played along, Toby might stop thinking I was a problem, and I could convince Aurora she was making the biggest mistake of her life.

I forced myself to smile. "We have a lot to catch up on. You have to tell me everything about the wedding plans. Why don't we go outside and take a walk?"

"There's plenty of time for that." Toby pushed his chair back and strolled over. "You do look delightful in that color, Tempest."

"Have you been here the whole time I've been getting changed?" I spoke through gritted teeth.

"Of course, he hasn't," Aurora said. "You changed upstairs, but the light down here is perfect to look at the color, and I wanted Toby to see you in your dress. Doesn't she look beautiful?"

"Almost as lovely as you, my dear." Toby wrapped a hand around Aurora's waist and pressed a kiss on her cheek.

I repressed a growl as Toby fawned over Aurora like a prized pony.

"What do you think about a tiara?" Aurora asked as she tore her gaze from Toby.

"For whom?"

She grinned at me. "You! I was thinking flowers, but something more traditional. One with tiny crystals that sparkle in the light will look pretty in your hair."

I wrinkled my nose. "I'm not sold on the tiara."

"Aurora's having one," Toby said. "It will make her look like royalty."

She smiled up at him. "You always treat me like a princess."

"As is fitting," he said.

Aurora simpered over Toby while I tried not to gag.

After several minutes of cringe inducing soppiness, Aurora glanced at me. "I'll get the flower samples, and we can match them with your dress."

"Great idea." The second the door closed behind her, I turned on Toby. "You won't get away with this."

He stroked a hand down his goatee. "What is it you think I'm getting away with? Making your sister happy? Ensuring she has the best life she can? Letting her spend time with the man she loves?"

"You're manipulating her, and you manipulated me." I stepped closer. "I know you have my hair. That's how you're able to influence me so easily."

He shook his head, an expression of innocence on his face. "Are you feeling quite well? I'm manipulating no one, and I know nothing about your hair. I was somewhat surprised when I saw you lurking outside the house like a thief, looking for a way in to steal my antiques. But it's only right that you come in and make amends with Aurora. She's been down since you abandoned her."

I hissed in his face. "I didn't abandon her. She'll come to her senses about you."

"She's perfectly sensible when it comes to our relationship," Toby said. "Aurora will be happy here with me. She'll have everything she needs and will worry about nothing. But that will only happen if you don't keep causing problems for her."

"She's my little sister, and you're taking advantage of her," I snarled at him. "You're using mind manipulation magic on her. How are you doing it? How are you making Aurora remain under your influence for so long?"

"You're making no sense. Aurora is here of her own free will. As are you."

My eyes narrowed, and I glared at him. Toby was lying. He'd done something to make me lose time and end up standing in his study wearing this ridiculous dress. And he was taking advantage of Aurora, despite her magic eraser pendant.

"Here we are." Aurora hurried back in the room with an armful of flowers. "Who knew there were so many shades of yellow and cream to choose from?" She scattered the flowers on the floor in front of me and began holding them up one after the other against the dress fabric.

"Where's Wiggles?" I asked sharply, suddenly aware he was nowhere in the room.

Toby turned away. "I haven't seen him. Perhaps he's outside."

"Wiggles can't come in here," Aurora said. "He'll be fine in the grounds. There's plenty to entertain him. So, which shade of yellow do you think goes best with your dress?"

I rubbed the back of my neck. This was too weird. Aurora was blind to what Toby was doing.

The sound of a thud outside had me turning to the window. Feodor lumbered past, swinging a huge club in his hand.

I hurried to the window and grabbed hold of the frame, gasping as I saw Wiggles belch a gout of flames at Feodor. "Call off your mad butler," I said to Toby. "He's trying to hurt Wiggles."

Aurora hurried over and stared out of the window. "They're just playing. Feodor's a sweetie."

"Feodor has a giant club spiked with nails in his hand. That doesn't look like playing to me."

Wiggles belched more fire at Feodor, hitting his club, and it burst into flames.

Feodor swirled it around his head before launching it at Wiggles.

Aurora gasped. "These boys do like their rough-and-tumble."

"Rough-and-tumble!" I gaped at her. "The zombie butler is trying to kill Wiggles."

Aurora glanced at me, worry shimmering in her eyes. "Maybe they do need to calm things down a little."

My hands clenched into fists. "Toby, call off Feodor. Now!"

A loud knock sounded on the front door.

"My dear, will you be so good as to get that?" Toby said to Aurora. "Feodor is otherwise engaged." He smirked at me.

"Of course, my love. I'll speak with Feodor as well and make sure things don't get out of hand with Wiggles." Aurora nodded and hurried out of the room.

"If your zombie butler hurts a fur on Wiggles' head, I'm coming for you," I snapped at Toby.

"I wish you luck with that," Toby said. "And a word of advice while your sister is not here. Stay out of our relationship. Aurora's mine. You're jealous because you no longer have any influence over her. She's moving on with her life and doing it without you. If you know what's good for you, you'll stop interfering."

I bared my teeth. "Or what? You'll use more of your mind magic on me?"

"It has its uses, but there are other types of magic I'll use if you don't stay out of our way. I want your sister, and I will have her. We'll be married, and there's nothing you can do about it. Keep away, and you and that revolting hellhound get to stay alive. How's that for a deal?"

I advanced on Toby, magic sparking from my fingers, fully intending to show him exactly what I thought of his deal.

Aurora returned to the room, followed by an anxious looking Sablo. "Darling, it's an angel."

Toby glanced at me, a warning in his gaze, before turning and smiling. "How may I assist you?"

Sablo glanced from Toby to me. "Actually, I'm here for Tempest. Someone saw her heading this way. There's an emergency."

I restrained from blasting Toby in the head with a spell. "What is it?"

Sablo played with the tip of her wing. "There's been another murder."

My eyes widened. "Who's dead?"

"Isadora Ash."

Chapter 15

I glared at Toby as I processed what Sablo had told me. I was torn between my desire to kill Toby and help the angels.

Isadora Ash was dead. She'd been my prime suspect. With her bad alibi and a strong motive for wanting Gretel dead, I'd been almost sold on her being the killer.

Sablo gestured for me to follow her. "Please, Tempest, we need you. We don't know what's going on."

"You'd better go," Aurora said. "We can finish the flowers another time."

I looked at the lemon-yellow dress I wore. "Where are my clothes?"

"Aurora washed them," Toby said. "They looked like they hadn't seen the inside of a washing machine for some time."

I glared at him. "They were fine. Those jeans had at least another two wears in them." I saw my boots in the corner of the room and pulled them on quickly. There was nothing for it. I'd have to go to the murder scene dressed as a bridesmaid.

I hugged Aurora tightly before I left. "Be careful," I whispered to her.

She pulled back, her expression curious. "Of what?"

I glanced at Toby. "Make sure you don't make a bad decision when it comes to the flowers."

She smiled and let out a sigh. "Of course, I won't. With your help, the wedding will be perfect."

I shook my head as I hurried out of the house with Sablo. This was one giant mess, but at least Toby was showing his true colors. There was no way I'd listen to his warning. I'd continue to mess with their relationship until Aurora came to her senses.

"Hold on a minute," I said to Sablo as we headed outside. I hurried around the side of the house.

"Wrong way," Sablo said.

"I just need to—" I ducked as a chunk of rock flew through the air and past my ear.

Feodor was still pursuing Wiggles around the garden, and he was gaining on him.

I hitched up the floor length dress and raced after them, conjuring a bolt of lightning as I ran, the pungent smell of ozone filling my nose as the air crackled with power. I pulled back my arm and threw the lightning. It sliced through the air and landed squarely between Feodor's shoulders.

He bellowed before crashing to the ground.

Wiggles slowed before doing a U-turn. He stopped by Feodor, who lay unconscious on the ground.

I hurried over and scooped Wiggles into my arms, my heart racing, and checked him for injuries. "Are you okay? I saw Feodor chasing you when I was inside."

"Of course I'm not okay." Wiggles squirmed in my arms, smearing mud all over the bodice of the dress. "I've been racing around the garden trying to avoid being slaughtered by this maniac. What happened to you? One minute, you were standing by the window, the next you were almost floating off the ground, a stupid look on your face. You went inside the house. I tried to follow, but the door was slammed in my face."

I placed him on the ground and knelt next to him. "Toby got me. He used his magic on me."

Anger bristled off Wiggles, and his fur stood on end. "That guy needs to be taught a serious lesson. He set this thug on me, and he manipulates you." His red-eyed gaze ran over me. "And he made you put on a hideous dress."

I looked at the dress, which was stained with muddy paw prints and fur. "This is Aurora's idea. She thinks we're friends again and wants me to wear this dress at her wedding."

"Yellow is not your color." Wiggles climbed onto Feodor's back and jumped up and down several times. "For a big guy, he's fast."

"He wanted you dead."

"He did. I was scratching at the door and trying to get in when he yanked it open and made a grab for me." Wiggles bounced off Feodor like he was a mini trampoline. "After that, he was roaring at me and trying to get me."

"Toby knows we're onto him," I said. "He's warned me off."

"Which you're going to ignore." Wiggles cocked his ears.

"Of course." I petted Wiggles on the head. "I was worried when I saw Feodor after you."

"I can handle one giant nightmare of a butler." Wiggles belched sulfur in Feodor's face.

"Tempest, we need to go." Sablo shuffled from foot to foot, choosing to stay well away from Feodor as she lingered at the edge of the lawn.

"What's an angel doing here?" Wiggles asked.

I tipped my head back. "There's been another murder. Isadora Ash is dead."

"No way!" Wiggles walked beside me as we hurried toward Sablo. "She was our prime suspect in Gretel's murder."

"Not anymore," I said. "Don't say anything to Sablo about what Toby's up to. I don't want the angels getting involved. We'll deal with Toby without their interference."

"Fine by me. If we need to break some rules to scare off Mr. Sleazy Goatee and his maniac butler, we don't need the angels figuring out what we're up to."

Sablo glanced down at Wiggles as we stopped in front of her. "Why was that giant man chasing you? Did you steal his food?"

Wiggles snorted and glanced at me. "He's not a fan of hellhounds."

Sablo tilted her head but then shrugged. "We need to go to the stone circle. That's where Isadora was found."

"What happened to her?" I asked as we hurried along next to Sablo.

She shook her head and grimaced. "It's not a pretty sight. Two walkers raced into the headquarters and said they'd found a body under a pile of rocks."

"Rocks! Did one of the stones from the circle fall on Isadora?"

"No. I wasn't there for long, so I don't have all the information, but it looks like Isadora was crushed by rocks."

"Multiple rocks? Not a single slab toppling and hitting her?"

"That's right. There are dozens of them piled on her. They look like they came from the chunk that was split from a standing stone a while back."

My stomach roiled unhappily. I wasn't looking forward to this crime scene, but then who could say they enjoyed poking around dead bodies? Necromancers, maybe?

We arrived to find Dominic and Cassiel already there. They stood either side of a pile of rocks in the center of the stone circle.

I decided not to get too close. I didn't have a strong stomach for murder, no matter how often I helped the angels.

"How do you know it's Isadora?" I asked Sablo as we stopped by the edge of the rocks. "I don't see anyone under there."

"If you go around the side, you'll see a hand. And we moved the rocks to make sure whoever was under there wasn't alive. It only took a couple of minutes before we revealed Isadora."

"Are there signs of a fight or a struggle?"

"Nothing like that," Sablo said. "As soon as we found the scene and figured out who it was, we didn't poke around, so as not to disturb evidence. We're not sure what to do next."

"Get on and do what you always do when you discover a dead body," I said.

Sablo's mouth twisted to the side. "Dazielle always tells us what to do. I figured, since you're in charge, you can suggest our tasks."

I rubbed the bridge of my nose. "Okay, so what would she tell you to do in this situation?" The angels were lost without their leader. As much as they frustrated me, I felt a bit sorry for them.

Sablo swallowed and glanced at Dominic and Cassiel who were deliberately not making eye contact. "Secure the scene so evidence isn't tampered with. Look around for any clues to suggest who killed Isadora. Remove the body and take it to be examined."

"Top marks! You know what to do," I said. "Get on with it."

Sablo nodded. "You're right. Yes, of course. I'll take a look around."

"Dominic and Cassiel, you stay here with Isadora," I said. "Don't let anyone near her body."

"Sure, we can do that." Dominic stood to attention, but there was a worried look on his face. "Who do you think did this?"

"I have no idea," I said. "I was thinking Isadora killed Gretel. Now, I'm not so sure." I walked slowly around the rocks, taking note of the hand poking out, palm up and fingers splayed. There was something horribly familiar about this scene.

"Are you looking for anything in particular?" Dominic followed closely behind me, his wings extended so I had my own private wind barrier.

"The way Isadora's been killed, does it remind you of anything?"

Dominic tugged on his ear. "It reminds me that there are a lot of sick people out there."

"Have you studied the history of witchcraft?"

Dominic shook his head. "It's not in our training syllabus."

"And Angel Ball is?"

He looked shamefaced. "I'm not much of a reader."

My thoughts were on the book Isadora had given me. "Hundreds of years ago, there were several ways people killed witches."

"Oh! The ducking stool in the museum." Dominic grinned. "I know about that."

"Well done. You get a gold star."

Cassiel smirked at Dominic. "That's not the only way to kill a witch."

"What are the other ways?" I asked her.

Her smirk faded. "Blast them with a spell?"

"No star for you." I pointed at the rocks. "People also stoned witches. Villagers would drag some innocent woman out of her house, surround her, and throw rocks at her."

Dominic looked at the pile of rocks, horror on his face. "Someone did that to Isadora?"

"It's a working theory," I said. "First the ducking stool and now this stoning. And two witches are dead. Maybe someone is targeting only witches."

"That's a relief." Dominic let out a sigh. "I'll sleep easy in my bed knowing I won't be at risk if it's only witches they're interested in."

I quirked an eyebrow. "As I said, it's a working theory. Don't forget to lock your doors at night."

Dominic's face paled. "Right. Of course. Always better to be safe."

I did another circuit of the rocks but didn't see anything helpful.

"You look lovely in that dress, Tempest, and you're so clever. You are the full package." Dominic's grin dazzled me as I stopped next to him. "How do you know all of this?"

I smiled at Dominic and stroked my hand down my ruined bridesmaid's dress. He was so gorgeous but so dumb. "It's no secret. And the details of witch stoning are in Isadora's book. If I remember rightly, she detailed the ducking stool method first and then the use of rocks. I think someone is re-enacting her descriptions."

Dominic's mouth dropped open. "Why would anybody do that?"

"As you say, there are some sick people around here." I looked for Wiggles and spotted him snuffling outside the stone circle. "Hey, come over here and see what you can find."

Wiggles trotted over and stared at the scene. "I've found a pile of rocks and a body underneath it."

"Get nearer and see if there's any magic around."

"What's in it for me?"

I glared at him. "I won't lock you outside for the next week."

He snorted. "You'd never do that. Make me an offer."

"No offer. Go smell the body."

"My nose has three hundred million receptors in it."

"I'm happy for your nose."

"And, I'll have you know, almost half my brain is dedicated to analyzing smells. Imagine what it's like for me, having to poke around near a corpse."

I sighed. "One bone."

"Ten bones. And a dozen cupcakes."

"One bone, and one cupcake."

Wiggles sat and curled his tail around his feet.

I growled at him. "Two bones and two cupcakes."

He tilted his head from side to side. "Triple caramel with frosting?"

"If that will make you move."

He hopped up. "We have a deal. I'll be your magic sniffing hero." Wiggles trotted toward the rocks.

"Should he be doing that?" Dominic asked. "We shouldn't let the evidence be tampered with."

"The worst he'll do is shed a few furs," I said. "Wiggles has a good nose. He often picks out different kinds of magic if it's been used."

"Wow! That's impressive."

"I'm not a one trick hellhound," Wiggles said. "I also belch fire in moments of crisis. There have been a lot of those recently."

"That's a neat trick to have," Dominic said.

I let Wiggles sniff around for a couple of minutes. "Have you got anything?"

"Magic was used. Nothing dark, but it feels like an immobility spell."

"I detected something similar on Gretel," I said.

"When did you detect the spell on Gretel?" Dominic asked.

I ducked my head. My illegal snoop around the ducking stool had just been revealed. "I felt it when the body was discovered, and it makes sense to use such a spell. I'm not sure how powerful Gretel or Isadora were, but they'd have a basic knowledge of defense spells. Someone used an immobility spell to prevent them from running, particularly in the case of Isadora. Unless they got a lucky first strike, she wouldn't have hung around while someone hurled rocks at her."

Dominic shook his head and smiled. "There you go again, being all brilliant and beautiful in your sunflower yellow dress."

Sablo returned from her walk around the circle. "I didn't find anything useful."

"Okay. Get Isadora uncovered and take her away," I said.

Sablo nodded and instructed Dominic and Cassiel to get to work. Some of the rocks were so large they needed two hands to roll them away.

"These rocks weren't thrown by hand," I said. "Someone used magic to propel them at Isadora. She must have been terrified. But what was she doing in the stone circle? The last time I saw her, she was focused on her work and didn't want to be distracted. What made her come here?"

"To have a break?" Sablo said. "All that research must get dull."

"Not for someone like Isadora. She was obsessed with her work. Jonah described her books as her children. That's all she cared about."

"It could have been for research," Wiggles said. "These old stones are full of magic. Isadora could have gotten excited about the stones for her new book."

"That's possible. Something drew her here."

We waited ten minutes for the angels to remove all the stones. I wandered around the stone circle again to see if anything had been missed but found nothing useful.

After the angels had uncovered Isadora's body, they placed her in a body bag, suspended the bag between their wings, and we headed back to the Angel Force headquarters.

I followed them at a short distance, Wiggles trailing behind me. I wasn't sure where to turn next. My prime suspect had been murdered. If it wasn't Isadora who'd killed Gretel, then I was back to square one.

Something else worried me. If my theory about the killer re-enacting the methods of murder in Isadora's book was correct, then they weren't finished. There'd be three more murders. Burning at the stake, hanging, and being bricked behind a wall.

I walked into the reception area, my thoughts on the killer's next move, and waited a couple of minutes until Sablo came through.

"What shall we do next?" she asked.

"You focus on examining Isadora," I said. "Also, go take a look around her room. She might have left a clue behind as to what she was doing at the stone circle. And you'll need to inform those working with Isadora as to what's happened."

"We'll get right on that," Sablo said. "We have to catch who's doing this."

I nodded. We did. I needed to speak to Dazielle before our killer struck again. She always claimed to be the expert when it came to solving a crime, and right now, I needed an expert. I had no clue what our next move should be.

Chapter 16

I'd left several messages for Dazielle the previous evening, and she'd returned none of them. Anyone would think she didn't want to keep her job.

I sat curled on the couch in my apartment, sipping coffee as I waited for my snow globe to connect. My gaze settled on the lemon-yellow dress sitting in a heap on the floor. It was destroyed. After the mad dash around Toby's garden to save Wiggles and the race to get to the stone circle and see what had happened to Isadora, I wasn't sure it could be salvaged. Wearing lemon satin when you investigated a murder was always a bad idea.

My snow globe finally connected, but I got the same message I'd heard the previous five times.

"Dazielle is not available. Please leave a message, and she'll get back to you. An angel's farewell to you."

There was no time for subtlety. "Having left three previous messages, we've all decided you're dead. Your possessions have been sold, and your apartment is up for sale. You'll be pleased to know the mayor has promoted me to your role. I'll be disbanding Angel Force within the next forty-eight hours and taking their salaries as my own. This could have been avoided if only you'd bothered to pick up your messages. A demon's farewell to you."

I shut off the snow globe and smirked. That might spur Dazielle into action. But her lack of communication was worrying, and, as much as I hated to admit it, she knew a thing or two about murders. Sablo and the others did their best, but I needed someone with a bit more clout to sort this mess out.

"It's no good," I said as I uncurled from the couch. "There's only one solution for this. We need breakfast."

Wiggles, who'd looked to be sound asleep on his bed in the lounge, leaped up and spun in a circle. "That's my favorite word. Alongside lunch, dinner, snacks, and treats. Oh, and belly rub. I love a belly rub."

We headed out of Cloven Hoof. The morning was bright and sunny with a hint of chill in the air as we headed to Unicorn's Trough.

I froze as I got to the door. Mannie Winter was inside at the counter.

"What are we waiting for?" Wiggles asked. "My stomach's growling like a frustrated fairy."

"Let's go elsewhere." I backed away from the door.

"No! Brogan's breakfast specials are the best." He pawed at the door.

I shooed Wiggles away and turned. "How about cupcakes from Sprinkles?"

"Tempest!" The door behind me opened. "I was just thinking about you."

I suppressed a groan as I heard Mannie's voice. "Good thoughts?"

"Come inside, and I'll tell you."

I took a deep breath, knowing I couldn't avoid Mannie, and walked into Unicorn's Trough.

"I've been waiting for an update from you," Mannie said. "I had to hear about Isadora from the angels."

"That is their job," I said. "They're trying to figure out what happened."

"And what about you?" Mannie stroked his eyebrows with the tips of his fingers. "You need to be on top of this. You're in charge of the angels until Dazielle returns."

"No, I'm in charge of what happened to Gretel. I signed on for one murder solving only. I didn't agree to be the big boss or have anything to do with what happened to Isadora."

"Come now, this must all be connected." Mannie patted his stomach. "One murder to solve or two, you can manage that."

"I'm doing what I can, but I'm no expert. You have the wrong woman for this job. I was leaning toward Isadora as Gretel's killer, but now she's gone, so I can't ask her what went on between them."

Mannie waved his hand in the air. "No, that's not possible. Isadora would never do anything like that."

"She had no alibi; she hated Gretel for attempting to ruin her career and had plenty of opportunities to return to the museum and drown Gretel. Isadora looked good for it. And she vanished yesterday. I was trying to find her and bring her in for questioning."

"Oh, well, when you lay out the facts, that doesn't look so good for Isadora." Mannie played with a button on his waistcoat. "You must see, she can't be involved now."

"She still might have killed Gretel."

"But who killed Isadora?"

It looked like this wouldn't be a quick conversation. I led Mannie to a quiet table in the corner, and we both sat. "I'd hazard a guess that it's someone she knew. Somebody must have tempted her to leave the house and go to the stone circle."

Mannie shook his head. "It's terrible what happened to her. A real loss."

"It's not a great way to die. Do you know much about Isadora's ability? If someone attacked her, could she have defended herself?"

"She had abilities, but she didn't use them that often. Isadora was more interested in exploring the old ways of magic rather than honing her power." Mannie stroked a hand down his beard. "Have you had breakfast yet?"

"No, that's why I'm here." I'd been so distracted by seeing Mannie that I'd forgotten the reason for coming to Unicorn's Trough.

"I've just placed my order," Mannie said. "You need fuel if you're going to solve these murders. I'm having an extra-large breakfast special."

"That sounds perfect," Wiggles said.

"Right you are. I'll be back in a moment." Mannie left the table.

I shook my head. For all Mannie's faults, he was always generous when it came to feeding me.

He placed our orders before returning to the table. "Whilst I'm mourning the loss of two dear friends, I do need this resolved swiftly."

"As you're aware, we're working on it."

Mannie tilted his head. "I need the museum open by the end of the week. The show must go on. You understand."

I shrugged. "That's not got anything to do with me. Any evidence that we need would have been collected from the ducking stool when Gretel's body was removed. If you want to reopen the museum, then you can."

Mannie smiled a little smugly. "I wasn't asking your permission, Tempest. I'll open the museum whenever I choose. But we can't have two unsolved murders hanging over Willow Tree Falls. That's terrible for business."

I raised my chin. Typical Mannie, always thinking about the bottom line before anything else. "With Isadora gone, I need to speak to everyone who knew her. The killer has to be someone who knew both women."

"That makes sense," Mannie said. "Although, her team is made up of decent people. I still can't picture any of them being involved with this."

This time, I was the one who felt a little smug. "You knew both of the women. Be honest with me. What was your actual relationship with them?"

Mannie lurched back. He cleared his throat several times. "Well played, Tempest. It's only right you ask me that question. I was friendly with Isadora. I considered her an asset and knew she'd prove a boon to tourist numbers, thanks to her book and its association with the museum. It's a tragedy what happened to her. She could be a little single-minded when it came to her work, but she was a decent woman. I will miss her."

"You didn't find her to be obsessed with her work? She didn't neglect your friendship because of it?"

"Not to a great degree. I always admire a feisty career woman. What's wrong with that?"

"It makes a person selfish if they single-mindedly obsess over a goal, excluding everything else."

"Oh! Well, no. I'd never describe Isadora as selfish. She was an academic. They tend to be eccentric and driven."

"And Gretel? Be honest. I haven't heard anybody say a kind word about Gretel other than you. Are you really going to tell me that you liked her?"

Mannie waited as our breakfasts were served before speaking. "I will admit to not being fond of Gretel."

"Why didn't you like her?" I sliced into a sausage on my plate.

He sighed. "She talked down to me. Have you heard that saying, never meet your heroes?"

"I have."

"Gretel Le Strange was a hero of mine. I thought she'd be a fascinating woman, full of interesting facts and sharing knowledge of ancient magic. Instead, she was shrill and unpleasant. She accused me of being a smug, fat dwarf."

Wiggles choked on the hash brown he was eating, and I averted my gaze and focused on my toast to stop from laughing. "Try not to take it personally.

Everyone said she was hard to get along with and could be rude."

Mannie patted his paunch. "I tried everything to get her to like me, but Gretel was having none of it. She wasn't interested in pleasantries or making people feel comfortable. She just cared about her work. If you didn't agree with her, you were dead to her. She wouldn't negotiate over anything."

"Which must have made her difficult to work with at the museum."

"Gretel's input was valuable, and we made relevant changes to the exhibits but not without extra expense being incurred." Mannie shook his head. "She was so rude to the staff that I thought they'd walk out. In hindsight, bringing her here was a bad idea."

"I expect she'd agree since she's dead."

Mannie nodded sagely. "You might be right."

"Since you weren't a fan of Gretel's, care to tell me where you were yesterday afternoon?"

His brow wrinkled. "I have no involvement in these unfortunate deaths."

"So, tell me your alibi. I believe the murders are connected. It's the same killer. If you killed Gretel—"

"Don't say that." Mannie flapped a hand in the air and looked around the café. "I can't let my constituents hear such a terrible rumor. It could ruin my re-election chances if I'm embroiled in a murder investigation."

"Especially if you did it," I said. "Where were you yesterday? I need your alibi to exclude you from Isadora's murder."

Mannie's lips pinched together. "I was with Trixie."

"All afternoon?"

He nodded, his gaze going over my shoulder. "In fact, you can ask her yourself what we were doing."

"Mannie! Sweetie pie." A tall, willowy goddess with jet-black hair and an ample cleavage wrapped herself around Mannie and kissed the top of his head.

"Trixie. We were just talking about you." Mannie's cheeks glowed as she continued to kiss his head, leaving hot pink lipstick marks on his forehead. "Tempest Crypt, meet Trixie Vermouth."

Trixie extended a ring covered hand to me. "Pleasure to make your acquaintance." She had a strong Eastern European accent.

"Likewise. I've not seen you around here before."

"We met online," Mannie said. "It was an unexpected treat. I made a trip out of Willow Tree Falls, and while I was there, a friend of mine suggested an online dating site for magic users. There's no point in trying that here because of our dubious internet signal. I was away for a few days and thought it sounded fun, so I signed up."

"And he found me." Trixie splayed her fingers across her chest. "True love."

Trixie looked at least fifteen-years Mannie's junior. I wondered what she saw in the wealthy, social climbing dwarf who just happened to be mayor. "Are you enjoying your time in Willow Tree Falls?"

"Very much. I have a job looking after cute animals. And I've been out with Mannie drinking and eating. And, of course, we make lots of boom boom." She winked at me.

Wiggles' head appeared from under the table. "Boom boom?"

Mannie cleared his throat. "We shouldn't talk about that, my dear. But since you're here, you won't mind telling Tempest what you were doing yesterday afternoon."

Trixie grinned. "Of course not. Making boom boom with Mannie all afternoon. He's a strong, lusty dwarf."

I grimaced. I needed no more information. "Great! Good to know. I'm happy for you both." I spotted a book under Trixie's arm. "What are you reading?"

"A copy of the dead witch's book." Trixie held it out. "It's signed. See?"

I went to take the book, but she pulled it back. "No, that's not for you to touch. No sausage grease finger marks on my nest egg."

Nest egg? "I just want to take a look."

Trixie shook her head and clutched the book to her chest. "I'm keeping this. It will be worth a lot of money now the witch is dead."

Mannie tutted and shook his head. "There's no need to talk about things like that in public. Remember to use your inside voice when appropriate."

Trixie scowled at him. "You said to keep all the signed books safe. Worth a lot of money."

Mannie glanced at me. "We need to wait awhile to see if Isadora's book appreciates in value following her untimely demise."

I saw a hungry glint in Mannie's gaze. He was hoping Isadora's fame would grow after her murder, and he'd be able to sell off her signed books for a fortune. It wasn't a bad motive for wanting Isadora dead, but he had a good alibi with Trixie.

"I'll be careful with the book." I took a few seconds to wipe my fingers clean. "I have a theory about the killings. I think there are more to come."

Trixie gasped. "More murders. This is such a small place. Why so much death? Mannie, you said this place is a haven."

Mannie glanced around as her shrill voice carried around the café. "Remember, inside voice, my sweet. Give Tempest the book."

"It's mine."

"It's ours." He tugged on the book. "There are other copies in the house."

Trixie pouted but handed over the book. "I get a treat for behaving?"

I ducked my head and bit hard on my lip.

"Of course. Why not treat yourself to an afternoon at the thermal spa? You can try that new bikini I bought you."

"You'll come with me? We can make boom boom in the water."

I tried not to gag as I studied the contents page of the book.

Mannie patted Trixie's hand. "That sounds delightful but another time. I have to finish my business with Tempest."

Trixie poked my arm. "No stealing my man."

I masked my snort of laughter with a weird sounding cough. "I wouldn't dare. He's all yours."

Trixie narrowed her eyes at me before kissing Mannie's cheek and flouncing out of the café.

"She seems nice," I said to Mannie.

He tilted his head. "She's a beautiful young woman with a lot of energy. I'm not sure I'll make her the next Mrs. Mannie Winter, but she makes me feel young again."

"I bet she does with all that boom boom." I turned to the description of the ducking stool in the book and handed it to Mannie. "This is what I'm worried about. Isadora described the ducking stool and being stoned to death as two popular ways to kill a witch."

Mannie nodded. "I've seen the book. I know the contents."

"Turn the page to the next method of murder. It's being burned at the stake."

He nodded again. "What does your belief that there will be more murders have to do with this book?"

"If I'm right, the killer is re-creating the different methods of killing outlined by Isadora. The way Gretel's body was staged on the ducking stool looks exactly like that picture, even down to the placement of the hands."

Mannie's eyebrows rose as he flicked back through the pages and studied the picture. "It's hard to say for certain, and I didn't look at her body for long. It does look similar, but maybe that's a coincidence."

I shook my head. "What if it isn't? Look at the picture of the stoning. See the hand poking out?

That's how Isadora was found. Just a hand visible. The palm up."

Mannie tugged on his beard. "That's concerning."

"What's more concerning is that there are five methods of killing detailed. The ducking stool was first, then the stoning—"

"Then burning at the stake, hanging, and being bricked behind a wall." He looked up at me, his eyes wide. "Someone's planning to re-enact all of these methods of murder?"

"I believe so."

"What can we do about that?" Mannie asked. "We don't know who it is, and we don't know who they're targeting next."

"We have to find out," I said. "This killer is just getting started. They've already killed two witches, and they'll be looking for their third victim. They might even have her by now."

Mannie turned the pages. His face paled as he read the description of a witch burning. "This can't be allowed to happen in Willow Tree Falls. Think of the bad publicity. It could ruin the museum."

I snatched the book from him. "More importantly, think about the dead witch."

"Yes, of course!" Mannie stared at me. "Tempest, what are you going to do to stop this?"

I didn't know. But I'd make sure no more witches lost their lives.

Chapter 17

After finishing breakfast with Mannie, I headed out of Unicorn's Trough with Wiggles. We needed as many eyes as possible looking for this killer to make sure they didn't snatch another witch.

I walked into the reception and found Sablo behind the desk.

"Not playing Angel Ball today?" I asked.

"We only play Angel Ball in the afternoon," Sablo said. The lack of sarcasm in her tone made me think she was being truthful.

"Did you get anything useful from Isadora's body?"

"There was nothing helpful from the study of her body or clothing," Sablo said. "Her chest was crushed. That's what killed her. She was most likely unconscious before that happened. She had several nasty wounds on her head."

I grimaced and held up a hand. "I've got an idea to share." I handed her the book I'd borrowed from Mannie and explained my theory about the killer's behavior.

Sablo's nose wrinkled. "Dominic mentioned your theory when we were having coffee. It's interesting, but I don't think it's right." She handed me back the book.

"Why not? Have you got evidence suggesting who's involved and why they're doing this?"

"We have a note," Sablo said.

"From whom? The killer?"

"From Isadora. As you suggested, I went to the house and took a look around. She left the note in her bedroom. It said she was sorry for her lies and betrayal and that she didn't mean to deceive anybody."

I rubbed the back of my neck. "What did she mean by that?"

"Isadora didn't mention any names in the note, but it sounds like she's been dishonest in her work."

"Dishonest about what?"

"Something that drove her to suicide," Sablo said.

My mouth dropped open. "You think Isadora crushed herself to death with rocks?"

"I didn't say it was an easy way to kill yourself, but she had magic. What's to say she didn't lie down and move the rocks herself?"

"Logic? Common sense?" I shook my head. "There are much less painful ways to do yourself in."

"Not if you're full of regret and feeling guilty," Sablo said. "Maybe Isadora felt she deserved a painful death because she'd lied."

"Let me see the note."

Sablo's mouth twisted. "It's evidence."

"And I'm leading on this investigation. Mayor's orders. I get access to all the evidence."

Sablo sighed. "Wait here." She returned a moment later and passed me a clear evidence bag with the note in it. It was typed, no signature.

"Anyone could have typed this," I said. "The killer included. Whoever it is, they want to push us in the wrong direction."

"You said yourself that Isadora was the main suspect in Gretel's murder. You had us looking for her to bring her in for questioning."

"When I met Isadora, she was stressed about her work but wasn't suicidal." My thoughts drifted to Jonah and how concerned he'd been about her. Was that what he'd been so worried about? He'd sensed she was close to the edge and might hurt herself?

"Those stones are full of ancient magic," Sablo said. "They could have sensed the darkness or deceit in Isadora and destroyed her."

My eyes bugged as my opinion of Sablo's detective skills plummeted to a new low. "You think the stone circle killed Isadora?"

"There's powerful magic there." Sablo sniffed and examined her nails. "If the stones didn't activate when they sensed Isadora's guilt, she could have encouraged them, activated them with magic, so they sought retribution against her deceit."

"The circle doesn't work like that. Isadora's death wasn't suicide. And the stone circle has never killed anyone before."

"It's alive, though. Maybe the stones were biding their time, waiting for the right amount of evil to step inside."

"Stop with this crazy stone theory!" I shook my head. The circle sometimes ejected people if they were trying to do harm to the stones, but that was about it. "The magic in the stone circle has nothing to do with what happened to Isadora."

"Then why the note?"

"The killer is playing with us. Whoever it is, they want us arguing." I gestured to Sablo. "They want to halt our painfully slow progress, so they can grab another victim while we're distracted."

Sablo tilted her chin. "Your idea about Isadora's book is as good as my theory about the stones."

"No, we're in different leagues when it comes to theories. We have to consider this a serious option." I tapped the book. "More witches will die if we don't find the actual killer."

Sablo shook her head. "The note means something."

"It means a big waste of time," I muttered. "There's someone out there hunting witches. We have to stop them."

"I'm right on this. I always follow my gut instinct, and it's telling me that there's a clue in this note."

I blew out a breath, seeing the stubborn glint in Sablo's eyes. She wasn't budging from her flawed idea. "Okay. Going with the crazy suicide theory for a moment, why choose that method?"

"Isadora knew that was what happened to witches," Sablo said. "She picked that method because she knew it was effective."

"And painful. There's no way she'd have been able to lie still and let that happen to her."

"I think she did," Sablo said. "We've solved this. Isadora killed Gretel then, full of remorse, she decided to end her own life."

"I'm not supporting this theory."

"You don't need to. Don't worry, Tempest. We've got this. I'll speak to Mannie and tell him the conclusion we've drawn. You'll get the thanks you deserve."

"Thanks?" Anger mingled with my frustration. "That's it? Murder solved? I'm guessing all those hours playing Angel Ball helped figure this out."

Sablo shrugged. "A fit body creates a fit mind. Exercise gets the blood flowing to the brain and makes new connections to help solve puzzles like this."

"Yes, but you need a brain for that to work. You follow that theory if you like, but I'm not giving up on this." I turned, my fists clenched, as I stomped out of the building toward the museum with Wiggles.

"Easy, Tempest," Wiggles said. "You look like you're about to blow."

"The angels are dumb at times, but this is beyond ridiculous." My anger made my voice sound growly.

"There's more time for fun if the angels aren't doing any real work," Wiggles said.

"And what are a few less witches in Willow Tree Falls?" I snarled. "They'd act differently if the killer was hunting angels to drown, stone, and burn."

"Not to mention hang and bury behind a wall."

"Every witch in Willow Tree Falls is vulnerable, even more so now the angels think they've solved this. They won't lift a finger to do any work. Our killer could be out there right this second, hunting for the next victim." I sucked in a deep breath to try to cool my anger as we walked into the quiet air of the museum.

I flinched as the peace was shattered by an ear-splitting squeal.

Cleo raced across the foyer and grabbed Wiggles, wrapping both arms around him and lifting him off the ground. "Puppy! You've come home. I knew I'd convince you to come and stay."

Wiggles struggled in her grip as she spun him around. "You've got it wrong, sister. I'm not moving in."

Cleo's gaze went to me as she continued to squish Wiggles. "Hey, Tempest. I heard about Isadora."

"That's what I'm here to talk about," I said.

"It's so sad. She was a nice lady. We had lovely chats about the past."

"It's a shame she's gone," I said, shoving down the last of my anger as the calming feel of the museum slid over me.

"I hope the museum won't remain shut for much longer," Cleo said. "All this beautiful history needs to be shown off."

"Mannie plans to open it by the end of the week," I said. "And the angels think they have everything sorted."

Cleo lowered Wiggles to the ground. She gave him one final squeeze before letting him go. "He's such a beautiful puppy."

Wiggles bounded away, his red-eyed glare fixed on Cleo as he disappeared into an exhibit room.

"He is that. Do you mind me asking where you were yesterday afternoon?" I asked Cleo. "I'm checking everybody's alibi, given what happened with Isadora."

"Of course. You must find out who did this. I was here with Jonah. I think he likes me. He was being very flirty." Cleo giggled. "He's cute, as well. Do you know if he's single?"

Cleo's alibi would be easy enough to check with Jonah. "He seems committed to his work. I'm not sure he has much time for love."

"Being committed to work is a good thing," Cleo said. "It's good to be involved with someone who has ambition. I dated a history professor once. He was cute in a nerdy kind of way. He had an interesting fetish for ancient Greek statues. Do you know the ones I mean, the ones with the women whose togas have slid down revealing their figures?"

"I think I know what you mean." I tilted my head. "What was his fetish?"

"Well, he never confessed anything to me." Cleo glanced around and leaned closer. "One evening, I found him standing by a statue with his pants around his ankles. He was—"

An enraged squeak was followed by the sound of hissing.

I spun on my heel to see Wiggles racing across the foyer. He was followed by three black fluffy blurs.

"Oh, look! Wiggles is making friends with my familiars." Cleo clapped her hands. "That's so lovely. I want them to be lifelong friends, so he can visit all the time."

Wiggles' paws skidded on the shiny floor as he rounded the corner and bolted toward a back room, the cats in hot pursuit. It didn't look like they were trying to make friends. Cleo's familiars wanted blood.

"Are you sure you can't loan him to me for a few days?" Cleo asked. "He's such a cute little thing."

"I'm not sure Wiggles is up for being loaned," I said. "And between you and me, he can be difficult to live with. He's got a problem with gas and doesn't understand boundaries when it comes to looting your trash. He's also obsessed with pillows."

"But he's such a sweetie. I can't imagine he'd be any problem," Cleo said. "I've even got him an outfit. It comes with a hat and boots."

"Wiggles will love that." I repressed a smile. Wiggles would rather shave off his fur than be seen dead in any item of clothing, other than his bow ties.

I winced as there were several loud crashes from the room Wiggles and the cats had raced into.

Cleo bit her lip. "I hope everything's okay. Does your puppy know how to play with familiars?"

"He's not a big fan of cats," I said.

"Get off me, you mangy beasts." Wiggles yelped, and more things crashed to the floor.

"My familiars are three hundred years old," Cleo said. "They've seen it all."

"Three hundred years old!"

"They're my eternal familiars. I got them from my granny when she passed. Old power from the Far East runs through their veins. They can tell you a story or two, when they decide to speak, in your head and usually when you're asleep. It gave me a fright the first time they all spoke to me. They talk about mice a lot and good places to use as a bathroom. And they often debate the merits of puddle water over tap water."

"That sounds intense." I hurried to the back room as something smashed on the floor. I poked my head inside.

The three cats sat at the bottom of a display of witches' hats. Somehow, Wiggles had gotten wedged on top of the tall display case, his butt hanging out and his back legs flailing.

"I didn't think you could jump high," I said to him.

"It's amazing what you can do when you're motivated." Wiggles grunted and squirmed some more. "Get those crazy cats away from me."

The cats hissed and narrowed their green eyes at him.

I stepped closer. "Cleo thinks they're making friends."

"If I need any more friends, I'll let them know." Wiggles squirmed on his belly, but he seemed well and truly stuck between the ceiling and the glass top of the cabinet.

I inched toward the cats. They turned on me, their hackles raised and eyes flashing with fury.

I raised my hands slowly. "I come in peace, fur balls. I need to rescue my hellhound before you make him your next meal."

The cats eyed me suspiciously as I inched around them to the display case.

I saw my family name in the next display case and paused to take a look. "Hey! This exhibit is all about our family." I peered at the huge family tree that branched off in all directions. "I'm on here."

"What about me?" Wiggles asked.

"You're not a blood relative," I said.

"I'm the closest thing you've got to a child," Wiggles said. "I should be on there."

"I'll make that suggestion." I tilted my head as I studied Wiggles' position. "I'm not sure how I can get you off there."

"You'll have to pull me out. My belly's gotten wedged."

"Too many cupcakes," I muttered as I wrapped my hands around his hips and pulled gently.

He slid back an inch but stopped. "Get those mangy cats out of here before I get down. I need a head start, so they don't catch me."

The cats all hissed as if they understood what he'd said. Maybe they did. Three hundred-year-old familiars must come with a hefty whack of power.

"Hold on." I grabbed a chair from the corner and stood on it. Up higher, I could grab a handful of warm, soft belly. I tugged on Wiggles again.

He popped out, his legs flailing as he flipped in the air. I grabbed hold of him before he hit the floor and hugged him to me.

The cats jumped to their feet and stalked toward me, their murderous gaze on Wiggles. I jumped off the chair and backed away quickly. "There's no trouble here. We're leaving. Don't kill us."

"Blast them with magic," Wiggles grumbled. "Evil little critters."

"Don't antagonize the ancient powerful familiars," I muttered.

"I'm not scared of them."

"You should be. They want to destroy you. I think they probably could." I hurried back into the foyer where Cleo stood, a concerned look on her face.

"Sorry about my girls. They can be feisty," she said. "I hope they didn't hurt you, puppy."

"You need to put leashes on them," Wiggles said. "They're out of control."

An angry hiss had me speeding to the door, Wiggles still in my arms. The cats clearly hated the idea of being given a harness and a leash.

I turned before we left the museum. "Where's the rest of Isadora's team? Is no one else working here?"

"I saw them all earlier," Cleo said. "They're staying at the house for now. They seemed a bit bemused. Since Isadora hired them, they're technically out of work. They're trying to figure out what to do next. I think Seth's setting up a memorial promotion for the book. He dazzled me with information, and I lost the thread when he talked about live chats and multi-channel social media options. It's something to do with capitalizing on tragedy so no one loses out."

Capitalizing on tragedy? Seth was a piece of work.

The cats advanced menacingly toward us. "Thanks, Cleo. It was nice to see you." I nodded at the evil cats. "You too, fur balls." I raced out and swiftly shut the door behind us before kneeling and letting go of Wiggles.

He shook out his fur and glared at the closed door. "We're never going back in there again."

I checked the door was shut tight. "I don't know. I've always been fond of cats. Maybe we can get a kitten."

"No cats. I'm the only pet in your life. You don't need anybody else. And I do not share treats."

I smiled as we walked away. "Fair enough. It looks like Cleo and Jonah are in the clear for Isadora's murder. All I need to do is confirm that she was with Jonah yesterday afternoon and we can tick them off the list."

"Cleo still doesn't have a great alibi for Gretel's murder," Wiggles said. "Didn't she say she was sleeping with her mangy moggies?"

"She did," I said. "And Cleo wasn't entirely honest with how Gretel had treated her. But I still don't get the sense she's a killer."

"It's her cats then," Wiggles said. "I can imagine them skulking in the shadows in the dead of night and taking down innocent victims. I bet they'd use their dark powers to frame someone else while they sit back, lick their paws, and plot their next evil deed."

"They were on the scary side." I slowed and turned away from the main street. "Let's head to the house and see how Isadora's team is feeling about her death. And we need to find out where they all were when she died."

Someone out there was a killer, and we needed to find out who it was before they struck again.

Chapter 18

The door in front of me opened, and Seth looked out. He smiled when he saw me and Wiggles.

"We figured you'd be by soon enough. The angels told us about Isadora." Seth turned and gestured for me to follow him.

I walked into the house and along the hallway. "That must have been a shock for you. I'm sorry for your loss."

"I'm hoping it won't be too bad for business."

"Bad for business?"

Seth turned, and his gaze ran over me. "That's why I'm here. Isadora was a client, not a friend."

Yep, it had just been confirmed. Seth was a Grade A piece of dirt. I followed him into the lounge to discover Lotus packing a bag. She glanced up, and her gaze narrowed as she saw Seth.

Wiggles took one look at the tense situation and trotted off toward the kitchen.

"Lotus, sweetheart, there's no need to do that." Seth walked over, his hand held out.

She backed away from him. "There's every reason."

"You're leaving?" I asked her.

She shrugged. "There's no point in staying. Isadora's dead. I have no boss. Besides, I was leaving anyway."

I was out of time when it came to playing nicely. "You have a good reason for wanting Isadora dead."

"What are you talking about?" Seth tried to place an arm around Lotus' shoulder, but she shrugged him off and moved away.

"It's true, isn't it?" I said to her. "You were angry with Isadora."

Lotus' shoulders sagged. "If only she'd stood up for me. All I needed was help to get rid of a problem." Her gaze drifted to Seth. "Just for her to intervene once. To lift her nose from her own obsession and help. If she'd done that, I'd have stayed. I enjoy my work. I don't want to leave."

"I have no clue what's going on here," Seth said. "If you have a problem, you can talk to me. We share everything."

"You're the problem, loser. Lotus is talking about you," I said. "She's sick of you sleazing on her. She's not into you."

Seth's eyes widened. "Of course she is! I'm planning to be with Lotus for a long time."

Lotus glared at him. "Not if I have any say in it."

I focused on Seth. "You lied to me the first time we talked. You told me you were in a serious relationship with Lotus, and you're planning to get married."

Seth's lips thinned. "I told you that in confidence. It was meant to be a surprise for Lotus."

Lotus snorted a laugh. "I'd never marry you. Tempest is right. Isadora saw you hassling me, and

I asked her to help me. She turned her back. She walked away. That's why I was mad with her."

"She knows what you're like." Seth touched Lotus' arm. "You're scared of committing to me. You shouldn't be. We're right for each other."

Lotus scowled at him. "I wouldn't date you if you were the last guy on Earth. We're not, and have never been, in a relationship."

"You're upset because of what happened to Isadora. You're not making any sense."

"Where were you yesterday afternoon?" I asked Lotus.

"She was with me." Seth stood next to Lotus. "We were together most of the day."

Lotus sighed and shook her head. "No, we weren't. You kept hassling me, and I kept telling you to get lost."

He grabbed her shoulders and turned her toward him. "Think carefully about what you say next. Isadora was murdered yesterday afternoon. Tempest is looking for her killer. You need a strong alibi, or you could be in trouble."

"What you need to do is tell the truth," I said. "Where were you both yesterday afternoon?"

Lotus shook Seth's hands off her shoulders and stepped away from him again. "I wasn't doing anything. Isadora wasn't around after about ten o'clock that morning. It wasn't unusual for her to disappear without telling anyone. She'd often squirrel herself away and focus on her work. Isadora could get lost in her research and forget to tell anyone where she was. I didn't worry when she wasn't back for lunch. I was here most of the day.

I went out a couple of times to stretch my legs but didn't see Isadora."

"Which means you have no alibi," Seth said. "I can be your alibi. Let me help you. If you don't, you'll find yourself behind bars."

Lotus crossed her arms over her chest. "I'm innocent. I'm not involved. I don't need an alibi."

"You absolutely do," Seth said. He turned to me. "I was here with Lotus. She doesn't always know I'm around, but I'm always watching her."

I grimaced. That wasn't at all creepy. "You were both in the house at the time of Isadora's death?"

Lotus scowled at Seth before nodding. "I didn't go anywhere near the stone circle yesterday. And yes, I was angry with Isadora. She did the wrong thing, but I'd made my decision to leave. I was moving on. There was no reason for me to kill her."

"Tempest, believe me. Lotus was here," Seth said. "And don't listen to her nonsense about us not being in a relationship. She's just stubborn and loves her independence."

"Give up on this dumb fantasy of yours!" Lotus shouted. "I don't love you. We're not together. And when I'm gone, don't you dare follow me, or I'll stake you."

"I'll follow you wherever you go," Seth said, seeming undeterred by Lotus' threat to puncture him with a wooden stake.

"You realize that's called stalking," I said. "Lotus has made it clear she doesn't like you. Back off, or you'll be the one behind bars."

"What for?" Seth sounded genuinely surprised.

"For being a sleazebag," I said.

Lotus nodded. "I'd rather tell the truth and have a lousy alibi than be vulnerable to Seth's advances because I owe him a favor."

Seth's jaw dropped. "I'd never hold this over you. I give you this alibi willingly."

"I know what you're like," Lotus said. "You still remind me of the time you loaned me some money. Even though I paid you back in full and on time, you still mention it, trying to get me to be nice to you because you did me a favor. That was the first and last time I asked you for anything."

He looked aggrieved. "I don't know what you're talking about. I've forgotten all about that loan."

Though Lotus didn't have a great alibi, I believed she was telling the truth. It would have been simple for her to accept Seth's alibi. If she was guilty, she'd have grabbed onto it, but she'd made the more difficult choice.

"What about you, Seth?" I asked. "Where were you yesterday afternoon?"

He scrubbed his chin. "Right here, as I said."

"Watching me." Lotus shuddered her gaze on Seth. "You have to see how weird that is."

"It's not weird. I need to watch you to make sure you're safe."

"From what?" Lotus asked. "I have one of the safest jobs in the world. I sit reading books all day."

"Some of those books can be heavy," Seth said.

Lotus threw her hands up in exasperation. "I give up. I'm packing my bag and leaving." She stomped out of the room and up the stairs, slamming a door behind her.

"Lotus! Wait!" Seth went to follow her.

I grabbed his arm and yanked him back. "Leave Lotus alone."

His top lip curled, exposing his fangs. "Keep out of this, witch."

"Not a chance." I shoved him away. "Lotus doesn't want you. Stay here. I'll make sure she's okay." I hurried after her. Lotus couldn't leave. I needed to keep everyone here until these murders had been figured out.

I opened the door I'd seen Lotus go through and eased it shut behind me. "How are you doing?"

Lotus stood by her bed, her hands on her hips and her back turned to me. "I've been better."

"Don't leave. Not yet. We have to find out who murdered Gretel and Isadora."

She spun toward me, tears in her eyes. "I promise this has nothing to do with me. They were complicated women and obsessed with their work, but I didn't want either of them dead." Her gaze drifted over my shoulder. "Seth, on the other hand. The day he's permanently out of my life is one I'll celebrate."

"I see what a problem he is. There are laws to protect you against being stalked."

"I've talked to the angels about it. But Seth's always so charming and convincing. He makes everyone believe I'm the neurotic one who's a commitment phobe. I've never once suggested to Seth that there's a chance of a relationship between us. He's obsessed with me. It's unhealthy, and it's not natural. I'm sick of it."

"Is he like that with everything?" I asked. "Does Seth get that obsessed with his work? Everything has to turn out the way he wants, no matter what he has to do to make that happen."

"You think Seth killed Isadora and Gretel because of a work glitch?" Lotus shook her head. "He's not a killer. He doesn't have the stomach for it."

"Gretel was putting together a case against Isadora and her work. Seth was dealing with the legal issues and trying to find a way out of it."

Lotus' eyes widened. "I didn't know that. What was the problem?"

"I'm not sure of the details. You've not heard anything about this? Isadora didn't mention her concerns?"

"No! This is news to me."

"Someone overheard Seth talking about dealing with the problem. It wasn't long after that, that Gretel died."

Lotus blinked rapidly. "I don't know. I mean, Seth's always working to get what he wants, and he normally gets it. But why would he kill Isadora? Her book will make him wealthy."

"Isadora was struggling with her work. Was she stressed about anything?"

Lotus brushed her fingers across her lips. "We were all being careful around her because she seemed a bit fragile. Apart from Seth, who never gets the hint when someone's unhappy. Jonah had even been treating Isadora to fancy food from Bite Me and trying to get her to take more breaks to see if that would help."

"Isadora was worried her new book would fail and was stressed about her new project. Was Seth unhappy with what she was working on?"

"I can't see why he'd have a problem," Lotus said. "I've done a little research on it myself. It's a follow-up to this book, focusing on powerful witch families and the evolution of their magic. That wouldn't bother Seth. I expect he saw dollar signs when he heard about the proposal. He could imagine it being another bestseller. He wouldn't block that by killing Isadora."

"The angels have a theory that Isadora might have killed herself," I said.

Lotus scraped her hands through her short hair. "No, she'd never do that. Isadora had so many plans for future publications. She had too much to live for. I can't believe she killed herself. And, although I despise Seth, I can't believe he's involved. He watches me all the time. He thinks I don't know, but I feel those creepy eyes staring at my back."

"And you felt that yesterday? He was watching you?"

She tilted her head. "Not for definite, but he's never far away."

I nodded. I wasn't as certain that Seth was innocent. He'd shown himself to be dangerously obsessed with Lotus, living in a fantasy in his head about them marrying and settling down, despite Lotus making it clear she hated him. What else had he imagined? That Gretel was planning to ruin his career? Isadora would fire him, so he'd lose all his money? Maybe he even believed they'd wanted to hurt him, so he'd struck first?

His alibi for Gretel's murder was also not solid. He could have slipped out of the Ancient Imp for half an hour and murdered her. And as for his alibi for the time of Isadora's murder, he was lurking in the shadows where no one could see him, watching Lotus. Again, he could have suspended stalking duties to go murder Isadora.

"Are you going to be okay with Seth?" I asked Lotus.

"I'll be fine. I'm so used to him being a lecherous creep, I'm almost immune to it. And after everything that's happened here, I'm glad to be leaving. I won't leave a forwarding address with Seth, no matter how much he begs."

"Stick around for as long as you can," I said. "I think someone who worked with Isadora and Gretel is involved in their deaths. You might remember something that leads to their arrest."

Lotus pressed her lips together but nodded. "I can wait around for a while. I'll help if I can, but I can't imagine who would do this."

"Thanks." I hurried out of her room. I could. I needed to speak to Seth.

Chapter 19

As I walked back into the lounge, I looked around. There was no sign of Seth.

"Wiggles!"

He appeared in the kitchen doorway a few seconds later, chewing on something. "What's up?"

"Have you seen Seth?"

"There are no smarmy half-vampires present in the kitchen."

"Search upstairs for him," I said. "We have to speak to Seth. I think he could be our killer."

Wiggles finished his mouthful and bounded up the stairs as I searched the rooms downstairs.

I checked the study, the kitchen, the living room, and a downstairs bathroom. Seth was nowhere to be found.

I met Wiggles back in the living room. "Any sign of him?"

"He's not upstairs," Wiggles said.

"He's gone on the run. Seth tried to use Lotus as an alibi for Isadora's murder. She refused to play ball, leaving him exposed to more questioning. We need to lean on him, see what he knows. He won't have gotten far." I hurried to the front door. "Let's find this sneaky half-vampire and get him to talk."

We raced out of the house. I looked around to see if I could see Seth walking along the lane. There was no sign of him.

I hurried toward the stores, wondering if he was planning an exit through the magic barrier. I'd be able to spot him from the end of the lane if we were quick.

I slowed as I reached Aurora's store and saw Jonah heading inside. "Wiggles, try to pick up Seth's scent out here. See which direction he's going. I'm going to speak with Jonah, see if he's seen Seth."

Wiggles nodded and snuffled on the ground.

I hurried into Heaven's Door and stopped on the dirty welcome mat. The store normally had a warm, welcoming environment, but the air felt cold, and half the shelves were empty. I was so shocked by how unfriendly the store felt that I forgot for a second why I'd come in.

"Tempest!" Aurora's eyes widened when she saw me. "I've been so worried about you ever since you raced out of our house."

"Our house?" My eyes widened. "You and Toby are living together?"

Her smile faded. "We're getting married. I don't see anything wrong with us sharing a home before our wedding."

I looked around the store, noticing Jonah studying a bottle and trying not to listen to our conversation. "Are you renovating?"

"No, why do you ask?"

"It looks like you're having a closing down sale. You never have empty shelves."

Aurora waved a hand in the air. "It's nothing, just a delay in getting new stock."

My eyes narrowed. I didn't believe her. But at least if she was here, she was away from Toby's influence. I checked and was relieved to see Aurora wore her magic eraser pendant.

Jonah glanced up from the herbs he held, his expression glum.

I had to focus on the task in hand. Catching a killer. I walked over to Jonah. "Have you seen Seth pass by the store?"

He shook his head. "I haven't seen him since this morning."

"I need to talk to him about Isadora."

Jonah sighed, and his gaze lowered. "I can't believe what's happened. We've been working side-by-side for such a long time. I considered her like family." He scrubbed a hand over his eyes.

"This must be hard for you," I said.

He nodded. "That's why I'm here. I need something to help calm my nerves."

"Those herbs won't help you." Aurora walked over and patted Jonah's arm. "You need something to help with your shock and the grief you're experiencing."

"I need to ask you some questions," I said to Jonah.

"Not now," Aurora said. "Can't you see he's upset?"

I took a step back, surprised by the sharpness in her voice. "I understand that, but there's a killer on the loose in the village, and we need to find them."

"Then go and look for your killer," Aurora said. "Stop bothering my customers."

What was wrong with her? She had to know I needed to talk to everyone who knew Isadora. Jonah had been Isadora's right-hand man for years. He probably knew her better than anybody else.

I chose to ignore Aurora. "Jonah, what's your opinion of Seth?"

Aurora tutted and crossed her arms over her chest. "Ignore my heartless sister. Let's get you some spells to help you relax."

"Thanks," Jonah said as he followed Aurora to the counter.

I hurried after them. "Seth might be involved in these murders."

Jonah turned and stared at me. "Really?"

"Has he done anything to make you suspicious of him? Anything that makes you think he planned to get Gretel and Isadora out of the way?"

"He's very determined when he wants something. Seth doesn't treat Lotus very well," Jonah said. "He's obsessed with her. He's upset her several times. I warned him off once or twice, but he said she was being stubborn and didn't want their relationship to go public."

"You believed him?"

"I wasn't sure what to make of their relationship. Most of the time, I'm too busy with Isadora to think about it. I'd often see them talking, and Lotus never seemed happy, but some relationships are like that.

Some couples love to fight. If you intervene, they turn on you."

"Seth's part of the reason Lotus is leaving," I said.

Jonah shook his head. "I know there's some problem he's hiding about the book. It was one of the things Isadora was stressing about. She'd heard Seth sending a message via his snow globe, something about needing the court summons to go away. When she quizzed him about it, he said it was nothing and he was sorting it out."

"Isadora didn't believe him?"

"She was torn about what to do. A part of her was worried and wanted to learn more, but she was already focused on her new book."

"Would Isadora have investigated the problem herself and found out what Seth was concealing?"

Jonah rubbed his chin. "It's possible. She was an independent woman, never scared to face a difficult problem."

"That's enough questions," Aurora said. "Jonah, try this tincture. Place three drops under your tongue and leave it for a moment. If it's effective, you should feel better."

I waited, my foot tapping as Jonah tried the tincture. I could tell from the glare on Aurora's face that she wasn't happy I was there. She'd have to suck it up. I had to do this.

"Tell me about your movements yesterday," I said to Jonah. "When did you see Isadora last?"

Aurora sucked in a breath. "Tempest, show some care. Jonah's grieving for someone he cared about. You should be more sensitive."

"And you should stop getting in my way when I'm trying to figure out who killed two witches in our village."

We glared at each other, neither one willing to back down.

Jonah shuffled his feet. "It's okay. I don't mind answering questions. Not if it helps you figure out what happened to Isadora."

I quirked an eyebrow at Aurora. "Thanks, Jonah. Your help is appreciated."

He nodded. "I saw her mid-morning, around eleven. Isadora said she needed time to work on new material. She told me to take a long lunch and come back in the afternoon."

"What did you do for your long lunch?"

"I went to the museum. I saw Cleo, and we chatted."

"What did you talk about?"

"Tempest," Aurora warned. "That's enough."

I kept my gaze focused on Jonah. Every time Aurora prodded me, I felt a flutter of Frank's energy. He was noticing her, and that meant trouble for everyone.

"Nothing important. We had a look at the exhibits and talked about places we'd visited. I like Cleo. She's quirky and cute."

That tallied with what Cleo had told me to support her whereabouts at the time of Isadora's murder. "Did you think it was odd when Isadora didn't show up as planned?"

Jonah shook his head. "It's not unusual for her to disappear so she won't be disturbed. She's a classic introvert. She can't work if there is any noise or distractions. Even me coming into the room can annoy her when she's focused. It was getting late, and I was beginning to wonder where she was when I heard the awful news." He sniffed and looked away.

Aurora patted the back of his hand. "How are you feeling?"

"I don't think the tincture is working," Jonah said. "Have you got anything stronger?"

"Of course." Aurora turned and rifled through her shelves. "I'm out of stock of lemon balm and valerian powder. That would have done the trick. We can try camomile tea and a spell of calm." She turned from the shelves. "I'll heat the water and you can drink it here, so I can monitor its effectiveness."

Aurora's look was full of warning as she glanced at me before heading out the back.

"Do you think Seth's capable of murder?" I asked Jonah.

His head jerked back. "I don't know. I mean I don't know him all that well. He's good at what he does, but I'm always wary around vampires."

"How much money was Seth making by doing this job?"

"Fifty thousand," Jonah said. "I handled the paperwork for Isadora when he came on board. Seth's also getting a percentage of the profits from the sale of Isadora's book and from her speaking engagements. That could easily add another hundred thousand to his deal. He was going to be wealthy, thanks to her."

"He won't see much of that money if the book can't be launched as planned."

Jonah nodded. "Seth will get his flat fee but won't get as much money if the book flops. He'd want this to be a success, just like all of us."

That left me with a puzzle. If Seth had killed Isadora, he was killing off his source of income. He needed this book launch to be a success. There was the possibility that Isadora's death would make her more famous. She could be like those starving artists who created masterpieces that no one bought, then when they died, their work sold for millions. Was that what Seth had been thinking when he'd killed Isadora? She was worth more to him dead than alive?

"Do you really think Seth's involved in these murders?" Jonah asked. "He's not dangerous to be around, is he?"

"He's not at the house. He left after I questioned him about his alibi, which is why I'm suspicious of him. If you see him, make sure you're not alone. I don't think you're his target, but he might not be finished yet. If he's going to kill anyone else, I think it will be another witch."

"Of course. If I see him, I'll let you know," Jonah said. "What if he comes back to the house when I'm there?"

"Don't let him know that you're worried," I said. "Get out and find me or an angel."

Aurora stomped back into the store and passed a mug to Jonah. "Drink that."

"Thanks." Jonah sipped from the mug.

"Tempest, it's time you left."

"You're throwing me out of your store?"

Aurora nodded. "You've interrogated Jonah enough. The poor man is upset. He needs to be in a relaxed environment to help deal with his feelings, not be harangued by you."

"I'm trying to help." Frank's energy curled up my spine as my anger grew.

Aurora raised her chin. "Where's the dress?"

"What dress?"

"The bridesmaid's dress you're wearing on my wedding day. You ran out of the house still wearing it. I need it back to complete the alterations, not that you deserve to be my bridesmaid, the way you're acting."

A trickle of guilt ran through me. "Oh, it's at my apartment." Lying in a heap in the corner with a rip in it and covered in mud. "I'll get it back to you soon."

Aurora's eyes narrowed. "We don't have long until the big day."

"You haven't even told me when you're getting married," I said.

Aurora's eyebrows shot up. "I have. We talked about it at the house. When you showed up and apologized and said you wanted me to be happy, I was overjoyed. I thought we'd put this nonsense behind us."

"We'll put this nonsense behind us when you wake up to what Toby's really like." Frank shoved up my spine, his dark, sticky power seeking out Aurora.

Aurora blinked at me rapidly. "You know what he's like. You hugged Toby and said all was forgiven. You were sorry for being so pig-headed and thinking badly of him."

I pressed my lips together. Toby deserved to feel some serious pain for making me do that. I had no recollection of that and no memory of Aurora telling me when their wedding was. For all I knew, they might be getting married at the weekend. This had to stop. I had to put an end to this madness.

"Get the dress back to me tomorrow," Aurora said. "I must make sure everything is on track. Getting married is stressful enough without you throwing up roadblocks and trying to ruin my happiness."

I leaned across the counter, fury spiking through me as Frank's energy continued to grow. "Sorry, little sister. I'm going to keep throwing up those roadblocks until you come to your senses. Toby's bad for you. Toby's deceiving you. Until you see that, I'm going to stand in your way. You're never getting married to that low life."

Aurora glowered at me and pointed at the door. "Then you're not welcome here, and you're not welcome at our wedding."

I sucked in a breath, and Frank tickled the back of my neck. I had to get out of here before the argument spiraled out of control and Frank broke free. I couldn't decide if he was spoiling for a fight because of what Toby was doing to Aurora, or if he seriously thought he had a chance to get his demon hands on her.

"Leave," Aurora said.

I stepped away. "I'm going."

Jonah cast a worried look from me to Aurora. "I should leave too."

Aurora grabbed his hand. "Stay right where you are. You're a customer. I'm helping you." She gave me a pointed look. "My sister is beyond saving."

"Fine, I'm leaving." I stamped out of the store, my nails digging into my palms and my blood boiling. I sucked in several deep breaths, pushing Frank down and getting control of my anger.

Aurora was so stubborn and blinded by Toby. How could she not see what he was doing to her? I rolled my shoulders, angry that Toby had driven such a wedge between us.

I spotted Wiggles trotting toward me. I had to focus on the immediate problem. The killer on the loose in Willow Tree Falls. That was something I could deal with.

"Any sign of Seth?" I asked.

"No. I couldn't find any new scent trails, although vampires don't always smell of much." Wiggles tilted his head. "Everything okay? You look flushed."

"Sure. No problems here." At least, there wouldn't be once I'd solved the Toby Matlock issue.

I had a killer to find, and Seth was in the frame.

There was only one way to find that out for sure. I had to find where he was hiding and force a confession out of him. The mood I was in, I felt ready to inflict some vigorous forcing.

Chapter 20

I'd been hunting for Seth all afternoon, and there was still no sign of him. Why did everyone keep disappearing on me?

Frustrated, with aching feet and a rumbling belly, I headed to the angels to give them an update.

The reception was empty, so I walked into the back room with Wiggles.

The place was almost deserted, other than two angels who had their feet up on the desks.

Sablo strolled in from the kitchen with a tray of takeout food in her hands. She slowed when she saw me. "I wasn't expecting you."

"Surprise! I have a new suspect for you to chase," I said.

"Is there enough food to share?" Wiggles hurried over to Sablo and sat at her feet.

She glared down at him. "No, there's not. We only ordered in for three."

"Those look like big portions," Wiggles said. "I'm sure you won't manage it all. I hate to see food go to waste."

Sablo placed the tray on a high filing cabinet. "There's nothing for you." She looked at me. "Who's your new suspect? I thought this mystery was solved."

"Not by me. I'm worried about Seth Fellows. I went to the house to speak to Lotus, and Seth was there. He tried to fake an alibi and claimed he'd been with Lotus at the time Isadora was murdered. She revealed his lie. When I went to talk to him about it, he'd gone. I haven't seen him since."

Sablo leaned against a desk and crossed her arms. "That doesn't make him guilty. I still think this note left by Isadora is significant. She killed Gretel and felt too guilty to carry on."

"Seth doesn't have an alibi for Isadora's murder, and he could have murdered Gretel. He has a lot riding on the book launch. If it goes wrong, he'll lose a lot of money."

"He's also a stalker." Wiggles' gaze hadn't left the food tray. "He's after Lotus, even though she wants nothing to do with him."

I nodded. "Seth isn't a stable guy."

Sablo picked up a french fry and popped it in her mouth. "I'm not buying this theory. Not when it's all sorted. Why go causing problems?"

Wiggles whined and raised a paw.

"You have to help me look for Seth," I said. "He's behind these murders."

"No, we've got this." Sablo dangled a french fry in the air before snatching it away from Wiggles. "I'll leave the investigation open until Dazielle returns, but I'm making a case for Isadora killing Gretel, just as you originally thought."

"If I admit I was wrong about Isadora, will you keep investigating?"

Sablo smirked. "It's tempting. It's rare to hear Tempest Crypt admit she messed up."

I gritted my teeth. "I'll do it. Willow Tree Falls isn't a safe place right now."

Sablo tilted her head from side to side. "I disagree."

"There's still a killer on the loose," I said. "A killer who'll keep attacking witches until they've fulfilled their sick fantasy."

"You've got no proof of that. It's a coincidence that the ducking stool and rocks were used."

It was too much of a coincidence for my liking. "Give me one angel. Even Dominic will do." He always did what I told him.

"Dominic is busy."

"Let me guess. He's making more angel balls."

"Nothing so important. Besides, his balls always come out lumpy."

"So, you can spare him?"

"Not for this."

I turned on my heel. I was done with these dumb bags of feathers. "Enjoy your food." I hoped they choked on it. Without Dazielle cracking the whip, the angels had gotten lazy. But I wasn't giving up.

I got to the door and realized Wiggles wasn't with me. He'd do anything to get his paws on takeout food. "Wiggles! We're leaving."

A moment later, he raced after me, a sullen look on his face. "They wouldn't even give me one lousy french fry. Did you see how piled those plates were? All I wanted was one french fry."

"We can have french fries later. We need to find Seth."

"We've looked everywhere. He's not coming out now he knows you're onto him."

"Then we'll stake out the house," I said. "He has to come back at some point. He won't have forgotten about Lotus that easily. I bet he'll try to convince her to run away with him."

"A stakeout," Wiggles said. "That always involves food. All goods stakeouts have plenty of food to keep you awake. I read about that in my private investigator manual."

I smirked. "Does your PI manual say what kind of food we need to get?"

Wiggles bounced around me. "Pizza!"

I shrugged, still angry with the angels, but I could do with something to eat. I'd also had pizza on my mind ever since talking to Lotus. "How about Mystic Mushroom?"

Wiggles danced around me. "I knew there was a reason I kept you around."

We didn't have to wait long to be served, and Tate was soon boxing two large pizzas, one covered in pineapple and mushrooms for me, while Wiggles ordered a meat feast with extra meat.

"Planning a fun night in?" Tate asked as he took my money.

"Something like that," I said.

"We're on a stakeout," Wiggles whispered loudly.

Tate's eyebrows rose. "A stakeout. That's an interesting way to spend your time. Sounds risky."

I glared at Wiggles. Nobody needed to know what we were up to. "Ignore him. He's been watching too many spy movies."

Tate nodded slowly. "If you need backup on this stakeout, you know where I am."

"Thanks, we'll be fine." We headed out with our pizzas and over to the house Seth was staying in.

After a few minutes of hunting for a suitable spot, we settled behind a large bush where we had a good view of anyone approaching the house.

I leaned back, resting against a tree as I made my way through my delicious pizza. Whoever said it should be illegal to have pineapple on pizza needed their head examined.

Wiggles had finished his pizza within minutes and was sitting next to me, his gaze not leaving my final slice.

"I'm worried about Aurora."

Wiggles glanced at me. "Because of Toby?"

"I have no idea about half the things we talked about when I was in his house. They've set a wedding date, and I don't know when it is. And Aurora was so spiky when I was in her store."

"A wedding date can be unset," Wiggles said. "As soon as you figure out what Toby's hold is over Aurora, you can destroy him."

"Rhett thinks Toby is after the demons. Someone's paying him to get access to our prison and using Aurora to help do that."

"Huh! What does Toby want with the demons?"

"Maybe nothing, but if the pay-out is large, he might be brave enough to mess with our operation. Somebody could be pulling the strings to break out a demon they want free."

"Or maybe they want to mess with us," Wiggles said. "Ruin the Crypt family name. What better way to do that than bust open the prison and point the finger at us for being incompetent?"

"Rhett also suggested that." I sighed as I wiped my fingers on a paper napkin. "Why do that? Who'd want to mess with us?"

"I imagine a fair few magic users aren't big fans," Wiggles said. "Anyone who's a friend of the demons won't be a friend of ours. There are loads of demons beneath the cemetery. Some of them have friends."

"So, they use Toby Matlock to cause us problems?"

"It's working," Wiggles said. "I've never seen you and Aurora argue so much. You used to be so close."

I crumpled the paper napkin and tossed it into the pizza box. "We still are. We just need to get Toby out of the way, and things will be fine."

"Easier said than done," Wiggles said. "Pretty soon, he's going to be your brother-in-law."

The thought made me queasy. "Over my dead body."

We sat in silence for an hour, my thoughts continuing to churn over the Aurora problem. There had to be a way to break Toby's hold.

"My butt's gone to sleep," Wiggles said. "It doesn't look like Seth's going to show."

I was also bored and getting cold. "Seth could have left something incriminating in his room. Evidence that will suggest he's involved in these murders."

"Are you thinking a little breaking and entering is in order?"

"It's in a good cause." I stood, grabbed the pizza boxes, and placed them in the nearest trash can.

"It looks like nobody's home. We haven't seen any lights go on and off since we got here. We can be in and out in ten minutes."

"Stealthy is my middle name," Wiggles said. "And now I'm fueled by pizza, I'm ready to go."

I checked the lane was clear before hurrying to the house with Wiggles. I tried the front door but wasn't surprised to find it locked.

We headed around the side of the house. I tested each window we passed, but none of them budged. However, when we got to the back door, it wasn't bolted. The handle turned, and we were straight into the kitchen.

I looked around the gloom and waited for any sounds of movement, but the house was quiet.

"Upstairs and straight into Seth's room," I whispered.

Wiggles scuttled along, his nose to the ground.

I checked in the lounge, and all was quiet. No one had been here for hours.

We raced upstairs, and after a quick check of the rooms, I figured out which one was Seth's. It smelt like him. It had the spicy whiff of his aftershave in the air.

I checked the closet. "His clothes are still here."

"There are loads of papers on this desk," Wiggles said. "He hasn't been back to pack his things."

"Maybe he's not coming back." I checked through the clothing and looked in the pockets. Everything was designer and tailored to fit. Typical vampire trying to be all debonair and sophisticated.

I walked to the desk and looked through the papers he'd left out. It was mainly information on schedules of appearances for Isadora and ideas for blog tours and book signings.

On a notepad, he'd written the words *legal issue resolved*.

I tapped my finger on the notepad. Seth had most definitely resolved the legal issue if he'd killed Gretel.

"We should look around the other rooms while we're here," Wiggles said.

"Good idea." We headed along the corridor and into the next room. "This must have been Isadora's room. I recognize that cream pant suit on the back of the chair. She wore it on the museum's opening night."

I looked through her bedside cabinet, checked the closet, and went to the dressing table. Everything was there. Nothing had been packed to send to any family.

Opening a drawer of the dressing table, I found a silver locket. I opened it and saw a picture of a baby wrapped in a white blanket. "I didn't know Isadora had kids." I showed Wiggles the locket.

"She never mentioned kids." Wiggles glanced at the picture. "Maybe it's a nephew or niece."

I snapped the locket shut and placed it back in the drawer. Next to it was a small book. I pulled it out and flipped it open. It was full of baby pictures. She had dozens of them, from the time the baby was first born until he was about six months old. I guessed it was a boy from all the blue he was dressed in.

"This must be her baby," I said. "Why keep so many pictures if he isn't hers? And why no toddler pictures or those cringey first day of school pictures? Every parent loves to torture their kids with them."

Wiggles snorted a laugh. "I like the one of you on your first day of school. Your hair looks like you stuck your finger in a power socket, and you were missing a front tooth."

I grimaced. "I've asked Mom to take that photo down so many times. I look like an ogre."

Wiggles nudged me with his nose. "An adorable ogre."

I flicked through the photos again. Someone clearly loved this baby.

"Maybe the baby died," Wiggles said. "That's why there are no more pictures."

I peered closely at the photos. "He looks like Isadora. They have the same chin."

"Someone on her team will know if Isadora has a kid," Wiggles said. "It must be hard to hide a baby."

"Why hide a baby at all?"

A knock on the front door made me jump, and the photo album fell from my hand. I grabbed it and shoved it into the dressing-table drawer before closing it softly. I crept to the front of the house and peered out the window.

"It's Cleo," I whispered to Wiggles.

"Don't let her anywhere near me. My ribs feel bruised from the last torturous snuggling session."

"What's she doing here?" I peeked out at her.

"Hunting for innocent hellhounds to hassle."

"Or looking for someone to tell her what to do. With Gretel no longer bossing her around and Isadora gone, she might be worried about her job."

I tensed as the door knob rattled but knew the door was locked.

She knocked loudly. "Jonah, it's Cleo."

"That's why she's here," Wiggles said. "She's looking for some hot lovin' with Jonah."

"Cleo said they'd been flirting when he paid her a visit at the museum."

A hand banged against the door. "Jonah! I got worried when you didn't show. Is everything okay?"

"It sounds like Jonah has stood her up," Wiggles said.

"The way he spoke about Cleo when I saw him in Aurora's store suggested that he likes her. I wonder where he is."

"Seth's done something to him, so he can't talk. Could Jonah be Seth's next victim?"

"Only if my theory is wrong. This killer is targeting witches."

Cleo knocked a couple more times before walking away and staring up at the house.

I ducked out of the way, so she wouldn't see me. After standing there for another minute, I saw her shrug and turn away from the house.

My gaze went to Isadora's room. I walked back into it and took out the baby pictures again. "What if this baby was a surprise? If she'd had him young, when she was starting her career, she might have felt unable to keep him."

"She gave her kid away?"

"Or maybe she tried to keep him, but it became too much for her. A young mom and no sign of a dad around, he's not in any of these pictures. Isadora had her future planned out, and it didn't include a surprise pregnancy." I flipped through more pictures and stared at the cute chubby-faced baby with his shock of blond hair and blue eyes. "You don't take dozens of pictures of your baby and then suddenly stop. Unless you no longer have that baby."

"Do you think Seth is related to Isadora? Is she his secret love child?"

"Not Seth. At least, this baby looks nothing like Seth. The coloring is all wrong. Seth is pale with dark hair."

"Unless he took most of his father's traits," Wiggles said.

My heart thudded. "Jonah was really upset about Isadora's death. How old do you think Jonah is?"

"Late twenties," Wiggles said.

"Look at these pictures." I showed him another one of a serious-faced baby with messy blond hair. "The baby has Jonah's chin and nose. What if Jonah is Isadora's son?"

"She would have told us they were related," Wiggles said. "Isadora made no mention of having a son."

My gut clenched. "What if she didn't know Jonah was her son? He said they'd worked together for five years. What if he'd been looking for his biological mom? Jonah discovered her and found she was looking to hire someone. He invented himself as this incredible assistant, so she'd take him on and he could get back into her life."

"It would have been easier to tell Isadora he was her son."

"Maybe Jonah didn't think he could," I said. "It must be tough on a kid to know your mom gave you up because she wanted her career more than her baby. That must hurt. He must have been worried that she'd reject him again. At least this way, he got to be in her life."

"Jonah thought he couldn't be in Isadora's life as her son, so he took the job as the next best thing?"

I chewed on my bottom lip. "Maybe he didn't come back into her life because he wanted to get to know her. Jonah came back into Isadora's life because he was angry. She'd abandoned him as a baby. She must have given him up for adoption. That could scar a child."

Wiggles stared at the pictures. "Jonah planned to ruin Isadora because she put her career before him?"

I nodded as I grabbed the locket and hooked it around Wiggles' neck. "Keep this safe. It's evidence." I headed to the door, the photo album in my hand. "Seth isn't our killer. It's Jonah."

Chapter 21

It had been hours since I'd seen Jonah at Aurora's store, but I raced back there with Wiggles, hopeful Aurora had insisted he stay until he felt better.

The more I thought about it, the more I was convinced that Jonah was Isadora's son. He was utterly devoted to her, and from the way he'd spoken about her, he'd do anything for Isadora.

But what if that devotion had become warped? What if Jonah had been sticking to Isadora's side and making her dependent on him because of what she'd done when he was a baby?

Wiggles panted as we ran. "I still think Seth's involved. He's too sleazy to be innocent."

"He's a moneygrubbing jerk, but all Seth's interested in is how much he can squeeze out of Isadora and how to convince Lotus to marry him. And, even with Isadora dead, Seth can still make money out of this deal. As Trixie suggested, people pay a lot for a first edition signed copy from a dead author."

"I still wouldn't trust him not to give me a nip with his vampy fangs when I'm not looking," Wiggles said. "I vote for Seth as the killer."

I checked the time as we approached the store. It should be open for another half an hour. Aurora had late night opening on Fridays. My hope fell as I saw the lights were off. It looked like she'd left.

"Tempest!"

I groaned as I turned and saw Mannie hurrying toward me. I could do without his interference right now.

"I've been trying to find you." Mannie puffed out a breath as he stopped. "I heard worrying news from the angels. They tell me they've solved the case, but you're still investigating. You're after Seth Fellows?"

"Forget about Seth," I said. "I'm more interested in Jonah Dragoon."

"Jonah! He's a charming young man," Mannie said. "Devoted to Isadora. He'd never kill her."

"Did you know he's her son?"

Mannie's eyebrows shot up. "That can't be right. Isadora never said they were related, and she didn't treat him like a family member. And, I don't think she had any children. I never thought to ask."

"I don't know if Isadora was aware that Jonah was her son."

Mannie shook his head. "No, you've got this backward. Jonah isn't involved in this. He's smart, hard-working—"

"And possibly a killer."

"It's time someone else took over this investigation. I appreciate everything you've done so far, but it's best to leave it to the experts. Sablo has an interesting theory about Isadora. She thinks—"

I grabbed his waistcoat and yanked him toward me. "Mannie, they're related. I found pictures of a baby in Isadora's things." I shoved the photo album I held in his face. "That baby is Jonah. He came back in her life as her doting assistant. He's anything but that."

Mannie looked at the crumpled waistcoat fabric scrunched in my fists. "You can't know that."

I shook him. "Look at the pictures. I've got evidence. If Jonah's intentions were good, he wouldn't have hidden this secret for five years. Imagine how mad you'd be if you were abandoned as a kid, all because your mom wanted to pursue a career and not have a baby under her feet."

Mannie spluttered and wriggled in my grip. "Well, I suppose I might be upset."

"Jonah's more than upset. He's raging mad. He wanted revenge. Jonah killed Gretel and Isadora, staging their murders so they looked like the pictures from his mother's book."

Mannie licked his lips, and his attention settled on the baby pictures. "Why would he do something so twisted?"

"We have to ask him that. But what better way to get revenge than to ruin the career his mom built up over the years? He said her books were her only love. Jonah hated Isadora's career, so he destroyed it. And he's not stopping. He's going to keep killing."

Mannie blinked up at me. "Are you absolutely certain of this? There's no chance the angels are correct?"

"I wish they were." I wasn't completely sure, not until I'd confronted Jonah, but I was willing to bet

Cloven Hoof on my hunch. "The last time I saw him, he was in Heaven's Door with Aurora." I let go of Mannie and turned back to the store.

Hurrying to the door, I tried the handle. My heart clenched as the door opened. Aurora never left the store unlocked at the end of the working day.

I swung the door open and stepped inside. My mind reeled, and I grabbed the wall for support. "What if Aurora's next? She was being kind to Jonah when he was here. He could have taken advantage of that. He claimed he was in the store looking for something to calm his nerves, but what if he was looking for his next victim?"

"My dear, I'm sure that's not true." Mannie stiffly patted my back. "Even if it was, Aurora has power. She can defend herself."

"No, she can't. Aurora's not herself. She's vulnerable. Jonah could have sensed that and targeted her." My throat tightened, and panic flooded through me. "Jonah needs another witch to re-enact the next murder from Isadora's book."

Mannie's face paled, and he tugged on his beard. "What's the next method of murder?"

I swallowed. "Burning a witch at the stake. That witch could be my sister."

"There's no need to panic. You don't know for certain that's what's going on."

I shoved Mannie out of the store and slammed the door shut. "We can't take that risk. Get help. Get the angels out looking for Jonah and Aurora. I don't care who they find first, so long as they aren't together."

Mannie staggered backward. "Of course. We'll find your sister. I'll get the angels right on it. Where will you be looking?"

"The forest. It's the perfect place to burn a witch."

Mannie nodded before turning and dashing away.

I sucked in a deep breath as blood pounded in my head. This couldn't be happening. I couldn't have left Aurora alone with a killer. If I hadn't been so wound up about her relationship with Toby, I would have spotted something was off with Jonah and stopped him. What if I was too late? What if he'd already killed her?

"Less thinking, more action," Frank growled in my head. His energy spiraled up to my neck and prickled across my skin.

I didn't even try to stop him from coming through. I needed everyone on my side if we were to hunt down Jonah and save Aurora.

"Let's go, Wiggles." I had to hope I could control Frank's rage, and his desire to rescue Aurora from Jonah would beat down his own lust to see her life drain away.

Wiggles sped along beside me as we raced away from the store.

"We will gut this monster." Frank's words rumbled through my head.

I tried to clear my panicked thoughts and figure out where Jonah would go. The forest wasn't big, but it would take too long to search without backup. Sweat ran down my back as Frank's energy pounded through me. He lingered just below the surface, ready to burst through.

I had to keep a sliver of control over him as we hunted for Jonah and Aurora. If Frank was pulling the punches when we found them, I wouldn't be able to protect Aurora.

We dashed through the trees, yelling Aurora's name.

I heard the sound of someone groaning and changed direction. Leaping around a bush, my fist raised ready to strike, I stopped. It was Fallon. She lay on the ground, blood seeping from a head wound and her eyes glazed.

"He got me," she whispered. "He was so fast."

I caught hold of her arm. "Can you stand?"

Fallon nodded as she staggered to her feet and touched her head injury.

"Did you see Aurora?"

She rocked back and forth unsteadily and groaned. "I'm dying."

"No, you're not." I steadied her, keeping my frustration in check but only just. "Think, have you seen Aurora in the forest?"

Fallon rested the back of her hand against her forehead. "There was a pretty blonde witch slung over this beast's shoulder. I halted him and demanded to know what he was doing."

"What did he do to you?"

"I'm not certain, but it hurt. I remember opening my eyes and finding myself on my back, having been knocked out cold. He must have dragged me behind the bush to conceal his evil deed." Fallon sank to the ground. "No one has ever beaten me before. I've failed my forest. If I wasn't dying, I would insist I get cast out for incompetence and forced to live in the bog lands of Tanith Mure."

"You weren't to know who you were dealing with. Jonah isn't a stable guy." I kept hold of Fallon's arm. "Which way did they go?"

She raised a trembling arm. "So, that's the monster's name. He went through the trees in that direction."

"Show us," I said. "He's got my sister."

Fallon nodded and stumbled a couple of steps before falling to her knees. "I can't walk. Leave me to perish. Save your sibling."

"Let's move," Frank growled. "This creep has a head start on us."

I glanced at Wiggles. "I know you'll hate me for asking, but can Fallon ride on your back?"

Wiggles' eyes flared red, and he bared his teeth. "I'm not a pony."

"Oh, yes!" Fallon waved a hand in the air. "That's my dying wish, to ride your special furry pony."

"We need Fallon to guide us safely through the forest," I said to Wiggles. "Remember, she has dangerous pits, magic arrows, and exploding webbing set up. If we stumble into that, we're goners. So is Aurora."

"I guarantee my magic will kill you," Fallon whispered.

"Wiggles! Please!"

Fallon held a hand out to Wiggles. "I'll show you exactly where they went."

Wiggles stalked over to Fallon and glowered at her. "You can ride me. But you have to say I'm not a pony."

Fallon tilted her head. "Then what are you?"

"Come on! We don't have time. Aurora's life's at risk." I hurried ahead of them, hoping I was going in the right direction.

I heard grumbling behind me and turned to see Fallon clambering on Wiggles' back and grabbing hold of his ears.

"Not the ears!" Wiggles flipped his head from side to side. "Wrap your arms around my neck if you have to hold on to anything."

Fallon grinned, suddenly looking much better. "I'll lead the way." She pressed her heels into Wiggles' sides. "Giddy-up, pony."

Wiggles growled and shot me a glare as they raced past.

I'd make it up to him. But right now, we had to find Aurora.

"Yee haw!" Fallon yelled. "This is everything I dreamed of. Faster pony, faster."

"Focus," I snapped at her. "Which way did Jonah and Aurora go?"

"Through that clearing. Straight ahead, pony."

Wiggles raced along, not seeming impeded by the extra weight on his back.

I kept up with them, drawing on Frank's energy as I raced past the trees. I slowed and raised my head. My stomach tightened, and fear flooded through me. "I smell smoke."

"So can I," Wiggles said. "It's stronger in this direction." He ducked around an enormous oak tree and sped along the path in front of me.

I followed, my stomach churning. If Aurora was dead, I'd never forgive myself. We'd had a petty argument, and I'd left her with Jonah. I hadn't paid enough attention to a suspect because he'd been polite and offered me cookies. I wouldn't lose my sister to him.

"I'm also not prepared to lose Aurora," Frank muttered. "We have unfinished business."

"Don't you dare talk about killing Aurora," I said to him. "Not now. You know how much she means to me."

"And you know how much she means to me." Frank's growl rumbled through me. "I'm in this for one reason. We're not friends; we've never been friends. I help you from time to time when your life is at risk. If you die, I die without a host, and that's not going to happen until I get what I want."

"Enough," I said. "We have to find Aurora." I swept aside a branch and followed the smell of smoke.

"You don't have to do this," a female voice cried out.

"That's Aurora!" I sped up, keeping up with Wiggles and Fallon as we raced along the path.

"Keep quiet, witch. Your death will be in the history books forever, just as it's supposed to be. Re-enacting the past is a way of bringing it back to life." That was Jonah.

"What are you talking about?" Aurora said, her voice sounding shaky.

"This is all she cared about, so this is what I'm doing. Bringing history to life."

I came to a stop as a clearing appeared, my throat tightening and my mouth going dry as I saw Jonah.

He prodded a flaming branch into a pyre. Tied above the pyre, standing on a wooden plank, her hands and feet bound behind her, was Aurora. Tears streaked down her face, and her eyes were wide with terror.

Lying on the ground next to the pyre was an open book. It looked like a copy of Isadora's book.

"Jonah, you need help," Aurora said. "Let me help you."

He pointed the flaming branch at her. "One more word, witch, and I'll end you."

"Please, I can fix this. You don't need to burn me."

"History must be served." Jonah jabbed the branch into the pyre.

"No, it doesn't." I raced out of the tree-line and slammed into Jonah, taking him to the ground in a bruising slam. I grabbed him around the waist and pinned him to the ground. "Keep away from my sister."

Chapter 22

I flipped over on the ground, keeping a tight hold on Jonah as he writhed in my grip. "Put out the fire," I shouted at Wiggles and Fallon.

"We're on it," Wiggles yelled.

Jonah swung a punch at my head, and I ducked, a deep laugh rumbling out of me.

He blinked at me, madness shimmering in his eyes. "What's gotten into you?"

"A demon." I growled in his face as I let Frank come through. "Jonah, meet Frank. Frank, meet the guy who tried to take Aurora from us."

Frank roared in my head, and I lost control as his energy poured over me. My eyes filtered the world through a red glow as my hands latched around Jonah's neck, and I squeezed.

Jonah wheezed and gasped. He grabbed the burning branch he'd dropped and swung it toward me.

I rolled away and felt the swish of flame pass my cheek.

Jonah jumped to his feet and clubbed me with the butt of the burning branch.

I felt the impact, but Frank didn't care about my bruises as I leaped to my feet and crouched.

Jonah rubbed his neck as he held the burning branch out in front of him.

I glanced over my shoulder to see Wiggles and Fallon pulling burning piles of wood away from Aurora as she choked on the smoke.

Jonah slammed into me, and we hit the ground again.

The roar that came out of my mouth wasn't human as Frank's rage flooded into my fists, and I fired bolts of black energy into Jonah's chest.

He yelped and flew backward, slamming into a tree.

I leaped to my feet and raced toward him. He rolled out of the way as another blast of Frank's energy spun from my fingers.

"What kind of monster are you?" he wheezed out.

"The kind you should never anger." I shoved hard against Frank's energy. I needed to maintain a fragment of control. Aurora was a few meters away, and she'd be a huge temptation for Frank, especially in her weakened state.

"We're here!" Mannie, Lotus, Cleo, and Seth emerged from the trees.

My mouth fell open. He was supposed to bring the angels, not Jonah's work buddies. "Where's the backup?"

Mannie's startled gaze took in the scene before it returned to me. "The office was closed. The angels weren't there. I wasn't sure who else to bring until I went past the museum and saw Isadora's team coming out. I grabbed them and asked for help."

"Jonah?" Seth stepped forward, a bemused look on his face. "What are you doing?"

Jonah snarled and raced toward Seth, head-butting him in the stomach as they made contact.

Seth gasped as they hit the ground and rolled around in the dirt, slapping at each other and grunting. For a half-vampire, he had a disappointing set of fighting skills.

While Seth distracted Jonah, I hurried to the burning pyre. Wiggles and Fallon had done an excellent job of stopping the flames from spreading, but the smoke was dense and choking.

I felt around for Frank's energy and paused. He was close, I didn't have him under control, but I couldn't risk waiting any longer.

I leaped onto the smoking piece of wood Aurora stood on and untied her hands and feet. "Are you okay?"

She nodded, but her jaw wobbled. "I don't understand why he's doing this. One second, he was being sweet and saying how helpful I was. The next, he had me in a headlock. Jonah moved so fast. He knocked me out."

My fingers went to her throat, and I stroked the soft skin, Frank urging me to continue.

"Tempest?" Aurora's eyes widened. "Or, is it Frank in charge?"

I bit my lip hard, and the pain helped me to keep control. "I'm still here. Tell me everything once we're safe." I helped her off the plank and away from the burning wood.

"Fallon, Wiggles, keep Aurora safe and away from me for now." I backed away from her and shook my head. Frank confused my thoughts and sent me disturbing images of how delightful it would be to choke Aurora.

"Tempest. You've got this. You can control Frank," Aurora said.

"I know. Just stay where you are." I held up a hand as she took a wobbly step toward me.

She nodded, a tear trickling down her cheek. She looked so small and lost.

I wished I could hug her and tell her everything would be okay, but it felt far from okay. My insides burned as Frank battled for control.

Turning away, I saw Seth still taking a beating from Jonah. This warlock had power.

Lotus, Cleo, and Mannie all stood watching, shock on their faces.

I gritted my teeth and growled. They were supposed to be helping, not getting a free warlock and half-vampire smack down battle to ogle. "Don't just stand there. Help me take Jonah down."

Mannie took a step back. "I don't have my weapons, and I've never been one to use my fists. Weak wrists, you see."

"Then strangle him with your beard!"

Mannie grabbed his beard, a look of horror on his face.

My gaze cut to Lotus and Cleo. "It's down to us, ladies. Are you willing to fight?"

Lotus' mouth twisted to the side. "I'm sort of enjoying watching Seth get a beating. I've dreamt about doing it myself on numerous occasions."

My eyebrows shot up. "Really? Now you want to get your revenge?"

She pursed her lips, and sparkles of magic glittered on her fingers. "I'm enjoying myself, but I didn't say I wouldn't help."

Cleo nodded, and magic swirled around her in a dusty cloud. "I'm ready when you are."

Jonah slammed Seth's head into the ground. His focus was on inflicting maximum damage to the half-vampire. It was the perfect time to strike.

"Now!" I yelled.

We launched our magic at Jonah's back. Cleo twisted her fingers as she directed her dusty blast at him. Lotus spread her arms, and a shower of vicious looking glitter appeared. My magic was a gray mix of my own powers and Frank's muddy energy. With our magic combined, Jonah was about to be in a world of hurt.

His back arched as our magic struck. His hands flew up and his head tipped back as our energy poured into him and held him in place.

Jonah writhed and bucked as Seth scrambled out from under him, his face bruised and battered and his suit torn. He staggered away before collapsing on the ground.

"Hold him," I said to Cleo and Lotus. "Don't let Jonah go." My magic felt too dark, and Frank added more heat to my power as Jonah struggled and bucked, breaking spells and inching toward us, a look of murderous hatred in his crazed eyes.

He snarled and snapped his teeth. "You can't take me."

"Yes, we can." I dropped a barrier and let more of Frank through. Sweat dripped off my chin as my magic united with Frank's demon energy.

Jonah roared as his hand reached for me.

Cleo and Lotus moved forward, flanking me either side. Magic flowed from both of them, their faces contorted with effort as Jonah's magic fought back.

"Stars! What is he?" Lotus gasped.

"Damaged," Cleo whispered. "I feel his anger. So much pain. He's broken inside."

"Don't let him fool you," I said. "Jonah will kill us if we let him loose."

Another tortured roar flew from Jonah's lips as he sagged forward.

I felt Jonah's dark essence drain away as he wobbled on his feet. He dropped to his knees, and his head slumped to his chest.

"That's it. We've almost got him." I pumped more energy into the magic that held him. Whatever power Jonah used felt dark and dangerous, and he didn't have complete control of it.

Only when Jonah was slumped on the ground did I pull back my magic.

Cleo and Lotus did the same, both gasping in relief as they drew in their powers.

Jonah lay on his side, his eyes fluttering and his breath panting out of him.

"Why was he burning that witch?" Cleo whispered.

"That witch is my sister," I muttered. "And Jonah is who we've been looking for. He killed Gretel and Isadora."

Jonah groaned and rolled onto his back, blinking slowly as he stared at the trees. "You've ruined everything."

I moved closer to Jonah, my fingers outstretched, a warning glimmer of magic lacing across my palms. "Why do this?"

He shifted his gaze to me, and his eyes narrowed. "I have to leave a legacy. I have to make sure my name is remembered in the history books."

Lotus stepped forward. "I don't understand. You were devoted to Isadora."

"Devoted!" Jonah snorted. "That cold-hearted witch wouldn't know the meaning of the word. I gave her everything, and what did she do for me?"

Lotus shook her head. "Paid you a decent salary?"

Jonah closed his eyes. "She was a monster."

I looked at the group and saw the confusion on their faces. "Isadora was Jonah's mother."

Cleo and Lotus gasped and grabbed for each other.

Jonah snarled at me as he pushed himself into a seated position.

I flicked magic at his feet. "No sudden moves, or we'll put you down for good."

He grimaced as he edged upright. "Isadora might have given birth to me, but she was no mother. She left me. She gave me up when it got too difficult. All she cared about was making a career for herself. Isadora couldn't do that with a brat by her side. Her ambition blinded her. She never loved me. She was no mother."

Mannie shook his head. "Well, I never. Tempest, who'd have thought it? You were right."

I was too angry and focused on Jonah to bite Mannie's head off.

Cleo walked closer to Jonah, her eyes full of compassion, and held a hand out. "Your mother abandoned you?"

"That's near enough," I cautioned her. "When I touched Jonah, I felt dark power in him. It will still be there."

Cleo moved away slowly. "I understand why you're hurting, but you didn't have to kill Isadora."

"She ruined my life," Jonah said. "She didn't want me. She left me in the care of others. I never found a home to settle in. I bounced from foster home to foster home until I was old enough to look after myself."

"That must have been tough," Cleo said.

"When I was eighteen, I began my search for her. It took a while, but she wasn't difficult to find. When I learned what she'd been doing all these years and how driven she was, I knew she deserved to be punished. Isadora was selfish."

"So, you waited until there was an opportunity to get close to her," I said.

Jonah nodded. "I watched Isadora for years and became familiar with her routine. I knew her favorite places to eat, what coffee she drank, what stores she shopped in. It was easy to fake a resume and submit it when she was looking for an assistant. You should have seen her, so eager for me to take the job. Mommy dearest kept saying that she felt as if she knew me and we had a connection." He scowled. "Little did she know what kind of connection we really had."

"Were you hoping she'd recognize you and welcome you back into her life?" Mannie asked.

"Of course not. I wanted nothing to do with that evil witch. All I cared about was getting justice. What kind of person abandons a child?"

"A desperate one," I said. "Someone young, inexperienced, and scared. Maybe someone with no support network. Your mom had ambitions, and you weren't a part of her plan."

"So, she discarded me like a piece of trash." Jonah swiped at his soot stained cheeks.

"Why wait until now?" Lotus asked. "You've been with Isadora for five years. You could have killed her any time."

"Five years ago, Isadora wasn't a world-renowned author, about to launch a best-selling book. She was just another lecturer, no one special. As her book took shape, I realized she had a hit on her hands." Jonah's gaze went to Seth, who remained on his back, panting. "Then Mr. Smarmy came on board, sending Isadora around the country on talks and generating a buzz. That was when I knew this was the right time to kill her. She'd spent every waking hour building her career, and I got to destroy it. I got a chance to make her pay for what she did to me."

"You talked about leaving a legacy," I said. "Was the plan to go down in history as some notorious witch killer?"

Jonah ran a hand down his face. "That's a bonus. Everyone will remember me for what happened here. My name will be linked to my mom forever. I have my own place in history."

"You set up the murders just as Isadora described in her book," I said. "People will think her work inspired you to kill."

He nodded. "Yes, but it was more than that. I wanted people to think she'd killed Gretel. I ensured Isadora had a lousy alibi on the night of Gretel's murder and that everybody knew they weren't friends. It was easy for me to return to the museum after it was shut. I knew Cleo would be in bed, and Gretel wouldn't be able to resist interfering when she thought no one was around. A blast of magic held her in place. You know the rest."

"The angels didn't arrest your mom, though. They pursued other leads."

"Or no leads." Jonah shook his head. "I've never met a more incompetent bunch of idiots. Everything was laid out for them, so they could arrest Isadora, but they refused to see it."

I bit my tongue. Jonah was good. I'd been well on the way to being convinced Isadora had murdered Gretel. "You planted that note the angels found in her room. The one suggesting Isadora might have killed herself."

"It was a long shot. Who'd be dumb enough to believe that was a good method of suicide?" He snorted a laugh. "I should have known the dumb angels would believe it."

Lotus shook her head. "Your mom didn't deserve to die."

Jonah glared at her. "And I didn't deserve to be discarded and not considered important."

Mannie shuffled his feet. "Why carry on? You killed Gretel in an attempt to frame your mother and then killed Isadora when your efforts to get her arrested failed. Why target Aurora?"

"Because he doesn't want to be forgotten." I looked at Aurora, her face soot stained and her eyes wide.

Jonah bared his teeth. "That's right, and I was enjoying myself. Mom had worked hard on her book, so I decided to re-enact every murder from it. It was only fitting, giving her a long-lasting legacy. Isadora Ash should go down in history as the author who inspired a serial killer. My name will be linked to her forever. She can never be rid of me, no matter how hard she tried."

I glanced at Cleo. "Your story doesn't fit. How could you have killed Isadora when you were at the museum with Cleo?"

Cleo's eyes widened. "Jonah was with me almost the whole time."

Jonah waved a hand dismissively at her. "When I met Cleo, I could see she was a weirdo. She's as obsessed with history as Isadora. I could also tell she was lonely. It was easy to flirt with her and get her attention. Soften her up so she'd be the perfect cover."

Cleo gasped. "You don't like me?"

"How can I like someone who smells like the pages of a dusty old book and recites Latin for fun?"

"Hey, that's rude!" Lotus wrapped an arm around Cleo's shoulders. "Ignore him. You're brilliant."

Jonah kicked his heels in the dirt. "Whatever. I was with Cleo most of the time, but I left for half an hour on the pretense of getting coffee and cake. I'd arranged to meet Isadora at the stone circle. I told her I'd found an interesting artifact buried there, and she had to see it. She totally bought the story. She had no reason to doubt me. I was her devoted employee."

I looked at Cleo. "Why didn't you say anything when I asked you about your alibi?"

She bit her bottom lip, tears in her eyes. "I didn't think it was important. We were together most of that day. Jonah slipping out to get us a treat seemed like a sweet thing to do. He wasn't gone long and seemed so calm when he came back. And he was happy."

"Of course I was happy," Jonah said. "I'd destroyed the woman who'd ruined my life. I wanted to dance and sing with joy because she was gone. Her life was over. Everything she wanted had been ripped from her. It was no less than she deserved."

Cleo shook her head. "You're a terrible person, Jonah."

"Because she made me terrible," Jonah said. "Isadora never cared for me."

"You're wrong," I said to Jonah. "Your mom loved you."

He scowled at me. "You don't know her. You know nothing about her."

"She had a locket with your picture in it," I said. "I found it when I was looking around her room."

Jonah blinked at me rapidly. "You're lying."

"Wiggles," I said.

He walked over, and I unhooked the locket from around his neck. "See for yourself." I dropped it on the ground and toed it toward Jonah.

Jonah grabbed it, a look of disbelief on his face. He opened the locket, and his eyes widened. He stared at the picture in silence for a moment. "This means nothing. That might not be me."

"Are you sure?" I asked. "Why else would Isadora keep that picture with her? She did love you, but she wasn't in the right place to look after you properly. She was trying to do the best for you."

Jonah snapped the locket shut and clutched it in his fist. "More like she couldn't be bothered to look after me. She only cared about herself."

"Where's the baby book?" I asked Wiggles. I'd dropped it in the dash to protect Aurora.

"Hang on a minute. I saw it by the fire." He sprinted away and returned with the small photo album in his mouth, which he spat out next to Jonah.

"In there, you'll find dozens of pictures of you," I said. "Your mom kept you for as long as she could. It looks like she tried to make things work for at least six months."

Jonah grabbed the album and flicked through the pages. He shook his head, the muscles in his jaw twitching. "I've never seen these pictures."

"Isadora had them with her. She had them in her room. She must have carried them wherever she went. Your mom loved you."

Jonah dropped the album and buried his head in his hands. "She hated me."

"She probably does now," Seth muttered as he pulled himself off the ground.

"You be quiet," Lotus hissed.

Seth looked startled but kept his mouth shut.

Jonah lifted his head, and I saw tears on his cheeks. "I didn't know," he repeated.

"Of course you didn't. Just as she didn't know you were her son. That's still no reason to ruin her."

Jonah slumped. "I got it wrong. She did try to raise me. She did love me." He clutched the album against his chest.

"Isadora wasn't perfect, but she didn't throw you away." I nodded as I looked at Mannie. We had everything we needed.

He returned my nod. "I'll go round up an angel. Let's finish this."

"Keep an eye on him," I said to Cleo and Lotus.

Lotus clenched her hands into fists, her gaze fixed on Jonah.

"We got this," Cleo said.

I rolled my shoulders as I checked Frank was back where he belonged. His anger still simmered, but he wasn't about to break through.

I let out a relieved sigh as I walked to Aurora and hugged her. "Everything's good. We're good. There's nothing to worry about."

She sagged against me, her thin frame shaking.

I kissed the top of her smoky smelling head. It was over. The killer had been found and the witches of Willow Tree Falls were safe.

Chapter 23

The sunshine felt great on my face as I headed out of Cloven Hoof with Wiggles for a late breakfast.

I skidded to a halt, and my eyes widened. In front of me was a very angry, very tanned looking Dazielle. The white of her angel's uniform made her skin glow.

"I thought you'd left for good," I said. "Where have you been hiding?"

"That's not your business." She crossed her arms over her chest. "What have you been doing while I've been away?"

"Keeping the village safe," I said. "Saving witches' lives. Stopping a deranged killer. I think that's about it. What about you?"

Dazielle arched an eyebrow. "Keep talking."

"I have to say," Wiggles said as he shuffled past me, "you look hot, Dazielle. I'm not a fan of feathers and blonde hair, but wherever you've been, it's taken five years off you."

A smile flitted across Dazielle's face before fading. "Time away has done me good. Now talk, Tempest."

"You can get the information from your angels. They were nothing short of miraculous while you were topping up that tan. I learned so many things, especially how to play Angel Ball and shirk responsibility whenever possible."

Her nod was curt. "I'm already having words with my angels. I've had several complaints about a lack of angels in the village while I've been away. They'll be undertaking intensive training, so they don't forget their responsibilities again."

"That sounds like the perfect plan. Good luck with that." I tried to step around Dazielle, but she blocked my path with a wing and shoved me back. "I'm not finished with you."

I raised my hands. "I don't know what to tell you. Mannie insisted I help, and he's our esteemed mayor, so I could hardly say no. You weren't around when the murders took place, so I was forced to step in. And you still haven't told me where you were. Why did I have to cover for you?"

Dazielle's nose twitched. "I was instructed to attend a transcendental yoga retreat."

Wiggles snorted a cloud of smoke from his nose.

I choked back a laugh, thinking she was joking, but the look on Dazielle's face was serious. "Wow! I understand why you had no interest in what was happening in Willow Tree Falls. You can't let a couple of murders in the village you're supposed to protect come between you and your yogic flying."

"Or your downward facing dog," Wiggles said.

"There was no flying," Dazielle grumbled. "But there were no external communications. Our mobile snow globes were taken off us when we arrived, and we weren't able to access them until the end of the retreat. When I found mine, I discovered dozens of messages from the angels, you, and Mannie."

"Did my message about taking your job and selling your apartment prompt your return?"

"I knew all of that was a lie. You'd never want my job." She had the decency to look a little ashamed. "I got back as soon as I could."

"We're so grateful you did," I said. "Everything's been falling apart."

Wiggles turned his back as he chortled.

Dazielle's mouth twisted to the side. "I owe you a favor for this, and I suppose I should thank you."

"That's very decent of you." I couldn't help but prod. "How's the temper? Did the retreat give you your mojo back?"

She sighed. "I hope so. My angels can be like naughty schoolchildren when not constantly supervised. I thought being away for five days wouldn't be a problem. How much trouble can they get into in such a short space of time?"

"They even surprised me," I said. "In Dominic's defense, he wasn't a total dunce. Sablo, she needs work, as does Cassiel. Everyone else, they all scarpered. You should fire them all and start again."

"Usually, the village is quiet. It didn't occur to me that the museum and its guests would cause problems." Dazielle turned and gestured with her head for me to follow her. "So, Jonah was the dead author's abandoned son?"

I glanced at Wiggles and shrugged before walking alongside Dazielle. "That's right. He'd convinced himself that his mom had abandoned him. The truth was, she did care for him but was too young to raise him alone. She focused on her career, determined to make a name for herself."

Dazielle shook her head. "And Isadora never tried to find him?"

"That's a question we can never answer," I said. "By the time Jonah found her, he was raging mad and determined to get revenge. He was obsessed with his mom's work and not only wanted to ruin her but planned to leave a legacy people would remember for hundreds of years. He found a way for the world to know he was her son and what she'd done to him."

"Jonah wanted a link between the two of them, so they'd always be joined."

"Sounds about right. Have you interviewed him?"

"I got back late last night," Dazielle said. "I spoke to Jonah briefly, and he's talking. He admits to everything. He had a ring in his pocket, which was the source of his dark power."

"I wondered what made him so strong."

"Jonah seems remorseful now he knows the truth about his mom. He's still going away for a long time." She glanced at me. "I heard about your sister. It sounds like a near miss."

I let out a sigh. "It was. She's unharmed, just shocked. She'll be fine."

"That's good to hear."

I stopped and turned to Dazielle. "Since you owe me a favor..."

Her eyes narrowed. "You're already calling that in?"

"It's about Aurora or, rather, who Aurora's dating."

Dazielle's eyes widened. "Go on."

"Aurora is getting married to Toby Matlock."

Dazielle grunted in surprise. "I hadn't heard that. Toby Matlock is old."

"And as shady as they come. He's manipulating Aurora. I don't know how he's doing it, but she's fallen for him in a big way."

Dazielle's nose wrinkled. "He's very rich."

"Don't go there. You know Aurora isn't that kind of girl."

"I'm just saying. I admit he's not her usual type."

"She thinks he is. Whatever I say, she's not convinced that Toby's wrong for her. He's also used his mind manipulation magic on me more than once. And, he's got a lock of my hair."

"Why would you give him a lock of your hair?"

"I didn't give it to him willingly. As I said, Toby's a shady warlock, and he's using his magic to get what he wants."

"He's ensuring an interfering big sister stays out of the way of his happy ever after with Aurora."

I glared at Dazielle. "Something like that."

"So, what's the favor?"

"I need to know everything you've got on Toby Matlock."

Dazielle shook her head. "I can't share details about an ongoing investigation. We've been looking into Toby for some time."

"I know that, which is why I'm so concerned about his manipulation of my sister. If you're having trouble pinning something on Toby, maybe I can help. I need to get him away from Aurora before she makes a terrible mistake."

Dazielle twisted her long blonde braid around her wrist. "It's against policy. You're not an angel. I'd be breaking the rules if I let you see what we've got on him."

"I did solve two murders for you and just about stopped Angel Force from imploding with incompetence. Your angels aren't as angelic as they appear to be. I could have walked away and left you to clear up this mess."

Dazielle tilted her head back before nodding. "You can't tell anybody about this. If you say I've shown you these files, I'll deny everything and make your life hell."

"My lips will be sealed. But I have to know how much trouble Aurora's in."

Dazielle turned in the direction of Angel Force. "You might think keeping Willow Tree Falls safe from Jonah and his crazed re-enactments of his mom's work was tough. You've got a bigger problem going up against Toby Matlock."

My stomach clenched as I followed Dazielle. "Whatever it takes, I'm bringing him down."

I spotted Mom and Granny Dottie heading toward the cemetery. It wasn't just Aurora at risk. If Rhett's theory was true, and Toby was after a much bigger prize, the whole village could be in trouble. Scrap that, the whole world.

Willow Tree Falls might be safe from Jonah, but we had a bigger snake living among us.

I'd fix this mess. I'd make sure Aurora got back to her happy, smiling self. Heaven's Door would open again, and Toby Matlock would be gone for good.

Dazielle opened the door to Angel Force and gestured me and Wiggles inside. "I hope you're ready for this."

I nodded at her, my expression grim. "I will be. No one messes with my family and gets away with it."

About Author

K.E. O'Connor (Karen) is a cozy mystery author living in the beautiful British countryside. She loves all things mystery, animals, and cake. When she's not writing about mysteries, murder, and treats, she volunteers at a local animal sanctuary, reads a ton of books, binge watches mystery series, and dreams about living somewhere warmer.

To stay in touch with the fun mysteries:

Newsletter:
www.subscribepage.com/cozymysteries
Website:
www.keoconnor.com/writing
Facebook:
www.facebook.com/keoconnorauthor

Also By

Luck of the Witch
Hell of a Witch
Revenge of the Witch
Curse of the Witch
Son of a Witch
Framing of the Witch
Trickery of the Witch
Wishes of the Witch
Harmony of the Witch
Remedy of the Witch
Gift of the Witch
Toil of the Witch
Jinxing of the Witch
Craving of the Witch
Union of the Witch
Chaos of the Witch
Sleighing of the Witch

If you enjoyed

Son of a Witch

turn the page to read an extract from the next Crypt
Witch Mystery

FRAMING OF THE WITCH

Chapter 1

"Tempest, if you want to take off for the evening, we've got a handle on things here." Merrie Noble nudged me with her hip as she leaned against the bar.
Whatever it took, this wedding wasn't happening.

"No, I'm good. Why do you ask?" I looked up from the notes I'd been studying.

She grinned. "That customer's been trying to get your attention for five minutes." Merrie nodded to the warlock standing at the bar with an empty glass in front of him.

I sighed. My head wasn't in the game tonight. I tapped my finger on the notes. For the past month, I'd become obsessed with finding out Toby Matlock's dark secret. Everything else had been put on the backburner, serving thirsty customers at Cloven Hoof included.

"And, I don't want to make you mad, but you look pale. Maybe you should take the night off if you're not feeling well," Merrie said.

I wasn't feeling all that lively. I'd been exhausted and grouchy for days. I also had a headache. "I'm fine." I made a move toward the customer, but Merrie stopped me.

"Don't worry. I've got this." She dashed over and swiftly served the customer, dazzling him with her easy charm and excellent bartender skills.

My gaze traveled around the bar. It was the usual midweek crowd in this evening. Everyone was here to kick back and enjoy themselves after work. It was only Merrie, Izzie, and me on tonight. I didn't want to leave them shorthanded, but I had two more piles of notes I needed to plow through before bed.

Whenever I had a spare moment, I'd been hassling the angels about information on Toby. Dazielle had stuck to her word and had given me access to the stacks of papers relating to the investigation they'd been running on him. They'd been trying to pin something on Toby for five years.

I'd initially scoffed at their incompetence, but having read through the files, the angels had tried just about everything to get him. As I was well aware, Toby was wily and excelled in covering his tracks. Although there were plenty of rumors about him and his underhanded dealings, there was no evidence to link him to any crime.

I turned my head as somebody cleared their throat.

Axel Shadowsoul stood by the bar, a sly smile on his face. Gone were the days of his slick, too tanned appearance. Axel came with a sharper edge, messed up dark hair, and a gleam in his eyes that suggested all his thoughts were impure.

"What will it be?" I shoved the papers under the bar.

"Are you studying for an exam?"

"My studying days are long gone." I placed an empty glass on the bar.

Axel's gaze went to the papers. "So, what are you up to?"

"Bringing down a problem," I said. "Although, it's taking longer than I thought it would."

Axel leaned his elbows on the bar, intrigue lighting his gaze. "What's the problem?"

I hadn't shared what I'd been doing with many people. Granny Dottie knew, as did Mom, but that was about it. If word got back to Toby that I was investigating him, he might try more of his mind manipulation on me. The last time that had happened, I ended up wearing a lemon-yellow bridesmaid's dress, declaring him to be my closest friend, and hugging him. I'd felt grubby for days after that experience.

"Have you ever had dealings with Toby Matlock?" I asked.

Axel's eyebrows rose slowly. "I can't say I have. Of course, I know about him. He's probably wealthier than I am, but his magic creeps me out. All that messing with people's minds. You need to play fair when you use magic."

"You're telling me you always play fair?"

He grinned. "I bend the rules a little. Why are you interested in Toby?"

"Because he's soon to become my brother-in-law, and I'm not keen on that prospect."

"Oh, sure, he's getting hitched to Aurora." Axel shook his head. "I never saw that one coming. Does she have a thing for older guys?"

"So she says. It's hard to know what's going on in Aurora's head these days." We hadn't spoken in weeks.

"I noticed that Heaven's Door has been closed for a while," Axel said. "Is Aurora giving up the business when she's married?"

"Definitely not." I ground my teeth. Toby had been slowly taking over every aspect of Aurora's life. She'd given up her apartment, not opened her store for weeks, and taken to wearing ridiculous flouncy dresses and high heels that weren't her style. It was all Toby's doing; it had to be. My little sister could be ditzy, but she knew her own mind and had never let herself get manipulated by a guy before.

"When's the big day?" Axel asked.

"If I have anything to do with it, never," I said.

Axel's gaze went back to the pile of papers. "Oh! I get it. You're digging for dirt on Toby."

I tilted my head from side to side, trying to work out the kinks that had been lodged in my neck for days. "There's something about him that sets my teeth on edge. The angels know he's dodgy, but they can't get evidence to take him out of circulation."

"What do they think he's done?"

"He's defrauded money from former girlfriends."

"Why do that?" Axel asked. "The guy's crazy wealthy. He doesn't need more money."

"Maybe he does it because he can. Toby could get a thrill from taking whatever he wants from other people. He's done that with my sister. The problem is, there's no proof. He's always insisted that these girlfriends gifted the money to him."

"What do the former girlfriends have to say?"

"They came forward with the same story originally but then changed it." My lips pursed. "Anyone would think their minds had been manipulated."

Axel smirked. "I'd place money on the likelihood of that happening. Have you talked to these women? Maybe their stories will be different now Toby's out of their lives."

"I'm having trouble getting hold of them. The first complaint was submitted by Marianne O'Hanrahan. She reported that Toby had taken over a million from her private account."

Axel whistled out a breath. "Surely that's enough to charge Toby."

"The angels were building a case, but Marianne suddenly withdrew her complaint. She said there'd been a mix-up and Toby hadn't taken anything. I've got contact details for her, but she's responded to none of my messages."

"What about the other women?"

"There's also Ava Capaldi. She had double the amount taken by Toby, but exactly the same thing happened. She complained and then withdrew her statement. Olivia Dearhart's the same."

"None of them have gotten back to you?"

"Nope. Much like the angels, I can't locate them."

"Are they hiding? Maybe they've experienced Toby's oily charm one too many times and want to keep out of his way."

"I wondered about that. Either they've gone to ground, or Toby's done something to them." I rubbed the back of my neck. The ache behind my eyes felt almost unbearable. It had been building all day. If I wasn't careful, I'd give myself a migraine.

Axel touched the back of my hand. "Is everything okay with you?"

I hadn't realized I'd closed my eyes until he touched me. I pulled my hand away and nodded. "Nothing that won't be solved once Toby's behind bars, but I could do with some fresh air."

"Merrie can look after me while you're gone." Axel looked over at Merrie and winked.

"About that," I said. "I hope you're treating her well."

"I treat all my women well."

"That's what bothers me. You've never been a one-woman kind of half-demon. Don't mess around with Merrie."

Axel's eyes narrowed a fraction. "I have no plans to mess her around. Merrie's great. She's cool and fun. We understand each other."

"This place would be nothing without her. If you go fooling around with Merrie and break her heart, she might not stay. You prop up this bar most nights, and she won't want to see your smug face here if you do anything wrong."

Axel raised his hands before placing one over his heart. "Merrie is safe with me."

"She's anything but that." I jabbed a finger at him. "I'm watching you."

"What a treat." Axel chuckled. "You have nothing to worry about. I like Merrie."

"Just so long as she knows the situation. You're known for overpromising and under delivering when it comes to relationships." Axel was something of a playboy. I'd never seen him stick with anyone for more than a couple of months. Maybe things could be different with Merrie. Just in case they weren't, I'd keep an eye on their relationship. If Axel messed up, he'd be in a world of pain. No one upset my bar staff.

After giving him one final stern look, I headed out from behind the bar.

Wiggles had been doing his usual social rounds all evening, chatting up the customers in the hope of getting a free snack.

He trotted over when he saw me walking to the door. "Are we going somewhere?"

"Do you fancy a midnight stroll?"

"Any time."

I waved at Merrie and gestured to the door to let her know I was leaving.

She waved back to show she'd seen me before turning back to Axel.

I sucked in a welcome breath of icy air as we got outside. My head instantly felt better as the music faded and the door swung shut behind us. I normally loved being in my bar, but not tonight. My eyes felt puffy, and my head was tender. Maybe I was getting sick.

"I saw you chatting to Mr. Smooth," Wiggles said as we strolled under the moonlight.

"Axel's not so bad. He seems sweet on Merrie."

"He's mildly less of a creep these days. Whatever his father did to him when he was out of Willow Tree Falls, it improved Axel."

Axel's father was Kroni, a powerful demon. After Axel had almost been killed, he'd recuperated with his dad for a couple of days and had returned a changed half-demon. It was a darker version of the half-demon I knew, which was another reason I was keeping an eye on him. My sideline was hunting rogue demons. I hoped Axel would never become one of those. I considered him an ally.

"Hey, look! It's your mom." Wiggles picked up the pace as he spotted Mom heading toward the cemetery.

She stopped when she saw Wiggles and bent to pet him. Mom stood as I got near.

"Hi, Mom. Have you got the midnight shift?"

She kissed my cheek. "That's right. I'm meeting your Granny Dottie there. How's everything with you? You look tired. Aren't you sleeping?"

"I'm good. The bar's quiet, so we're just taking a stroll," I said.

She tilted her head. "Have you heard from your sister?"

I frowned. "She's not been in touch."

"Have you been in touch with her?"

"I don't dare go near Toby's house after the last time," I said. My visit to Toby's had involved an unpleasant experience with mind manipulation, almost tearing Toby's head off when he'd revealed his true colors, and Wiggles facing off with Toby's terrifyingly large butler.

"I wish you two would make up," Mom said. "There are only three weeks until the wedding."

"Which I'm no longer invited to." I tried to pretend it didn't hurt that Aurora had sent me a letter telling me I was no longer welcome at the celebration. Before that, I was to be her only bridesmaid. Not anymore. I wasn't even allowed to go to the reception. There would be no wedding cake and buffet for me.

"I keep asking her to change her mind, but Aurora has dug her heels in." Mom patted my arm.

"I've been watching her store, hoping she'll stop by," I said. "It's neutral territory, so I planned to go in and speak with her."

"If it's about what happened to the dress, Aurora will understand if you apologize." Mom knew all about me ruining my bridesmaid's dress. It hadn't been deliberate, but I wasn't sad that I'd no longer have to prance around looking like a giant ear of corn in lemon-yellow.

"It's so much more than the dress." I kicked my foot through the dirt. "This wedding can't happen."

Mom clasped her hands together. "None of us are thrilled about what's going on, but it's Aurora's decision. And so far, you haven't found anything against Toby. There's nothing to prove that his intentions are dark."

"Mom! You have to admit Aurora's not herself."

Mom sighed. "I agree, but I can't get her to talk about it. Every time I mention she seems different, she tells me it's wedding jitters. She's so busy planning everything and making sure their big day is perfect. Maybe she's right. A bride-to-be gets nervous about her big day."

"Aurora's not letting anyone help," I said. "She's keeping us away for a reason. I understand why she kicked me out of the wedding, but none of you have done anything wrong. You hardly see her."

"Which I don't enjoy, but I do understand. I have managed to corner Toby on two occasions and see if he's up to anything dubious. Nothing he tells me sets off alarms. He always has Aurora's best interests at heart."

I shook my head. "It's not in her best interest to abandon Heaven's Door. And it can't be good for her to live with Toby."

"We just have to accept that we're adding Toby Matlock to our family."

"I can't accept that," I said. "If I can speak to the three women he's already messed with, I'm sure this will be resolved. Maybe they'll speak to Aurora and tell her what Toby's really like. She'd have to believe them."

Mom hugged me. "Keep looking, but I'm trying to fortify myself that this wedding will happen. You have to be prepared for that, too."

"I won't be." I pulled back from the hug. "We could always kidnap Aurora. If we can get her away from Toby, we can break his hold on her."

"Kidnap your sister!" Mom chuckled and shook her head. "She'd never forgive us."

"I'm willing to do it. She already hates me, so it can't get any worse. She's not walking down that aisle with Toby."

"Aurora doesn't hate you," Mom said. "It would be so good if you reunite before the wedding."

"Aurora won't let me anywhere near the wedding. She knows that, if I'm there, I'll do everything I can to stop it."

"Tempest! Don't do anything rash. Think about this. Your sister's happiness is at stake."

"It's all I've been thinking about." Toby had become an unhealthy obsession. Nothing else mattered. I had to get people to see the real Toby Matlock and get Aurora away from him.

"I'd better go," Mom said. "Granny Dottie's all alone in the cemetery. You know what she's like when she gets bored."

I grimaced. Granny Dottie was worse than an unsupervised school child on a sugar high.

"I'll see you later." I walked away with Wiggles, not going in any particular direction. I just needed quiet time to think about this wedding.

"We could sabotage it," Wiggles said. "I could get some buddies together. We could sneak in and eat the food."

"How is that sabotaging the wedding?"

"Everyone will be miserable because there's no nice food."

"Aurora and Toby will still be married."

"There's no food at the actual wedding ceremony, is there?"

"I don't think so."

"There's no point in me being there then. Eating is what I'm best at."

I sighed, not able to work up the energy to warn Wiggles away from the wedding buffet. Every bone in my body ached like I'd had a wrestling match with a giant demon.

He nudged me with his nose as we continued to walk. "I get it. It sucks being excluded. I love Aurora, too. She's making a huge mistake, but she can't see it."

I nodded. "It's a good job we can. If being excluded from Aurora's life is what it takes to stop Toby Matlock from marrying her, then that's what I'm prepared to do."

"I still vote for the buffet sabotage."

"You focus on the buffet. I'll figure out how to get Aurora away from Toby."

Whatever it took, this wedding wasn't happening.

Framing of the Witch is available in paperback and ebook.